I0668930

MADELEINE ABDUCTED
(Estate Series – Book 1)

By M.S. Willis

ISBN: 978-0-9915666-1-7

mswillis@mswillisbooks.com

www.facebook.com/mswillisbooks

OTHER BOOKS BY M.S. WILLIS

Control Series

Book One – Control

Book Two – Conflict

Book Three – Conquer

Coming in 2014

Because of Ellison

Hope Restrained (Estate Series #2)

Captured (Control #4)

Changed (Control #5)

Table of Contents

Madeleine Abducted is dedicated to the poor fool who currently occupies my old desk. Good luck to you.

Prologue

This is a story that is not meant for the faint of heart. If you are looking for inspiration, if you are looking for light, if you are looking for something that will help you sleep and dream, you've come to the wrong place.

Within these pages you will find a tale typically left unsaid in polite society because of the formidable fear and striking sorrow its events evoke. It is a story about abduction, enslavement, and the moment when a life is delivered into darkness.

There is no neat and tidy ending, no white knight that rides in and delivers freedom, nor salvation — there is no escape. Like life, stories don't always end with elegant edges.

A weak woman at one time, she fell victim to evil, disappeared on a fated night never to return to the world again ... but not for the reasons you might think.

Her name is Madeleine Clark, and when she was abducted, she was not only dragged into hell ....

She took over.

1

Chapter One

Madeleine stared out over a sea of shadowed faces. From where she stood, the conversations between the audience members were nothing more than gentle murmurs adding white noise to the barely lit concert hall. Her stomach knotted as she paced the long white corridor between the stage and the rear practice room; her eyes flickered out through the small, square windows to the audience below. Other musicians passed her as they moved about, waiting to take their places on stage. Discordant sounds and brief glimpses of shuffling sheet music escaped the practice room door each time a musician passed through. Her head pounded and her chest constricted as she felt the time grow closer to her performance.

Deep breaths, Maddy ... you can do this ....

Her long, black gown flowed around her feet like liquid onyx, shimmering in cadence with her steps, swallowing her small stature. She pulled at the high neckline and longed for the comfortable t-shirts she normally wore. The rhythmic click of her heels reminded her of a metronome keeping time with the beat of her heart. Her breath was irregular; her skin was sticky with nervous perspiration. Surprise overtook her when, suddenly, a friendly voice invaded her panic.

"I should probably remove that bow from your hands before you snap it in two." Jeremy's mouth curved up into a genial grin, his warm brown eyes looked down on her with a glint of humor.

She wrung her hands across the smooth wood of the bow; her fingers covered by rosin dust from the horsehair. Releasing her tight hold on the thin bow, she politely smiled in response to his jest. Jeremy reached down to take it from her hands and said, "Maddy, you'll be extraordinary. You have nothing to worry about." Continuing, he laughed. "You can't hide behind the walls of a studio forever, people want to see you play."

That was the problem. Although Madeleine didn't mind people hearing her music, but she did not like being seen; preferring instead the protection of her studio or home, where she could remain invisible to the eyes of the world. Her voice came out in a mousy whisper, fear evident in her tone, "But I'll feel so naked ... so exposed ...."

Her hands moved over themselves, the trapped blood looking pink within the pale white of her taut skin. Jeremy placed his hand over hers and said, "If I could remove your hands to protect them as well, I would."

Madeleine looked up into Jeremy's face. He was a close friend, one of her only friends. He understood her introversion and didn't hold her lack of social skills against her. If not for her need to remain emotionally distant, she may have considered Jeremy for more than friendship. He was handsome in the most classical sense of the term: dark chestnut brown hair; eyes a shade of warm mahogany; and she knew he was tall, but at

3

5'2", most people were tall compared to her. Jeremy's body was long and lean, his upper body and arms toned from the decades he'd spent mastering the violin. Standing before her in a coattail tuxedo, he exuded masculine elegance and refinement. He was friendly to a fault, a person she could rely upon to understand her and guard her secrets.

"Besides," he said, beaming a grand smile, "you've played publicly before. This should be no different."

But it was different. Tonight was her first solo performance using *her own* music, not something from a popular composer. This music came from within her, revealing her innermost thoughts and desires in the form of melodies and sounds. If the audience could decipher the hidden meaning of those notes, they would discover the true person within her.

"Yes," she said, "but when I played before, I was unseen, buried within the orchestra." She turned to look out over the audience and continued, "Tonight, I'll be the focus. Tonight, there's nowhere for me to hide."

His hand came up to softly brush along her cheek. He moved to stand next to her, his eyes also taking in the sea of people. "Nonsense, Maddy. With your size, that cello covers most of you," he teased. "Or you could just close your eyes and hide within the music. It's beautiful. It makes you beautiful. You should be proud, not shy."

4

The practice room door swung open as the stage director walked into the hallway, the light trill of a flute escaping as he passed through the door. "Fifteen more minutes before showtime," he said. "I'll need the two of you to return to the backroom. You'll be going on stage last."

Jeremy nodded to the director before he reached down to gently take Maddy's hand. She could feel his breath brush across her cheek as he leaned down to whisper, "When you take the stage, Maddy, just know that I am there with you. You have nothing to fear."

A nervous wave rolled up her body and escaped her lips as an anxious sigh. She squeezed Jeremy's hand, released him, and turned toward the backroom. Walking into the room, her ears were assaulted by the discordant sounds of multiple musicians readying their instruments for their particular parts. Maddy knew that while the noise was grating as it occurred in this instant, once on stage, each piece would perfectly fit together. Her heart tightened with the realization that her part would be heard above them all.

Fighting the rising bile in her throat, Maddy sat down to tune her cello. She'd already tuned it five times since arriving at the concert hall, and she would still make final adjustments once on stage, but she had to do something with her hands to keep her mind occupied. A pair of black leather shoes, shined to the point she could see her distorted reflection, appeared in her view. Looking up, she was once again met with Jeremy's friendly eyes. He reached down to hand her the bow he'd taken from her in the hallway.

5

"You'll be needing this, little one," he said.

His hand lightly tapped her on the shoulder in an attempt to comfort her. "Remember to breathe, Madeleine," he said, "The rest will come easily. You were meant to play ... remember that."

Maddy watched as Jeremy turned to take his place at the end of the line with the other orchestra members.

Breathe ....

The doors rushed open and the line of musicians moved forward into a black abyss. Pushing herself up from the chair, Maddy straightened out her gown, picked up her instrument and moved to stand behind Jeremy. He turned to her and quickly winked before saying, "Showtime."

Training her eyes on the back of Jeremy's jacket, Maddy attempted to hide herself as they took the stage. When Jeremy moved to stand by his seat, she was left alone, exposed to the rows of attentive people. As the spotlight shone down upon her, she felt like her throat was closing, blocking off the air she so desperately needed. When a single, lonely note filled the auditorium, the murmuring white noise from the audience ceased; all eyes turned toward the stage.

Maddy took her seat, her eyes trained to the strings stretched taut across her instrument. Pulling the fine hair of the bow across the strings calmed her suddenly, the sound becoming a soothing reminder that soon, when she became

6

lost within the music, the audience would cease to exist.

Two taps of the conductor's wooden wand, two hands raised, and silent anticipation overtook not only the musicians, but the audience as well. One held breath ... two hands begin to move.

Her eyes closed.

Three fingers pressed down on the strings, her arm pulled the bow slowly but powerfully, producing sound. One lonely, low-timbered note started softly, building in intensity as a wave of melancholy wrapped itself around the large theater. Delicately, a higher pitched note accompanied hers. The light pull of a violinist's bow added a quiet smile to the sadness of her song. One by one, the other instruments joined her, providing a background to the haunting melody she manipulated from nothing more than metal pulled tight along a wooden frame.

Building to a sudden crescendo, the sound of the cello swiftly filled the large space, eliciting a collective gasp from the audience. Inspired and lost within the resounding harmony produced by the other performers, Madeleine let go; finally her spirit was revealed and it emerged dancing within the music she played. Her heart began to sing and her eyes fluttered open and then closed again as she was overtaken by the naked beauty of the piece. The feeling of freedom drove her, harder and faster, the melancholy now changed into a desperate need, a heartfelt longing for resolution. Maddy wondered if those who listened would recognize the hidden meaning of the melody. Two

7

lovers, bonding in the most passionate of encounters, become one. She'd never truly known that moment, but she could imagine what it felt like to give herself to another person; to find shelter in something other than her own heart.

Separated from the concept of time, she powered through the climax of the piece, eventually weaving her way back to the melancholy from which it began. The rhythm slowed, the heartbeats of each person in the room thumped in time with the music. Quiet reentered the space as the song was, once again, brought down to a single, solitary note, pulled tight against the strings of her instrument.

Her eyes opened.

The audience seemed to swell as bodies rose to their feet, a deafening boom of applause struck her, snapping her back to the present. On shaky legs, she pushed herself to stand up. She nodded her head in acknowledgment, relief flooding her every nerve.

~ ~ ~

Following the end of the performance, Maddy sat in the backroom, packing her cello into its large black case.

Jeremy walked over to her and said, "You were amazing, Maddy. I was impressed by your performance."

Jeremy stood above her, his pride in her evident as his eyes twinkled with delight. Maddy stood up, her hands instantly moving to brush down her gown. A smile escaped her lips and her cheeks heated in response to his praise. With nothing more than a raspy whisper, she responded, "Thank you. I took your advice and lost myself in the music."

Jeremy wrapped his arm around her shoulder, dwarfing her by his large size. His warm brown eyes smiled down at her as he said, "I'm going with a group of people to celebrate tonight's success. Would you join us for once?"

She instantly looked away before returning her shy eyes to her friend. She shook her head "no" in response to his invitation, immediately feeling his disappointment in her refusal.

His smiled turned into a mock frown. "Oh, come on, Maddy! You can't remain a recluse your entire life. I promise you, I won't leave your side."

She cleared her throat before summoning forth a weak apology. "You know I can't, Jeremy. I need to go home. I'm tired. It takes so much ... it drains me to perform. Please understand."

Jeremy looked instantly apologetic and was about to respond when he heard another throat clearing behind them. Turning suddenly, they discovered a strange man standing there holding a single red rose. Maddy looked up from the rose and froze when her gaze was met with a pair of the most brilliant green eyes she'd ever seen. The man's hair was black as a raven, shining like smooth silk trained back into a short, yet messy style. The lights and shadows of the room emphasized the cut

9

of his strong jaw. She looked down to see that he was dressed elegantly in a tuxedo, his strong, broad shoulders evident underneath the clean lines of the material. When her eyes returned to his, he was staring intently at her. Another blush reddened her cheeks as she was caught gawking. Her breath hitched; her skin tingled. He was the most beautiful man she'd ever seen. He exuded a graceful masculinity; powerful and strong, but with an underlying hint of a sharp and lethal edge.

Jeremy took a protective step in front of her, challenging the stranger who'd mysteriously appeared in the room. "I'm sorry, sir, but you're not supposed to be back here," he said. "This is for orchestra members only. You need to leave." Jeremy's voice was calm but firm.

The man's eyes never left Madeleine as he flippantly responded to Jeremy's request. His voice rolled through her, the tone reminiscent of the instrument she played. "I'll leave in a moment," the man said. "I wanted to deliver this rose to Ms. Clark." Reaching out to hand her the flower, his eyes intensified as he stared down at her. "Your performance was an absolute joy to experience. I've never been as moved as I am when I hear you play. It *truly* is an honor, Ms. Clark."

Maddy's hand hesitantly reached out to accept the rose, her voice nothing more than a whisper as she thanked him before turning her eyes downward, away from his burning gaze.

Jeremy repeated his demand, "You need to leave, sir."

10

She could feel the man look her over for another second before returning his attention to Jeremy. Maddy felt like she was in the company of darkness. Her skin prickled from his observance of her, she felt timid and nervous about his presence in the room.

"I'll be leaving now. There is no need to follow me. I can see myself out." Like the soft caress of fur against her skin, the tone of the stranger's voice was pleasant and soothing. But there was a dangerous edge to his words that acted like an unspoken warning. The stranger looked at her once more before turning and slowly departing through the exit doors. Maddy peeked up through her lashes and watched as he walked away, graceful and sure in his steps. It was only when he was gone that she released her held breath.

Jeremy looked back down at Maddy and said, "Are you sure you don't want to come?" Before she could decline again, Jeremy waved away the question. "No need for an answer. I can at least stay behind and help you to your car."

Her eyes looked over to the group waiting by the doors. She smiled up at Jeremy. "Thank you, but no. They're waiting on you; you should go join them. I'll have no problem getting to my car." He hesitated, before finally relenting. Nodding at her once, he turned and moved to join the departing group.

An hour later, Madeleine carried her instrument through the large, nearly empty parking lot, struggling not to break the rose given to her by the beautiful, yet intimidating stranger. As she approached her car, a limousine pulled up beside her. She looked over to see the rear passenger window rolling down. Holding her breath, she wondered if this was the same man from backstage. When the window finished lowering and revealed the passenger on the other side, she felt oddly disappointed to discover it was someone else entirely. The man behind the window was older, his handsome face made even more distinguished by the silver streaks at his temples. He was obviously wealthy, exuding an air about him of authority and prestige. Madeleine wasn't shocked when he called out to gain her attention: she simply believed that he was another admirer wanting to congratulate her on her performance.

He opened the door to his car and stepped out and she was instantly impressed with his choice of tuxedo. He looked debonair, moving with a swagger that gave away his refined taste and upbringing. He was definitely sure of himself and the slight smirk to his mouth gave him a boyish charm. Two large men stepped out of the car behind the first. After unfolding their large frames and exiting the vehicle, they took their place behind the older man. Maddy's heartbeat skipped from nervous energy as they approached, but she swallowed down her concern, assuming the man to be a politician or other well-known public figure.

The men approached and once they were within close proximity, the older man reached out his hand as if to shake hers. Maddy wiped her hand down the side of her gown to remove the moisture on her palms before reaching over to accept. As soon as they touched, his grip tightened around her hand and his smile dripped with malice.

"Good evening, Ms. Clark," he said. "I wanted to introduce myself to you and let you know how impressed I was by your performance." The words were polite, but there was an undertone of cruelty. Madeleine's heart pounded against her chest as she forced a smile.

Her voice was laced with trepidation when she responded, "Thank you. I believe it was one of the best I've given to date. Are you a fan?"

She attempted to pull her hand from his grasp, but his grip tightened in response. He pulled in closer and said, "I have not always been a fan, but I came here tonight because my son has a huge appreciation for you. His birthday is coming up, you see, and I was hoping you wouldn't mind giving him a private performance." His eyes seemed to darken as he spoke and the two men behind him moved so that they were on either side of Maddy. Suddenly, their hands came up, grabbing her arms. Before she could react, one of the guards covered her mouth so that she could not scream.

The man's smile faded once his guards had her secured. "There is no need to struggle, Ms. Clark. It won't do you any good." With that, the man turned and started making his way back to his car. One guard lifted Maddy while the other retrieved her instrument. She screamed into the guard's hand, but knew that there was no one around to hear her pleas for help. She was dragged to the car and shoved into the back while the other guard took her instrument to the trunk.

13

Desperately kicking and flailing her arms, she attempted to break free, but once she was placed in the car, more hands grabbed onto her, and a cloth bag was thrust over her head. She felt rope being tied around her arms and legs. Finally, something hard hit her in the back of the head, and her body instantly went limp. Madeleine realized, as the blackness slipped in and stripped her from consciousness, that tonight, the stage was not what she needed to fear.

Chapter Two

Madeleine woke up to discover herself locked inside a dark room. Groggy and slow moving, her head was pounding and she was disoriented from the lack of light. The normal symptoms of panic were oddly absent; her mind struggled from the lack of adrenaline pumping through her body. Slowly, she moved her hand to her head and pondered how her body could feel so weightless, but unusually heavy at the same time. As she tested her ability to move, the squeak of metal could be heard. She reached down to find what felt like canvas pulled taut beneath her. Her hand slid across the canvas, the sound reminding her of the same serrated harmonic you would achieve by lightly sliding your finger along the string of an instrument. The sound was oddly comforting in its familiarity. Abruptly, her hand came upon a cold metal bar, to which the canvas was attached, and Maddy deduced that she was lying on a simple cot.

Rolling onto her back, she felt something cold against her leg. Slowly, she pulled her leg up to investigate and discovered a metal shackle locked around her ankle. She reached down and gave the chain a hard tug and quickly determined that the binding was secure.

She laid back down, the throbbing in her head increasing from her movement. Her thoughts were slow and jumbled and she felt numb in some areas, while tingly in others. It was difficult to move

15

her appendages and oddly, she felt like giggling. As she laid there in confusion, her mind traipsed back to her performance at the concert hall. Her thoughts briefly touched upon events from that evening: the solo performance; Jeremy's smiling eyes; the green-eyed stranger; and finally, the older gentleman in the parking lot. She remembered being grabbed and forcefully shoved into the back of a limousine. Her nerves started to regain feeling, the synapsis in her brain communicating once again. Adrenaline began to finally wind its way through her veins while fear tugged at even the deepest recesses of her mind.

She opened her mouth to scream, but her throat was so dry and raw that she couldn't get out much more than a raspy whisper. She wondered if this was the type of nightmare where she was paralyzed, unable to free herself from some unseen force. Her body felt languid and she wondered if she'd been drugged or if this was an aftereffect of the blow to her head. A cold breeze caressed and prickled her skin. Her hand reached to investigate, delivering the realization that she had been stripped of her clothes.

She wanted to be strong. She wanted to think that she was adjusted well enough to be able to face her circumstances with determination and courage. But as understanding seeped into her mind, fear consumed her, leaving her feeling helpless, reducing her to tears. Although it's easy to scream for a victim to run or fight when you see them in a movie or read about them in a book, the futility of the situation is far more evident when you find yourself in their place. Maddy curled herself into a tight ball; her body shook as she sobbed. The heat from her tears slowly cooled, leaving icy trails from the paths they traveled down her cheeks.

After regaining consciousness, time snuck by as Madeleine lay unaware of its passage. The lack of light or sensory stimulation kept her mind stagnant and confused. Second, minutes, hours or days could have passed and she wouldn't have known. Desperate for sound, she kicked out her leg at times just to hear the rattle of the chain, or she would move on the cot to hear the thin aluminum bars groan from her weight. Any noise was welcome within the suffocating silence of her dark space. At some point, her eyes dried up and she reached a numb state. She wasn't afraid, she wasn't happy, she wasn't sad; she just was. Her mind wandered from why she'd been captured, to the identity of her abductors, and on to the question of their intentions. But even those thoughts were smothered under the weight of the hopelessness she felt.

As her mind aimlessly drifted, a solitary note lightly played within the recesses of her mind. Like a small glimmer of light and warmth, Maddy chased the note within her thoughts as it grew in volume and intensity. That note slowly changed into another, and then, blessedly, another. She tried to let herself be absorbed in the haunting melody of the cello's song that played within the confines of her imagination; an escape from the tragic circumstances of the present. She was most likely hallucinating, but it didn't matter. The song was a gift, a distraction, and she was swept up in the feelings it elicited. Her body floated with the waves of sound as it rose and fell. At times it was so loud, it caused her heart rate to increase with its intensity, but when it dipped back down to only a slight, soft reverberation, she felt like she was sinking into nothingness with its threatened absence. Her breathing began to keep time with the tempo of the melody. She became the music, losing herself within the ethereal plane it produced.

One song gracefully ended, allowing another to begin. Each piece, wrapped within melancholy and despondency; but the absolute perfection of the harmony within the notes, the sharps and the flats, combined with everything in between, added beauty to the evocative and emotional depths of that sadness. Was this her soul speaking to her from within? Or had she simply lost her mind to the environment that surrounded her? In truth, the cause of the music didn't really matter; the freedom she found within it was the only thing for which she cared.

As she continued to be carried within a musically induced trance, a sliver of light appeared before her. It was distant and faint and she blinked repeatedly, thinking visual illusions had now joined her auditory manifestations. She held her hand out above her, sweeping it along as she created the music from air. Her other hand moved as if playing an instrument that did not truly exist. She didn't pay much attention as that sliver of light became wider and she all but ignored the creaking hinges as a door was being opened. Still lost in her fantasy, she didn't notice as a large man entered through that door and walked over to her. A beam of light hit her face just before the force of the man's hand rocked her head sideways.

"Snap out of it, bitch!" he yelled.

She was instantly removed from her reverie and her jaw stung from the impact of the slap across her face. Tears sprang from her eyes and her mind was suddenly stripped of any happiness she'd gained in her delusional state. Before she could react, a large hand painfully gripped her arm and pulled her up from the cot. The chain around her ankle rattled as she was forced to stand; her legs threatened to give out from their lack of use.

Another vicious slap impacted with her face and the force of it knocked her back. Her neck craned and her head spun in the direction of the blow.

"You need to wake the fuck up. It's almost time for the party." The man's voice was rough and menacing and it was followed by a sickening chuckle. Maddy instantly recoiled at the sound, but his grip around her arm was so tight, there was no means for her to escape.

As her body reawakened, her bladder suddenly screamed with the need to release. She wasn't able to hold it in the vertical position she now found herself and a warm trail dribbled down her leg.

The beam of the man's flashlight traveled down her body, stopping suddenly on the puddle forming beneath her. "What the fuck?! You sick bitch!" Maddy was thrown back suddenly, landing in

19

the urine that now spread along the floor. She watched the beam of the flashlight as the man turned and left the room; closing the door, he returned her to the pitch-black darkness. Multiple nerves called for her attention: her head and neck ached from being struck in the face; her body retched from being soaked in her own foul-smelling fluid; and a sharp pain shot through her hips and back from being thrown to the ground. Before she could process anything more, the door once again flew open and Madeleine was struck with the ice-cold spray of a fire hose.

A scream tore out from her throat as the deluge of water bore down on her body. The icy temperature of the water only adding to the pain caused by the strength of the hose's spray; she felt like someone was dragging razorblades across her skin. Within minutes the onslaught of frigid water stopped, but her skin continued to sting. Her body began trembling, now completely soaked, in the freezing cold of the room. The door closed and she was consumed, yet again, by the void and unrelenting darkness. Her arms folded across her chest in a pathetic attempt to warm herself as she sank to the floor.

The door swung open again, but this time, a different man entered. He was backlit for the most part, shadows hid the discernible features of his face, but she could see that this man's frame was thinner than the first. His shoes slowly clicked as he walked, finally stopping just short of the puddle of water that surrounded her.

"Are you going to continue sitting there crying?" he asked. "Or are you going to be a good

20

girl and get up to follow me? I'll be extremely disappointed if I have to get my shoes wet grabbing ahold of you and forcing you up."

His voice was smoother than the first man's, almost consoling in the depth of its tone. The only response she could manage to his words was the chattering of her teeth.

"I'll ask you one more time, Cricket, are you going to get up on your own, or do I need to force you?"

Cricket??

Her body was frozen ... in motion and temperature ... and she wasn't able to respond to him or the odd name with which he'd referred to her. Even if she had been able to respond: What do you say to a strange man who's been holding you captive? It's not exactly like a person can simply blurt out *'No, thanks, but I'm happy sitting here freezing on the wet concrete floor.'* It didn't matter. Fear was constricting her body in such a way that even an attempt at movement or response would be feigned at best.

The man let out an exasperated sigh, "I guess we'll do this your way." Then he called for someone outside the room, "Marcus!"

Her body flinched when he raised his voice, almost as if, subconsciously, she knew what was about to happen. As feared, the first man came lumbering back through the door. A whimper escaped her trembling lips as she shook her head and cowered back from his approach.

21

"No." Her voice was whisper soft and barely discernible, even to herself.

"Ah, she speaks. It's a miracle." His droll words were spoken with obvious condescension. "Stand, Cricket, or else Marcus here will have to *assist* you."

She had no other choice but to do as the man ordered. Yes, technically, she could resist, but the last thing she wanted was for Marcus to touch her again. She peered up at the backlit silhouettes of the men standing above her. Her hair hung in damp clumps in her face, which, thankfully, was long enough to hide her breasts. Uncurling herself from the ball she'd formed on the floor, Maddy pushed herself up, despite the disputes of her body and mind. She stood on shaky legs and nearly fell over from the lack of muscle strength. Once she was standing, the smaller of the two men stepped around the puddle and gently took her arm in his hand.

"Marcus, leave us," he said.

The large man let out a huff at having been dismissed, but turned around and did as he was told.

She was pulled closer toward the door, her legs resisting the movement. Pulling a key from his pocket, the man bent down to remove the shackle from her leg. Once she was free, he forcefully shoved her toward the door. Maddy stumbled over her own feet and the man's grip tightened around her arm to keep her from falling. Tears began pricking at her eyes and she considered fighting back. Realizing that any fight she could put up would be a weak attempt in her condition, the uselessness of such an effort was not lost on her. She was a gentle person. She played music, that's ALL she'd done; she began to lament the life experiences she passed up as she realized the likelihood of *ever* experiencing them had been taken from her.

As they neared the door, the man stopped and moved in closer to her. Maddy flinched back as his grip tightened, but he pulled her in closer, so that he could speak softly into her ear. With a business-like tone, he said, "Listen, Cricket, once we walk through that door, your acts at resistance need to stop. I'm somewhat more forgiving than your Master will be and I'm certainly more patient than his father. If you want to make it through this with the least amount of pain possible, I suggest you do as you are told without fighting. You will not win against them, so you need to accept your circumstances and make the best of it."

The grit in her voice sounded as painful as it felt when she asked, "W-why … why are you doing this to me?"

He took a moment to consider his words, before responding, "This is your fate, Cricket. Asking why isn't going to do anything for you except make that fate a much more painful journey. You need to learn the rules of your position and learn them quickly if you want to make a smoother transition into your new role."

"And what is my role?" she asked. Her voice was stronger this time and she would have been glaring at him, if she could actually see him.

Pulling her close once again, he warned. "I will tell you this one more time: asking questions will only make this more difficult for you to survive ... "

Maddy flinched at the word 'survive'; it was an open confirmation that her life was endangered. Her mind could no longer hide behind the mask of denial that it used to defend her sanity.

" ... but maybe, it will help you to know this sooner, rather than later. You are a slave. You caught the attention of the man to whom you now belong. You are to do as you are told *without* asking questions and you are to follow instructions *exactly* as they are given. Obedience is paramount from this point further. Any infraction on your part will provoke dire circumstances. Do you understand?"

She was able to nod her head in response, even though the rest of her was paralyzed by the realization that she was now a missing person. She'd seen notices about them all the time: on the news, in the paper, on the internet, and on those flyers she received in the mail. Never had she imagined she would become that random face plastered across the media. Those things always happened to someone else; someone less careful than her; someone less scared of life outside.

The man must have been satisfied with her silence because he turned and moved swiftly to the door, dragging her along as he walked. The door swung open and she was momentarily blinded as he dragged her out from the darkness and into the light.

Chapter Three

The girl looked like shit and Xander was instantly pissed that she would need to be cleaned up before she could be *presented*. Her skin was literally blue from having been sprayed down in that meat locker they called a room. He felt sorry for her as he watched her feet trip over themselves, desperately attempting to match his pace. He wanted to be kind and slow down to accommodate her weakened condition, but his kindness would only work against her in the end. She needed to learn now that she was no longer a free person, and that she should no longer expect compassion or understanding from any of her *superiors*.

Xander knew Aaron wasn't going to be pleased with this turn of events and he was not looking forward to Aaron's reaction when his new slave was discovered. If Aaron were to have his way, his birthday would have been forgotten. He would have been left alone to tend to his own interests. Unfortunately, his father, Joseph Carmichael — also known as the head of this Estate — was a cruel bastard and had learned to take anything of enjoyment to Aaron and turn it into something dark and disturbing. It was a subtle manipulation tactic on his part, and Aaron was powerless to fight against it while his father still held the reigns.

Xander's eyes couldn't help but take in the small girl walking ahead of him. He inwardly

26

chuckled at the irony that such a little person would have absolute mastery over an instrument that was damn near the same size as her. Unfortunately, it was that very same talent that caught Aaron's attention. Xander had to admit, Cricket was beautiful. Even with her small stature, her body was a sight to behold with the perfectly proportioned curves of her chest and her ass. If a man had to have a slave, she was definitely not one to be passed up. Regardless, he worried for her. Even though Aaron never intended to enslave her, he wouldn't exactly be the type to set her free. No concessions would be given to this little beauty and he knew Aaron would not stand for any questions or rebellion on her part. Aaron was a good man, but lacked the patience it required to train a decent slave. Believing that Cricket would, most likely, be passed to him for training, he decided to pity her this one time and prepare her for what was to come.

He pulled her petite body close to his and leaned down so that he could whisper to her as they walked. His gait was made awkward by the position he was forced to take because he practically had to bend in half to reach his mouth to her ear. "You are going to be cleaned up very shortly. You do not want to struggle against it or display any modesty by attempting to cover yourself. There will be several large men in the room who would be perfectly willing to correct you for any acts of disobedience."

Her tiny frame trembled violently and she reminded him of an excitable Chihuahua. Except for the trembling, she remained still as he spoke to

27

her. Xander was impressed that she hadn't yet broken down into absolute hysterics. Typically by the time a woman had been made aware of her fate in this place, it was a matter of seconds before the true histrionics began. The fact that she wasn't throwing herself on the ground in a fit of self-pity made him think that there might be more strength to the little sprite than he believed.

Leaning down to speak to her again, she turned suddenly, looking him dead in the eye. Xander was instantly struck by the dark blue hue of her gaze. Almost a cobalt color, yet there were tiny specks of a lighter color that resembled starbursts. The light hit her eyes in such a way that he was reminded of the way the sun reflects off of turbulent water; blinding and beautiful one second, gone the next. Her gaze was so disconcerting in its depth, it seemed like she was looking beyond his physical eyes into something much more private and personal. He shook himself of that thought and held her stare as he gave his final instruction: "Do NOT fight against them, Cricket. They will not redirect with words. They prefer a more ... *physical* ... approach." Another tremble, and it was time to push through those doors.

Xander led Maddy into the dressing room that had been designated for her. In order to keep her presentable for Aaron, he'd requested that only other slaves or he be the ones to handle her. He noticed that her cheek was already marked from her run in with Marcus and he was going to be sure to speak with Aaron about Marcus' inability to follow strict orders. Even though he was nothing more than a bodyguard and henchman to Aaron, he still carried weight in the Estate due to his closeness to the second in command. Mr. Carmichael and Aaron may run the Estate and businesses, but Xander was one of the best when it came to the rest of the underlings, and he wasn't about to put up with Marcus' transgression.

As soon as Maddy passed through the double doors, she froze at the sight of the other slaves and their guards. Her sudden stop was unexpected and Xander almost knocked her over when he collided with her back. He knew she was scared and didn't like to speak much, but was a warning too much to ask? Stepping around her, he continued dragging her to the open shower in the room. He looked down at one of the nameless slaves and ordered, "She is to be cleaned up with warm water. We can't exactly gift wrap a *smurf* and expect Aaron to be happy."

The little blonde slave followed his instruction without question, taking Maddy from his arm. When Maddy resisted, Xander stepped toward her to redirect her behavior, but stopped when he saw her shoulders drop in defeat while she held her chin up in silent defiance. He was instantly intrigued by her actions and considered her fate to be a waste of such an interesting person. Talented, beautiful *and* the inner-strength of a champion; it was a shame to have to break her down further. It was obvious that she was not the type to stand naked in front of a group of men and women, yet she did so without so much as flinching. She had the instincts of a survivor.

Once she was cleaned and her skin had taken on a pinkish color, she was removed from

29

the water and set aside to be dried and prepared. Xander's eyes wandered over her ample breasts and perfectly flat stomach. Her waist looked cinched in comparison to the well-rounded curves of her hips; his dick twitched at the sight of her. When they dried her and began applying scented oils to her skin, he had to look away so as to avoid any embarrassment from his body's reaction. He couldn't help it. He was a man and before him stood one of the most beautiful women he'd ever seen. The only problem being that she was Aaron's and he couldn't act on the overwhelming urge he had to throw her down and claim that tiny body for himself.

Once Maddy was oiled and Xander felt like he had regained control over his manhood, he turned back to monitor their progress. Her eyes were trained to the floor, but within seconds they suddenly shot up to him. There was no fight in her stare; she appeared to have already accepted her fate and he didn't know if he was heartbroken over how easily that had occurred, or relieved to know she wouldn't endure as many beatings in her training. Her eyes silently pleaded with his, but not for release or mercy; no, she pleaded with him to maintain their connection, almost as if she was looking at him as a distraction from the other people in the room.

Very Interesting.

It seemed as if he'd somehow earned a small token of trust from her. Xander decided to grant her the comfort to which she was attaching herself, but eventually she would need to learn that eye contact was only permissible when requested.

30

However, if it kept her calm for now, he was willing to condone it. The poor thing was about to be shoved into a box; it was best to keep her pliable until it was time for her to be degraded even further.

"Now, Cricket, you need to remember that you are a gift to someone very special and if you were to ruin the surprise by moving or making noise, I'm positive you would not like the results. Your arms and legs will be bound and you will be in a tight space. You are to remain perfectly still and perfectly quiet and it will all be over with before you know it. Understand?"

Her eyes continued to hold his as he spoke. He expected her eyes to narrow, her eyebrows to furrow, or to see even a small spark of rage develop in her stare — some kind of response to his instructions — but there was nothing. She simply put her hands behind her back, waiting to be bound. The position caused her bare chest to pop out and he groaned as his pants tightened again. He couldn't watch as they bound her and placed her in the cardboard container, so he simply turned and walked to the door. Once it was stated that she was ready to be moved, his arm went up against the door and he pushed his way out into the hallway.

Chapter Four

It was a simple sequence of events that led to the moment when Madeleine ended up naked, bound, and gagged in a box. It was a little anticlimactic. There was no true struggle: no fight to keep herself clothed, or unbound, or to even keep herself in an upright position. There was no dramatic plea for her freedom. She just let them do this to her. She could have fought, or screamed, but really, would it have done any good? Do bad men ever really let someone go when begged?

Maddy still had no idea who these people were or why they chose her, but she knew she was targeted, watched, maybe even followed at some point or another. Maybe if she'd been more diligent, paid better attention to her surroundings, this wouldn't have happened. Truthfully, she could come up with a thousand different decisions she could have made that would have changed the circumstances leading up to her capture; but ultimately, would those decisions have changed her fate? Or would they have merely delayed the inevitable?

As Maddy remained crouched and silently crying inside her tiny cardboard prison, the partygoers were becoming more drunk and obnoxious. Laughter from women turned into small screams and moans. She didn't even want to know what was going on outside the four cardboard walls and she began to appreciate her hiding place, despite the pain and discomfort. Her mind drifted over the events that had occurred since she'd awakened to a nightmare. The two men: Marcus and the other one. Marcus was an obvious monster, but the other man, he was more deceptive. He was the kind of monster that you didn't see coming; his demeanor refined and calm so that there was no visual warning of the evil lurking within.

She remembered when she first turned to him after they'd exited the dark room. The beauty of the man who'd informed her that she was a slave instantly struck her. His face was chiseled and his jaw line was sprinkled with the shadow of a beard. He was dressed well, much like a businessman, but more casual as he lacked a tie and the top buttons of his shirt had been casually left undone. His clothes screamed wealth; he was not the image that typically came to mind when she imagined what a kidnapper might look like. It was his eyes, however, that struck her to her core. Even as he maintained a matter of fact, almost pragmatic, composure, his eyes told her a different story altogether. When she first gazed into those dark blue eyes, she noticed flecks of green that added life and vitality to his stare. Within the depth of his gaze a far more sinister side was revealed of him, a side that remained hidden, waiting for the chance to strike. Even as she trembled, frozen in place by his gaze, she was captivated by his beauty.

"HAPPY BIRTHDAY!!!!"

She jumped at the booming salutation and was instantly dragged from her thoughts by the shouts and bellows resonating throughout the room. Laughter erupted, followed by crude comments and jabs at the man who'd entered. From what Maddy could hear, the man who'd entered was not happy to be there as he was teased for not donning a smile. Her heart skipped and the violent shaking of her body returned. Her breathing quickly became labored and the thick air in the box was making her lightheaded. If he'd arrived, that meant she would soon be *unwrapped* and she wasn't particularly interested to know what would happen to her next.

"Aaron. I'm so glad you could join your own party." A man's voice rose over the others.

Aaron?

"Smile, son. Everybody is gathered to celebrate your life ... the least you could do is look like you *enjoy* being here." A veiled threat was evident in the man's words. The room grew eerily quiet; so quiet, that Maddy swore others would hear the pounding of her heart.

"I apologize father, but I had business to attend to." Audible contempt rolled off those words. The man's voice was so familiar; she couldn't place where she'd heard it, but she was sure she recognized the voice. Even though her mind couldn't place the sound, her body froze to hear it. Instinct was more aware than intellect in that moment.

"Of course, Aaron. I understand you are a busy man, so let's get right to it. I have a very special gift for your twenty-fifth birthday. I thought long and hard trying to decide the perfect gift for a man turning a quarter of a century old, and I believe I've found exactly what you wanted."

Her body clenched to a point of pain. Her breaths coming out in short pants as it felt like her heart would tear through the walls of her chest. A soft whimper escaped her, so overtaken by fear that she was losing control. Panic set in. This was the moment she would finally face the man to whom she now *belonged*. She would never be used to those words; *slave, master, belong*; she was now property and nothing more.

The room grew quiet and Maddy could hear slow, steady footsteps approaching her. Curling herself tighter, she was desperate to hide from what she knew was to come. Two quick taps sounded against the walls of the box.

"Let me guess, father, you bought me a pony." The voice was a deep baritone, the tone mocking and resentful.

That voice ... so familiar ...

She could hear the soft swish of material, just as the box was jarred sideways and the walls began to fall. When the perspiration of her skin met with the chilled air of the room, she shivered from the sudden change in temperature, not daring to uncurl herself from the tight position she held.

"What is this?!" Cold anger saturated those words; spoken softly, they were made even more terrifying.

Fingers entwined themselves in the back of her hair just before her head was pulled upwards,

35

pain splitting along her scalp from the forceful hold. An intake of breath, fingers loosening in her hair, she slowly opened her eyes and was met with the emerald greens eyes of the man who'd given her the rose on the night of her performance.

"Madeleine Clark?" His voice was a whisper drowned in disbelief and shock. His eyes changed from confusion to anger almost instantly, but became blank as a mask fell over his face, effectively hiding his thoughts. Turning in the direction of the older man from the parking lot, he released his hold on her hair, only to replace the grip of his large hand around her arm. Maddy flinched not knowing what he intended to do next.

A cough sounded from within the room and Madeleine forced her eyes off of the man who held her and turned to look at her surroundings. The sheer opulence of the room was unexpected. Madeleine gasped when her eyes were flooded with the decadent dark wood furnishings and the collection of luxurious fabrics used to fill the large space. The vaulted ceilings rounded into a dome, with dark wood beams running evenly spaced, all meeting at the center. Below the point where the beams met hung a large, breathtakingly elegant chandelier made entirely of fine crystal. It filled the top space entirely, the lights dancing off the multi-faceted crystal; small rainbows of color cast upon the cream paint of the ceiling.

Maddy's eyes traveled down, taking in the burgundy red of the walls. The richness of the dark color was broken apart by exquisitely detailed tapestries and large oil paintings in gilded frames. The stark beauty of the room was inspired, every

36

detail obvious in the loving touch of its designer. Maddy couldn't make sense of how such beauty existed within the same place as the dark and damp room in which she'd awakened.

For a fleeting moment, she was relieved of her fear, her embarrassment and her torment as her eyes danced along the wonder of her surroundings. However, she was quickly pulled back to her nightmare when she heard laughter erupt within the space.

Turning back, she remembered her nudity and attempted to curl back into herself, attempting to hide from the surrounding people.

"Surprise, Aaron! I do hope you like her. I thought long and hard about your *gift*." The father's voice rattled Maddy's nerves. Forcing back a whimper, she closed her eyes to block out the stares of the audience around her. Her skin crawled as Aaron's father continued the sardonic explanation for his gift to his son. "I've noticed that you've never taken interest in the slaves kept by The Estate. It's concerned me, to say the least." His father laughed a humorless laugh before continuing in a threatening tone, "I've even wondered if it was possible that you fancied Xander a bit too much."

The partygoers quietly laughed at the father's teasing remark. He waited for silence to resettle over the room before he continued again, his voice booming throughout the large room. "I struggled with what to get you, Aaron; but then, it was brought to my attention that you had an appreciation for this particular woman ... that you'd even approached her on the night of her

37

performance. Once I learned of your interest in her, I was delighted to finally find the perfect gift."

Aaron stood perfectly still, like a coiled snake, muscles tense and ready to strike. His hand gripped Maddy's arm tighter, causing her to wince in pain. Almost instantly, he loosened his grip. His voice was smooth and controlled as he responded to his father's explanation, "Thank you. I shall see to her now if it pleases you."

After another soft wave of laughter, the partygoers were not sure whether they should believe Aaron's words. He pulled on Madeleine's arm, urging her down from the table upon which she was displayed. She resisted, every instinct within her begging her to scream ... to fight against being pulled along to the next attack she would face. His head whipped around to look at her before he leaned down to whisper in her ear. His voice was rough with anger, a subtle threat wrapped within his tone. "You will get down from that table and follow me if you know what's good for you. DO NOT fight against me, Madeleine. It will bring you more harm than good."

Her body convulsed with terror, her muscles suddenly becoming weak. Fearing the sting of another beating, she slowly uncurled herself, tears seeping from her eyes from the shame of her unclothed state. When her eyes met Aaron's, Maddy thought she saw a small glimpse of compassion; but when she looked deeper, she saw nothing more than the lethal edge of a honed blade. Aaron's beauty was a wicked veil; mystifying and lulling those that looked upon him into a false sense

38

of awe, only to have that security ripped from them when they saw the menace lurking beneath.

She turned and moved her legs over the edge of the table. Pushing down, her feet met with the cool stone floor. Violently, her body shook as she steadied herself on legs burning from the cramped conditions and uncomfortable position she'd been forced to hold in the box. Once she was standing, Aaron pulled her to him, his warmth enveloping her skin where they touched. She was sickened by her enjoyment of that warmth, wanting to feel nothing more than revulsion at the man holding her captive. She kept her eyes trained on the floor as they moved through the space. Walking along a center aisle, she knew she was in full view of every soul within that room. Aaron's father sat at a center table along the left side, his voice booming out as they passed.

"She is a slave, Aaron. I want to make sure that you understand that fact." It was a warning Maddy could not fully comprehend. "I expect that she will be trained accordingly."

Maddy looked up at Aaron, noticed the curt nod of his head toward his father before he pulled her along to the door. Aaron stopped, turning suddenly, his eyes met with those of the man that had removed her from the dark room. The silent exchange between the two men was understood as the man moved to take up his position behind them.

The silence between the three was only broken by the sounds of the men's shoes along the floors of the hall; each step echoing back steadily

39

and in perfect time with the other. Maddy's heart felt like it would tear through her skin, her throat closing, making it difficult for her to breathe. Her bare feet ached from the chill of the stones upon which she walked as it seeped past her skin into the delicate bones. Her neck hurt and felt locked, her body continued to tremble from fear of where she was being led. Desperately, her mind ran back to any memory that would help her escape the present. She thought about the fear she'd felt before her performance that night, about how silly that fear seemed in comparison to her current circumstances. She forced her thoughts to a place far from where she stood, to a time when she was safe within the confines of a sheltered life. Her uncle had raised her in a meager home after her parents died when she was young. Their home could have fit within the ballroom she'd just occupied, but it was warm, filled with love of each other and the love of music. She'd never understood wealth growing up, never knew the need of anything beyond the warmth of the home her uncle had provided her.

They stopped suddenly, causing Madeleine to bump against Aaron's back before she could stop herself. Peeking up through her lashes, she watched as his eyes moved to hers; her fear returning in a dizzying wave when their gazes locked. Instantly she felt violated by his stare; his eyes seemed to penetrate the hidden depths within her.

Xander stepped around them, his hand grasping the handles to the large, rounded set of doors. He pushed down on the handles and against the doors, both opening to reveal another large room on the other side. Aaron turned his attention away from her, pulling her with him as he entered the room.

Her eyes were assaulted by the continued theme of decadence and luxury that permeated every corner of the space. The room would have been foreboding in the choice of dark, rich colors and dark wood furniture, if not for the lighter colored accent of silk throw pillows and the cloth spread along a large dining table. They entered into a living room area that was offset by the elegant dining area to the right. The living space was filled with plush leather couches, the leather stained to a deep red brown. Wing-backed accent chairs were set amongst the sofas. The walls of the living area were lined with floor to ceiling bookshelves with expensive, superb decorations perfectly placed among the large leather bound tomes.

Two sets of rounded, wooden doors set opposite one another on either side of the living space. This room, just as the last, was large with high ceilings that also curved into a dome. However, unlike the other room, the chandelier in this room was formed from dark iron, one large circle that hung heavily upon four chains, lights fashioned to mimic candles dotting along the circular frame. Unlike the splendor of the crystal from the other room, this chandelier held a far more mystical feel, masculine in its formation, casting shadow rather than light.

"Sit here." Maddy was shoved down onto one of the large couches in the room. Instinctively, she folded over herself, the feel of leather against

41

her skin reminding her of her nudity. She flinched when Aaron's hand came down to move her hair away from her face. His gentle touch was striking in its contrast to the cold and unfeeling expression painted across his face; his eyes only momentarily widening at the mark left on her cheek. His tone was abnormally soft as he instructed, "Stay on this couch, Madeleine. The doors are locked, preventing your escape. You will only anger me if you attempt to move away from where I've placed you." Like fur along her skin, his voice soothed her. Her brain raged against the comfort, finding it disconcerting, given the monster that must reside within his exquisite beauty.

He removed his hand from her, only to turn in the direction of the other man. "Xander, follow me." Walking through one set of doors, the two men left her alone. She cowered in fear, trying to bury herself within the folds of the leather couch.

Chapter Five

Aaron watched as Xander closed the doors behind them. Once the large wooden doors were secured, Aaron's eyes narrowed on his best friend and guard. "Did you take part in this?" Seething anger rolled off the carefully spoken words, Aaron's inquiry carrying an underlying question of Xander's loyalty.

"No."

Aaron looked over his friend and saw nothing but honesty in Xander's casual posture and in the calm manner of his response. "I wasn't informed of her presence until she'd arrived to the compound. There was no time between my becoming aware and the event for me to tell you what your father had done."

Every muscle in Aaron's body clenched with the thought of his father's *gift*. He'd known for years that the old man's mind was slipping into a cavern of deeper depravity, but he'd never imagined he could sink to this depth. The capture and enslavement of an innocent woman; she had nothing to do with his family; she owed nothing to The Estate. The heavy blanket of guilt settled over his thoughts; Aaron knew this woman had been stripped from her life due to his interest in her.

His mind drifted to the small woman, currently cowered like a cornered mouse in his living room. "What are we to do with her, Xander? You heard what my father said; she is to be treated

43

like a slave and nothing more. Has he lost his fucking mind?!" Aaron's hand shot out beside him, violently knocking aside the papers and objects littered along his desk.

Xander winced at the sound of the breaking glass. His face remaining trained on Aaron's, a fierce determination within him to calm the raging bull. "He lost his mind many years ago, Aaron, you know that."

Fury, like a poisonous river, coursed through Aaron's veins, splintering and fracturing within the capillaries of his skin. Fists clenched at his sides, he could feel the pins and needles from the blood loss to his hands. With steps, pulsing and heavy, he paced along the dark wooden floors of his office.

Xander's voice broke through the pounding of blood within Aaron's head. "He seeks to control you, Aaron; to tame you by forcing you into corruption. It is the same game you've played with him since the beginning." Xander's posture relaxed as he brought his hand up as if to inspect his fingernails. "I don't understand how you can be so shocked."

Aaron glared at his first guard for the flippancy of his statement. Yes, his father had grown madder with age; once keeping his crimes within the dealings of business, he'd eventually moved on to cruelties only possible for those who'd lost all sense of morality. Dipping into the shallow dealings of drug trades and prostitutes, murder and conspiracy, his father had kept his crimes limited to the lowest of society, to other criminals who knew beforehand what they were getting themselves into. But this girl? She did not belong in this world. She had done nothing to deserve this fate. The cobalt light of her eyes flashed within his mind, the gleam he'd seen as she'd spoken to him backstage. Even then, she appeared afraid, but nothing like in the ballroom, the gleam all but removed by the dark tint of fear within her wide-open eyes.

"I'm not shocked that my father has acted against me, yet again. His obsessive need to drag me to his level has grown old. He knows I will not reduce myself to garbage. I will not mess with innocent lives!" The walls shook from the strength of Aaron's voice, he grimaced at the thought that, perhaps, the mouse could hear him through the walls.

Xander chuckled, further enraging Aaron. No other man could get away with Xander's actions; but the two men had grown up together. Xander was Aaron's friend before he became his guard.

"Well, what do you suggest we do with this new development? If you free her, we die. It's the only reason we remain locked up in this hell hole ... our lives are at stake." Xander's voice lowered on those last words, not wanting to vocalize the futility of their plight.

A lengthy pause before Aaron's words rolled from his lips. "I will die. Your use of the word 'we' is erroneous."

45

Their eyes met and each man's posture straightened from the exchange. The silence between them was as palpable as was Xander's loyalty to his friend. "You are mistaken, Aaron ... " His words spoken smoothly, pointedly, " ... if not in this hell, then I will exist in the one that welcomes you upon death."

Aaron turned, raising his hand to brush aside Xander's words. "No need to rush the inevitable. For now, we'll deal with this one." Picking up a pewter letter opener from his desk, he pressed his finger to the pointed tip, calculating his next step. Silence fell heavy upon the two men before Aaron finally spoke again. "I won't train her. That bastard looks to corrupt me, but I'll have nothing to do with this game. We need to decide on another approach. I want nothing to do with that woman; not in this place."

"If you feel nothing for her, why did you approach her backstage at the concert hall? Why not just accept what your father has given you, play along until we can ensure that more men are loyal to your side? We've been working toward ending that asshole! We can't afford to screw it up over that woman."

With unspoken threat, Aaron stepped forward toward Xander. His hands were again itching to strike out, to show Xander that under no terms would he defile Madeleine. Aaron was not a good man. He'd cheated in business, he'd killed when it was required, but never had he acted against an innocent person; and never had he taken a woman against her will.

"You can't ignore her. She has been gifted to you as your slave. I'm sure you understand exactly what is entailed in the role of her Master. If your father suspects you've disobeyed his directive, I hate to think what consequences will follow; not only for you, but for the girl."

Like the sharpest of blades, Xander's words instantly sliced through Aaron's resolve, reminding him that his decision would not only bring torment to his life, but to hers as well. Aaron loathed the choice he would have to make. Madeleine would need to learn the expected behaviors of a slave and the hierarchy of the Estate. She would endure ridicule and humiliation in her role, the injustice of being forced to act against her own will. Aaron wasn't sure such a small, innocent thing could survive the role that even the most corrupt and sinful of women could barely tolerate.

"Fine." One word, gritty against his throat, swelled closed from contained rage. "We'll train her; but she will not endure the abuse of the other slaves."

Xander's expression betrayed his confusion and disbelief at Aaron's words. "And how do you expect to pull that off? You know we are constantly watched. Your father's men will never let even the slightest infraction slip ... "

"We're not watched here." Aaron's rage finally overwhelming him, his tone was raised, yet cold; each word spoken slowly, effectively: "She's safe within the confines of my apartment. There's plenty of space."

47

"But, he will want her displayed, Aaron. You cannot hide her away in here forever. He will want to see that his *gift* has been accepted ... used ... *properly.*"

Aaron stomped toward the doors, the weight of his feet sending tremors through the wooden floor. "This discussion is over for now. She will be trained, but do NOT violate her, Xander. You are a better man than that." His hand slammed down upon the handle. A gust of wind blew against his face as the air objected to the movement of the large wooden doors. His eyes instantly sought her. She remained where he'd left her, balled tightly in the middle of the large sofa. Even if you weren't looking for her, you still wouldn't be able to miss her; the dark mahogany of her hair and the alabaster tone of her skin helping her contrast sharply against the rich, brown leather.

As Aaron passed, he noticed how her body would flinch with each approaching footstep, how her skin was prickled from the cold of the room. Cursing the situation, he turned to enter his bedrooms through the opposite set of doors. He walked the long corridor, finally bursting through the door at the end of the hall. His bedroom was another large, ornately decorated space; lavish fabrics and dark woods softened by the elegant touch of fine metals and plush carpeting. He only used the room for sleeping, spending much of his time outside of the large compound, or buried deep within business in his office. Marching toward the bureaus, he ripped open a drawer to grab a pair of sweat pants and a black t-shirt. The clothes would swallow her, but he couldn't let her sit around pissing herself from the frigid air in the rooms.

The back of the bureau collided heavily with the wall as Aaron closed the drawer. Spinning on his heel, he noticed Xander standing quietly in the doorway to his room. "Who are the clothes for? Please tell me you're feeling the need to dress more casually."

"They're for the girl." Noting the disapproval in Xander's expression, Aaron quickly added, "Has she eaten, or gone to the bathroom; hell ... or been bathed?" Before Xander could respond, Aaron moved his hand dismissively to his own question. "The concert was last night, it hasn't been twenty-four hours since the time they could have grabbed her." His words came out a tired mumble, as if thinking aloud rather than attempting communication.

"She was bathed before the party. She ... pissed herself when Marcus tried to pull her from the room."

Aaron's voice thundered at what Xander had just explained, "Marcus?! What the fuck was Marcus doing anywhere near her?! Is he the reason for the mark on her face?"

Xander let out a calming breath. "Yes. Marcus was placed on our team today. He'll be removed and never allowed near her again for his inability to follow instruction." Xander's eyes looked directly into Aaron's, his honesty and intent evident, but a touch of guilt darkened his gaze. "I requested that Marcus retrieve her; I didn't consider that he would be violent in his task."

Brushing past Xander, Aaron exited the room and walked briskly through the corridor, back out into the main room. He approached Maddy, but stopped short when her body began to visibly tremble at his close proximity.

"I've brought you some clothes." His voice thundered through the room causing Maddy to whimper at the sound. Aaron's head tilted as he stretched his neck, relaxing the taut muscles. Lowering his voice so that it was softer, he said, "They're likely too big for you, but they will warm you up."

Madeleine continued to quietly shake, Aaron's patience waning with each passing second that she didn't respond. He opened his mouth to command her, scare her into submission, but his compassion got the better of him in that moment. She was so small, so absolutely terrified that she was nearly catatonic. Xander entered the living room and Aaron walked past him, forcefully shoving the clothing into Xander's hands. "Make sure she puts these on. See to her basic needs, but let her sleep after that. I'm in no mood for defiance tonight. We'll start the training in the morning." He began to walk away, but stopped abruptly, turning to quietly ask, "Has she spoken since she's been here?"

Nodding in response, Xander's eyes flicked to the huddled woman. "She spoke to me very little, but she spoke."

50

One curt nod and Aaron moved toward his office, disappearing behind the large wooden doors before slamming them closed.

Xander moved slowly toward Maddy. His steps were soft against the floor, not wanting to startle her as he approached. In a soothing voice, he cooed, "Tsk, Tsk, little Cricket. That is not the way we treat our Master."

Chapter Six

Madeleine had heard bits and pieces of the men arguing behind those large doors. The angry tone of Aaron's words was terrifying, only punctuated by the high-pitched splinter of crashing glass, the heavy sound of the larger objects hitting the floor. Her muscles quivered and rippled in revolt of their constant constriction from fear.

Her mind was tired, flooded with chemicals, drowning in panic and dread. However, even as terrifying as the heated argument had been, it compared little to the moment he passed her by. Each step echoing, brushing against her senses, warning her of his approach. Adrenaline coursing through her veins, screaming for her to run even though she knew there was nowhere for her to go. Her mind, racing with ideas and images of what he would do next. She'd tightened into herself, pushing past the exhaustion of her body; but he'd kept walking ... without a touch or a sound. When he'd walked through the opposite set of doors, she forced back a sob, finding that the waiting, the not knowing, was the most terrifying part of all.

"You'll need to stand and get dressed, Cricket. There is no tolerance for disobedience where you are concerned."

Cricket ....

That name he kept calling her, a false semblance of affection. It was the type of name you were given as a child: from a man to a girl; from a

52

father to a daughter; from an uncle to a niece. It sickened her to hear the pet name, knowing full well this man held no affection for her at all.

Xander's hand came down to brush against her face. Moving aside the clumped and knotted strands of her hair, he removed her from the only hiding place she had. He brought her back to the present, to the undeniable truth of the nightmare from which she couldn't wake: staring squarely into the beautiful faces of the monsters that held her. Growing up, her uncle always warned her that evil hid itself within the most enticing of forms, drawing its victims in with a false sense of wonder … of hope. Madeleine now understood his warnings, wishing she'd never ventured out of their small, warm home, into the night that would grab her and never let her go.

"Stand, Cricket. NOW!" His voice shook her small frame. If not for her fear of being struck, she would have remained wrapped within the cocoon of her body. Forcing herself into an upright position, tears leaked from her eyes, small bits of heat sliding along her cheeks, turning cold before running along the crease of her lips. The salty taste seeped into her mouth; another reminder of her pain. Her muscles screamed in objection as she stretched out her small frame. Her arms instantly moved to cover her breasts, shame once again enveloping her thoughts. Xander remained quiet, allowing her the time to adjust, to come into compliance with his request.

Shakily, her legs held her as she stood at full height. Much shorter than the man who stood before her, she could only see his chest, his pants, his shoes; not daring to look up into his watchful eyes. He extended the clothes to her, holding them low so that they would be within her line of sight. "Put these on and then I'll escort you to the restroom. Are you hungry?"

Maddy shook her head, the movement barely visible, but Xander still noted her refusal to eat. "Very well. Take the clothes." His hands pushed them forward, causing to her to jump back when they came in contact with her skin. She forced out a breath before reaching out to accept his offering. Her modesty got the better of her as she turned herself to get dressed.

"No." His hands came up to gently grab her shoulders, turning her back to face him. "You must learn to accept your nudity. Outside of these walls, it will be the only thing you know. Your Master is being kind by providing you these clothes, but do not expect that same level of kindness from anyone else within The Estate. You should appreciate him. He risks himself by allowing you this small comfort." Xander's words were spoken in a soothing voice, but still the words cut like a razor.

Anyone else ... so she was to be passed around to multiple people; a plaything and nothing more.

Another rush of air, her breath quickly left her as she accepted her fate. She placed the clothes on the table beside her, choosing to pull on the large t-shirt first, effectively covering herself as quickly as possible. The t-shirt could have been a dress. Hanging down to her knees, it swallowed the majority of her small frame. Xander chuckled

54

softly. "With as small as you are, I see no need for the pants, but I'm sure you would like as much covering as possible."

Her hand stilled over the pants while she waited for him to finish his remark. As soon as the last syllable had left his tongue, her hand grasped the fabric, pulling it to her. Putting the pants on one shaky leg at a time, she pulled the full length of the material over her body. Xander chuckled again when he noticed how the waistband met with her chest. "It appears I need to go shopping. It'll be interesting trying to smuggle clothes in unnoticed."

Maddy jumped again when his hands gripped the waistband of the pants, his knuckles brushing across the tips of her breasts through the thin material of her shirt. Arching away from his touch, her eyes peeked up into his. Her breath caught at the sight of his blue eyes; the color reminiscent of a stormy sea. Perfectly white teeth appeared as he grinned. His hands moved the waistband of the pants to the widest part of her hips; his fingers pulled the drawstring tight before tying it in place.

"Those should do for now. Follow me." Xander's lean frame moved with feline grace as he led her down the corridor of a long hallway. The flexion and contraction of his muscular form clearly visible beneath the black shirt that he wore. Like Aaron, Xander exuded a quiescent danger, the same as that of a sleeping tiger. She broke her gaze from him, her eyes moving to take in the expensive wallpaper and chair rails that lined the halls. Stopping suddenly, Xander turned, extending his hand to direct her to a room on her right. "The restroom is in there."

55

Maddy began to brush past him to enter the room when his hand came up to grip around her bicep. His lips tickled against her ear as he spoke. "There is no way for you to escape that room. The window is sealed and I will wait outside this door. Use the bathroom, wash your face, and brush your teeth, then return to the hallway." Maddy nodded her head in understanding before Xander would let her go. Without a word, she entered the bathroom and closed the door behind her; her continued silence the only escape she had from the hell in which she'd found herself.

Like the other rooms, the bathroom was large and magnificent. Maddy briefly wondered what amount of money it took to maintain a home like this. The floors of the bathroom were the same dark slate grey stone as the hallway leading into Aaron's apartment. Black granite was used for the counters, bathtub and shower. Glass brick walls were used to separate the different spaces. Scattered throughout the large room were plush carpets that felt soft against Maddy's bare feet. The walls were a muted grey but the darkness of the room was broken apart by the dancing light reflected off the polished silver fixtures and crystal soap dishes. Even this bathroom hadn't been spared the fine works of art that had adorned the walls of each room she'd seen within the estate.

She moved quickly across the room, having needed to relieve herself for several hours. The sensation of such a simple thing as emptying her bladder was a welcome gift, a thing she'd never considered would one day be something of a courtesy bestowed upon her by another individual.

She grimaced to realize that even the most basic human needs could be denied upon the whim of her captors. Two taps on the door alerted her to the fact that she'd apparently taken too long. Hurriedly, she moved to the sink, splashed warm water on her face before unwrapping one of the guest toothbrushes and cleaning her mouth. The feeling of clean teeth was suddenly a luxury that she had, up until her capture, always taken for granted.

After placing the toothbrush on the counter, Maddy returned to the hallway as instructed. Silently, Xander led her deeper down the corridor to another room. He opened the door and motioned for her to enter. Maddy's steps failed her, causing her to stumble at the sight of the large bed in the center of the room. Her head spun to look at Xander, a silent question of his intent. His eyes looked deep within hers; his lips, a pinched line across his face.

"Tonight, it is for sleeping only, per your Master's instructions."

A relieved sigh racked her body, a shiver snaking along her spine. However, still not quite trusting Xander's words, Maddy moved to the opposite corner of the room, as far from the bed as possible. She watched as his shoulders shook with silent laughter. "If I wanted to take you, Cricket, the distance you put between the bed and yourself wouldn't prevent me from doing so." Flashing her a quick grin, he turned and sauntered out of the room, closing and locking the door behind him as he left.

Her posture relaxed at his absence and, suddenly, her eyelids felt heavy. As exhaustion consumed every muscle in her body, Maddy's eyes set upon the soft blankets of the bed. Sleep. She needed sleep, but she knew that the fear of what she would awaken to in the morning would keep her from ever crossing that blessed edge between wakefulness and slumber. Still, lying down would bring her some peace, another small courtesy extended by Aaron. She wondered about his intentions. Was he being kind now, only to gain her trust so that his eventual violation of her would be easier to accomplish?

The plush carpeting rubbed against her feet, forcing itself up between her toes as she slowly crept toward the bed. Reaching out, she ran her hand along the soft fabrics, the quiet only amplifying the sound of skin sliding against silk. She was hesitant as she climbed up onto the mattress, not sure if Aaron's kindness would be rescinded. The exhaustion finally taking over, Madeleine curled up with the velvety throw blanket that had been spread along the base of the bed. The thick material instantly warmed her.

As her eyes drifted closed and she hovered between consciousness and dreamless sleep, she heard the door to her room open, a familiar rattling soon followed. She was pulled violently from her lethargic state, her heart skipping slightly due to its sudden return to a fast pace. She pushed up on the mattress with both arms, instinctively forcing her body backwards off the bed, and moving to crouch in a corner at the farthest wall.

58

A dark laugh, Xander was amused at her behavior. "Ahhh, my little Cricket, whatever will I do with you?" The loud clatter of chains hitting the floor. "I thought I'd bring you something else to wear. You do remember the shackles, don't you? Unfortunately, little one, you'll be wearing these tonight as well. We can't take the risk of your escape."

All hint of affection gone, Xander bent down, retrieving one end of the chain before moving to secure it to the heavy foot of the bed. The threat of tears burned Maddy's eyes as she put her hands out and shook her head; silently begging for him to leave her unchained. A sympathetic mask fell over his face, but was quickly replaced with an expression of disinterest.

He moved quickly across the room, catching her as easily as if she hadn't moved at all. His speed was disorienting, catching her off guard before she could even react. She screamed, the volume of her cry scratching painfully against her already raw throat.

"Cricket, calm down!" With a quickness akin to that of a snake, Xander pushed Maddy face down across the bed. Pressing one large hand against the center of her back, he used his other to restrain her legs. His chest heaved against her shoulder as he leaned over her. Maddy screamed again, unable to simply accept what was being done.

The bedroom door burst open again. "What in the hell is going on in here?!" Aaron came marching through the open door, stopping

59

suddenly when he saw Xander pressed down against Maddy's back. "Xander. Explain, NOW!"

A tiny, metallic click as Xander finished locking the shackle around Madeleine's ankle. Pushing himself up, he smoothed down the front of his shirt and pants, his already messy hair made even more so by the struggle. "I was attaching a chain to the woman, ensuring that you and I sleep well tonight, not worrying about whether she would attempt escape." Seeing the rage behind Aaron's eyes, Xander quickly realized what it must have looked like when Aaron walked in. "I promise you, Aaron, that is all that was happening in here. You can ask the little cricket yourself ... if she'll speak, that is."

Aaron's eyes narrowed; rage, a smoldering ember building within him. "And who instructed you to chain the girl?" The tone of his words sent chills over Maddy's skin; dark and lethal, Aaron's voice betrayed the menace within his thoughts.

Xander stood speechless for several seconds, finally brushing off Aaron's veiled question and the implied threat. "No one, Aaron. I assumed ... "

"YOU ASSUMED WRONG!" His voice boomed throughout the room, rattling the windows, causing Maddy to jump from the sudden anger that rolled from his voice. "Now remove that fucking chain before I shackle your ass to a bed tonight!"

Maddy was sure Xander would flinch at Aaron's threat, but when she dared look up at him,

60

she noticed a coolness about him that was unexpected. Xander simply nodded at Aaron and reached down to remove the shackle from her ankle. After he'd removed the chain, he let it slip from his hand to the floor. "Aaron, I do not want to question you in front of the woman, can we speak privately in the hallway ... please?" Disdain dripped from that last word, his lack of trust in Aaron's decision evident in his tone.

Aaron's hand reached behind him, finding the handle to the door and forcefully pushing the door open, before stepping backwards out into the hall. His eyes never left Xander as he exited the room. Once Aaron had moved to accept Xander's request, Xander walked swiftly across the room, exiting through the door before shutting it silently behind him.

Maddy could not hear the discussion between the two men, but instead, she used the opportunity to remove herself from the bed, moving to the corner of the room where she sunk to the ground, curling herself back into a protective ball. Her heart pounded against her chest and her chest heaved from her heavy breath and the sobs she attempted to suppress. Her muscles, once again, screamed at the constriction of being curved in on herself; the tight ball she assumed, an unforgiving position that her body had never known until arriving to this place.

The door swung open again; both men, silhouettes against the bright light of the hallway. Xander silently marched around the bed picking up the chain and moving back to the door. He brushed past Aaron as he exited out into the hall. Aaron stepped into the room, slowly closing the door behind him. Once closed, the room was reduced to darkness, only the moonlight from the windows providing enough light so that Maddy could track him as he crossed the room. He stopped just short of her, his tall frame hovering over her like she was a child.

Her sobs finally broke free of her throat and tears that she wasn't sure she could produce trailed down her cheeks. Fear crippled her body as Aaron stood above her. After a few moments, he reached down, stopping suddenly when her body trembled violently in response to his movement.

"I'm going to lead you back to the bed, Madeleine. You need sleep. I have ordered Xander to leave you unchained, however I will tell you that your escape is impossible from this room. The windows cannot be broken and the door will remain locked from the outside."

His large hand wrapped around her upper arm as he gently pulled her up from the floor. She attempted to stand, having no choice but to comply, but her muscles failed her and were unable to hold up her weight. She dared look up into Aaron's eyes and was surprised to be met with compassion behind those gorgeous green orbs. His smooth voice softly rubbed against her as he said, "I'm going to pick you up. Nothing will be done to you, except to be placed back in bed. Do not scream."

Madeleine stared up at him, confused as to why he protected her. He was, after all, one of the monsters, one of the men who were holding her against her will, forcefully taking her freedom. Curling up into herself, she dared not move, too afraid that he would change his mind; too afraid that she would not escape being beaten or raped by either of the men who'd been handling her.

After placing her on the bed, he immediately released her, backing away so that distance was between them; but he never left the room. He watched her, his broad shoulders, thin waist and hips, silhouetted by the hallway light behind him. She wanted to beg for him to let her go, convince him in some way that she deserved her freedom, but her voice failed her. Frozen in place, she remained huddled, knowing full well she was at the mercy of the man that stood before her.

Chapter Seven

Aaron stood watching her as she lay perfectly still on the large bed. Not wanting to further torment her with his touch, he'd placed her down and immediately stepped away. Although she would need to learn to accept the touch of a stranger, to obey his commands; tonight, he would let her sleep, so that she could better accept the fate that had been handed to her.

Her entire body was bathed in shadow, only a large black mass existed where he knew she lay; but still, he couldn't look away. Achingly, his heart went out to this gentle musician; one who'd done nothing wrong, who'd dedicated her life to her music. She knew nothing of the evils that awaited her, the futility of existing as nothing more than property ... an object to be used and tossed aside. Aaron knew he had to do something for the poor mouse, anything that could keep her moderately safe, while not seeming to defy his father's instructions. Even though she was veiled by the cold, darkness of the room, he could see her body tremble at his presence.

"I truly am sorry for this, Madeleine." His voice was nothing more than a whisper as he stepped out into the hall, softly shutting and locking the door behind him.

Aaron's steps were surefooted and strong as he marched down the corridor to the living room. Xander silently fell in step behind him, matching each of Aaron's steps with his own. Shutting the doors to the hallway, Aaron continued forward, directly through the living room and through the doors of his office. He took a seat behind his large desk, leaning back into his chair while steepling his fingers before touching the tips of his index fingers to his mouth. Xander moved to sit in one of the large wingback chairs opposite Aaron, the smooth surface of the desk creating a barrier between the two men.

Silence, a heavy weight hanging over their heads, Xander finally spoke. "I'm sorry for my actions earlier. I thought you would want the woman bound. She could easily break the windows to attempt escape."

Aaron's eyes ran over the tapestries and paintings that adorned the walls of his office. His mind was a ticking machine as he pondered how he would handle his father's gift. Finally coming to a decision, he turned suddenly to face Xander across the large wooden expanse of the desk. "Even if she were to able to break one of those windows, we both know she would not make it off the grounds of the compound. She would be found ... returned."

"But in what condition?"

A humorless laugh escaped Aaron as he responded, "Now, THAT, Xander, is something I intend to take care of this evening." His movement was fluid as he stood, crossing the room, expecting fully that Xander would follow. He stopped suddenly, twisting to look over his shoulder at his best friend. "Don't tell me you meant to protect

65

her with those chains .... " His voice carried an air of mockery. "Have you come to care about our little mouse?"

Bowing his head slightly, Xander responded, "She is so weak, Aaron. I wonder how she will survive." Aaron was shocked at Xander's confession. Although he knew his best friend and first guard was, at the core, a moral man, he'd never witnessed him show concern for anyone's safety but Aaron's.

"She'll survive; but I'll need to speak with *daddy* to make sure of it." Xander's eyes widened in response to Aaron's statement, but he faithfully fell in step behind him nonetheless. The two men traveled the distance from Aaron's apartment to the ballroom where he knew he would still find his father, piss drunk and covered with whores. Now was the perfect opportunity to cement another rule in this game. His father wanted nothing more than to corrupt his son with his gift, but Aaron wanted to publicly ensure that no one was to touch Madeleine beside himself. If he could get his father to agree to the new condition in front of the members of the Estate, his father would have to honor that condition, forbidding every man at the compound to touch that which was Aaron's.

Two men, both dressed in black on black suits, moved to open the large, double doors so that Aaron and Xander could pass through. After their grand entrance, the chaos of the room quickly hushed when the revelers noticed who had returned to the party. As expected, his father sat upon his would-be throne; one woman massaging his shoulders while another had her head buried in

66

his lap. His face showed no reaction to the bobbing of her head, his shame at public displays such as this, lost years before. Eyes the color of steel moved to look at Aaron; the father finally acknowledged the presence of the son.

"Aaron ... " His slurred words reverberated throughout the hushed silence of the room, " ... so good of you to return to the celebration of *your* birth. I do hope you've found ... enjoyment from your *gift*." Laughter, drowned in mockery and disdain rolled from his father's lips; his sloppy movements and slurred words made his inebriation blindingly apparent. "What brings you back? I thought for sure you'd be riding her raw this evening." Another dark laugh. "Or, has it been so long that you're all dried up?"

Aaron waited for the responsive shouts and jeers by the men in the room to simmer down before answering. "I thank you for the gift, *father*, however, I have a condition I'd like to request before I agree to use her as you require. You see, I prefer my dick not shrivel and fall off my body, so I have a thing about not fucking whores who have been passed around liberally."

A perfect eyebrow arched quizzically on his father's brow. "And what, exactly, is it you're requesting, Aaron?" His father's voice deepened as he spoke. Aaron hoped that his father believed he'd succeeded in finally corrupting him; however, he knew the man was far too shrewd to believe that he had caved so easily. They'd been playing this game for too damn long.

67

"I'm requesting that the slave is mine, alone; that you order your men not to touch her while she remains in my service."

His father's hand grabbed the head still bobbing in his lap, wrenching the woman back by her hair and tossing her aside like nothing more than garbage. She'd cried out at his father's actions, but knew better than to move away. Crouching at his feet, the woman remained motionless, her eyes lowered to the floor, as she waited for when she would be made to continue. Aaron kept his eyes trained on the steel grey eyes of his father, not wanting to look down to see his father's unabashed display.

His father took a moment before responding. Suspiciously eyeing his son, he finally spoke. "I have to admit, I'm a little shocked by your request. I thought for sure you would have tossed her aside, refused my offering."

Rolling his shoulders back, Aaron carefully chose his words. Madeleine's safety was at risk, he needed to ensure she would be viewed as his. "I assume, father, that you located this woman due to my interest in her. Perhaps, you had me followed the night of her performance. Given that to be the case, you know I was interested prior to your gifting of her to me. It would make no sense for me to turn her away now." He made sure his voice was purposeful and strong, showing no signs of his desperate need for his father to agree publicly to his request.

The frantic beat of his heart echoed through Aaron's ears as he waited for his father's response. White noise, a pulsing sound, as the blood rushed through his head. The silence of the room was only disturbed by the shuffle of feet, a cough or the sound of a throat being cleared. It was not only Aaron that waited, but the entire party, as well. Never before had these men seen Aaron take part in the depravities of The Estate, in the cruel and sadistic actions of his father. Yes, Aaron had killed, had taken the lives of those who threatened the network that, over the years, had been built by his father. However, Aaron had acted only against other criminals, other people who'd committed enough evil of their own, that the world would never rue their absence.

If it hadn't been for his father's inebriation, Aaron knew his motives would have been further explored. As it stood, his father could barely remain sitting upright, much less have enough mental function to see past Aaron's intent. "And is it your request that she remain untouched by all of the men in this room? Is she a toy kept for your pleasure alone?"

Weighted was the question his father asked; one intended to goad Aaron into a mistake. He knew his father was placing him in a position to, once again, be reminded who ruled this network of murderers and thieves. If Aaron gave the wrong answer, Madeleine would be dragged out here now so that his father could show him who sat at the top of The Estate. "No, father. I am still well aware that nothing within this compound shall be denied to you. I'm simply requesting that all others be restricted from touching what is mine."

Silence, pregnant with the anticipation of his father's approval, was deafening against Aaron's thoughts. No man spoke, even the short coughs and cleared throats were absent as Aaron awaited his father's directive. Standing firm, his blue eyes never looked away from the scrutiny of the steel grey.

"Well done, Aaron, it's good to see you understand who still sits at the top of this food chain." Shifting in his seat while tucking himself back into his pants, his father raised his hand and snapped, summoning forth Emory, his most trusted man.

"There will be a new decree that needs to be delivered as quickly as possible ..." Emory lowered his head, indicating that the decree would be made known. "... No man shall touch Aaron's slave."

Relief flooded Aaron's body as he fought to keep his stance firm, not wanting the drop of his shoulders, or the relaxation of his muscles to betray his feelings to the group. That relief, however, was short lived.

"However, although no man may touch the slave, it does not mean she can be hidden away." He turned to Aaron, amusement evident in his dark gaze. "She will be displayed when requested by me. It would be a shame for your plaything to be kept, locked away from the enjoyment of The Estate." Lowering his voice to a dangerously low level, he added, "Do not forget that we are a community, my son. One in which, only one man is allowed selfishness."

70

It was not a complete win, but it would do. Aaron lowered his head in silent acknowledgment of his father's directive. The tension between father and son was palpable, causing Emory to clear his throat in order to interrupt the unspoken exchange.

"And if a man breaks the decree, touches the woman without Aaron's permission?"

The steel grey eyes finally released Aaron, redirecting their focus on Emory. "Then that man shall lose whatever part of his body it was that came in contact with her."

Silence again as the group of men took in the seriousness of his words.

Having received what he'd come to request, Aaron inclined his head before turning to leave.

"One more thing, son ... "

Aaron turned back, his eyes meeting the coldest of steel.

"You have five days. I expect that within that time, she will be brought under control, taught the ways of her new life. When that week ends, I'll be calling upon you to display your pet before me, for you to show me how well you can train a slave."

Aware that his father's statement was a command more so than a request, Aaron simply turned to continue his path out of the room, a response was not required.

71

The large doors closed behind them as Aaron and Xander wordlessly traveled down the long hall back to Aaron's apartment. Once they were safely tucked back within the walls of his private space, Aaron moved to the side bar, pulling out a crystal decanter containing the finest scotch money could buy. Filling his glass, he turned to offer a drink to Xander.

"No, thank you. I believe one of us needs to have his wits about him tonight, should our guest attempt her escape." Xander's deep gritty voice carried an air of sarcasm.

Aaron brushed off Xander's remark. He knew the little mouse was most likely tucked safely within sleep's strong arms; she'd been close to collapse even before they'd first reached his apartment.

The liquor bit at the back of Aaron's throat as it went down, distracting him momentarily from the present. A sigh escaped his lips as he moved to sit on the large leather sofa, the same sofa that had earlier held the trembling, terrified woman.

"I'm not worried about her escaping ... not any longer, at least." With words saturated in arrogance, Aaron held the drink up to eyelevel, swirling the liquid within the glass. "It wasn't a complete win, but it will do. I was hoping the old man would have been too drunk or high to remember to correct me on HIS right to her. Even with a whore in his lap, a few bottles down his throat and the drugs he is always taking, his mind is

72

still as shrewd as a viper." Alcohol slowly seeped into his bloodstream and his muscles relaxed as he sank into the thick cushions of the couch. He turned his head to look at Xander. "At what age does dementia start to set in? Is the old man close?" He chuckled. "It certainly would make bringing his ass down a hell of a lot easier."

Xander fought to keep his expression impassive, yet the slight curve to the corner of his mouth gave him away. "I believe we have a few years before we can rely on old age as our ally." He paused, choosing his next words. "What are my instructions for the girl? Am I to start training her in the morning?"

Aaron's brow furrowed in consideration of Xander's question. "No." He sat up to place the glass on the table in front of him. "I think I'll handle her in the morning. She seemed more *receptive* to my company than yours during our last little encounter."

"And what are your plans for her? She's found her voice, apparently. Should I purchase some earplugs for us?" Xander smiled.

Rubbing at the tight muscles of his neck, Aaron chuckled at Xander's joke. In reality, it wasn't funny, they were discussing teaching despicable things to an innocent woman who didn't deserve the horrors she would soon face. "No. I don't think it will be necessary. I have a week to get her ready for her presentation. I believe this can be done with as little fight as possible. Hopefully, we can coax her into submission rather

73

than forcing the issue. However, my instruction still stands that she not be violated in any way."

Nodding in acknowledgement, Xander responded, "Of course."

Exhaustion battering at his body, Aaron stood to walk toward his bedroom. "We'll reconvene in the morning, but, for now, I need my sleep. I'll have my hands full come tomorrow." Sluggishly, Aaron traveled the long corridor until finally reaching his room at the end of the long hall. Stripping off his clothes, Aaron's thoughts continued going back to the small woman currently sleeping in the room down the hall. He thought about how beautiful she'd been when he'd presented the rose to her the night of her performance. Inwardly, he cursed himself for that offering, blamed himself for the events that would soon occur. Walking across the room, he turned on the stereo in his room and was reduced to shame when the lonely and haunting sounds of a cello sprang forth from the speakers. The quality of the music was exquisite, but it was the soul of the musician that called to him from within those notes. Melancholy like he'd never experienced, a kindred spirit singing to him with wordless sound. Images of a beautiful, chestnut-haired woman mastering an instrument, backed by a full orchestra came into his mind. He swore he could feel each touch of her finger to the strings, each pull of the taut hair of the bow. It wasn't just music that was elicited from the combination of wood, metal and Madeleine, it was emotion, thought, a message only understood by those who could appreciate the fine combination of the sea of notes, blended together into an intoxicating song.

Crawling into the warm softness of his bed, his mind drifted with each note of the instrument, as he was lulled into slumber. His heart constricted at the thought that he would end up breaking her, possibly ruining the very thing that had brought him comfort in the unending nightmare he called life.

Chapter Eight

Light flickered in through the window; thin fingers of orange and red touching her face, gently waking her to a new day. Gradually, Maddy was brought from the comforting blankness of slumber's void, back into a nightmare that existed in her waking life. Groggy, she pushed herself up, her muscles protesting the movement, begging for more time to remain slack and immobile. Almost to a point of being closed, her eyes were swollen from tears shed the previous day. Hair clung to her skin, sticky from fearful sweat. Had she been home, she would have crawled into a bath, soaked in the luxury of warm waters. But as it was, she could only wait for the beautiful monsters to return, to claim her once again as theirs.

The room was quiet and sound did not invade from the hallway she knew to exist outside the door. Her eyes traveled around the room that acted as her prison. This space wasn't as elaborate as the other rooms she'd seen; the walls were bare, not even adorned with the rich colors of the other rooms of the apartment. The walls, carpeting and fabrics of the space were cream, bland in comparison to what she'd seen before.

Fear continued to hold her body hostage, but curiosity rubbed along the back of her thoughts, driving her to crawl down from the bed to tiptoe to the expansive window. Pulling the thick curtains aside, her eyes were met with nothing more than trees; their leaves, a symphony of color:

76

reds, oranges, and golds as nature pushed forward into the slumber of winter.

Despite the large grounds, not a single sign of life stirred before her eyes, the scene, nothing more than a painting, one solitary moment frozen in time. Her fingers, long and thin, those of a musician, touched the frost kissed glass as she lamented her captivity. As she was lost to thought, she noticed how quick bursts of wind broke up the scene, creating small cyclones of fallen leaves dancing in its path. Only a week before, she'd looked forward to the coming season, a fond memory of a childhood spent enjoying the serenity of the earth as it laid itself to rest with promises of life beginning again with the coming Spring.

Warmth trailed down her cheeks; her tears were a physical manifestation of her pain. Never again would she return to that time in her life, to a time where she'd taken her freedom for granted.

A soft sound of metal sliding against metal alerted Maddy that her time of solitude had expired. She continued staring out the window, not caring to see who walked in through that door. Another click and the swish of the door brushing across the carpet and Maddy knew she was no longer alone. She waited for a command, braced for the sting of someone's hand across her cheek; but mostly, she grieved for how easily she'd been broken.

A minute passed, and another. No command came. Her body was left untouched. Curious, she turned to peek out from behind a tangled curtain of brown hair. Her breath caught;

Aaron stood silently within the doorway. He held his body with perfect posture, however his hands were casually tucked inside his pockets. The material of his white dress shirt pulled at the broad expanse of his chest, hiding nothing of the toned physique underneath. The tails of the shirt were tucked into the slate grey slacks that hung perfectly from his narrow hips. Her eyes slowly moved back to his face where she was met with eyes the color of a rainforest after a storm; different shades of green blended perfectly from the light bouncing off the leaves. The perfectly straight line of his nose ended at full lips, the kind that make women think sinful thoughts.

She expected him to speak, to demand something from her, but only silence followed. Returning her eyes to the window, she watched him through the reflection in the glass. Minutes passed, tense and foreboding, as she watched him stand motionless. Her fear was soon tainted by wisps of confusion and anticipation; an undercurrent of curiosity calling for her to turn, ask him why he'd made no move to approach her. The silence was heavy, only the sounds of her breath and the beat of her heart interrupted her quiet expectation of violence.

Another minute ...

Another ...

Madeleine lost track of time as she waited, but Aaron simply stood in the doorway, never changing position, never uttering a single sound. Through his transparent reflection in the glass, she watched the leaves dance within the blowing winds

— a kaleidoscope of colors — telling her that fall was turning into winter. The longer she waited, the harder her heart pounded, the faster thoughts and questions flooded her head. The tension between them built to a point of palpable discomfort, yet Aaron never moved, never spoke, just stood there watching her, waiting for her. Slowly, her head turned, her eyes peeking out from behind the thick curtain of matted hair. The swirling greens of his eyes held her gaze, penetrated deeply, as if he knew her on a deeper level than she understood.

Her voice, so quiet, almost a whisper, finally broke the tense exchange. "Why are you not moving?"

A crooked grin finally broke free of his sculpted mouth. "So, Xander was correct. You do speak."

Anger tore through her body at his levity. He'd taken her life, her freedom from her, and all he could do was mock her for her silence. Never before had she felt such insolence from another person. He sickened her, this man that portrayed beauty and refinement, while hiding poison and death … darkness … within him.

Her head spun back to the window favoring the transparent apparition of the monster to the physical threat lurking in the doorway. Blood rushed through her head, the pounding white noise only building her anger, her absolute disgust with the man standing behind her. Never moving, not speaking again, Aaron stood … waiting.

Like a string pulled too tightly, her patience

snapped, striking at her with the sting of indignation and insult. Whereas the others had made their intentions known, had struck her and insulted her and demanded her obedience, this man left her in a stagnant void, depriving her of even the faintest hint of her fate. His was the worst offense, not allowing her the knowledge of what was to come. Her only defense was to force the issue, take away his control, and give him no choice but to act.

Turning to him, her eyes burned into green eyes filled with malice and mirth. "Tell me what you want, or go away! Just do whatever it is your sick mind can come up with!" Her small body shook from the force of her anger. The feeling was alien; she'd never been driven to a point where rage drowned every nerve, every cell within her body.

Impassive and neutral, his eyes held hers. The only thing betraying his thoughts was the slight tick of his jaw. Trapped by his inaction, suffocating within the void of not knowing, Maddy lost herself, moved to approach him in demand of his intent. A burst of surprise was quickly seen in the slight widening of his eyes as she approached, but he remained still, waiting to see what she would do. When she was in range of him, her hands came up to wrap themselves within his shirt. Her strength was not enough to move him, but she pulled and pushed at him anyway, attempting to goad him into action.

"Just tell me what you want, you bastard!"

Fire flashed through his eyes, smoldering and bright, it burned into her as she exhausted herself in futility and fury. Finally his hands came up to hers, quickly enveloping her small form, removing her grip from his clothes. His fingers wrapped tightly around her wrists. She could feel the bruises form from his strong hold.

Razor sharp and controlled to a point of lethal resolve, his words were spoken with warning. "I recommend you never attempt touching me again without permission, Madeleine. Acts such as those will likely get you beaten or killed."

Rebellion and contempt darkened her gaze. "Then why not just get it over with?"

Like lightning on a clear day, he struck quickly and without notice. Curling his fingers deep within her tangled hair, he pulled her toward him, bending down so that his lips were pressed against her ear. Menacing and cruel, his voice shook her, igniting within her the terror that should have crippled her long before.

"I warned you," he said.

Three words were all he spoke before pulling her behind him as he walked out of the room and down the long corridor to another doorway. His free hand slammed down on a handle, freeing the closed door and revealing the bathroom she'd been led to by Xander the night before. Crying out in pain, her hands went to his, trying desperately to free her hair from his grip. Tears cascaded from her eyes, the earlier swelling and burn relieved by the sudden return of moisture. She was nothing more than a doll being

81

dragged along the bathroom floor, her efforts at escape useless against the strength of his hold. While she struggled and while she screamed, she became aware of the sound of water only moments before she was shoved into the shower.

So cold, the water that saturated her clothes, wrapping her in a blanket of ice, causing her to scream even louder from the feeling of knives being dragged across her skin. Her muscle spasms tightened and convulsed until she could barely move, barely fight against what he was doing. Finally giving in, she dropped to her knees as sobs escaped her, causing her body to thrash violently against the smooth tiles of the shower floor. She felt as his hands came down to the waistband of her pants, pulling them easily off her before tossing them to the opposite side of the bathroom.

"No! … Please! … " She begged while he let go of her hair to use both hands to tug away her shirt. Once removed, he tossed it aside and turned his eyes back to her huddled form.

"If you'll promise to behave, I'll add some warm water to your bath." His words were matter of fact, lightly brushed with humor as he offered her relief from the freezing water.

Hurried footsteps could be heard as another person approached the room. Aaron tore his eyes from her to look behind him for a split second before turning back to her.

"Aaron …? " A hesitant question. Xander stood in the doorway, obviously confused by the scene playing out before his eyes.

Ignoring the concerned man behind him, Aaron reached down to once again take Maddy's hair into his hold. Wrenching her head in his direction, his eyes burned down on her, demanding compliance. "Apologize to me and I will give you the heat you need. Your skin is already turning blue, Madeleine. Apologize and let me correct that."

Her teeth chattered violently in response to the deluge of water. She could feel her skin becoming numb, tightening to a point of discomfort against her muscles and bones. "Please … " Barely a squeak as her breath grated against her cracked lips. "Please … "

Aaron released her hair, allowing her to fall against the tiles again. "'Please' is not an apology, Ms. Clark."

On her hands and knees she attempted to crawl along the floor, only to be pulled back underneath the spray of the shower by Aaron. Spasms shook her convulsing muscles again when the water met her skin. She cried out from the pain.

"Aaron … "

Aaron turned to Xander and yelled, "Leave now!" Rage boiled and burst from each word he said to his friend. Xander responded by quickly turning and exiting the room; his eyes momentarily meeting Maddy's as he left.

"Apologize, Madeleine." Aaron's terse words were a command that would have to be

83

followed if she was to find relief from the agony of the frigid water.

It took her three attempts to finally be able to rasp the words, "I'm sorry, please, I'm so sorry."

Warm tendrils of water found her skin, caressing her, inducing the blood to begin circulating through her restricted veins. She sat still under the water, waiting as Aaron stood above her. At a slow crawl, the minutes ticked past as she allowed the warm water to erase the bite of the cold. Steam quickly filled the air, rolling with her and Aaron's exhaled breath.

Softly, she felt hands slide along her skin, starting at the bottom of her back, moving it's way along her spine, eventually touching her, holding her at the base of her head. Her body flinched at his touch, tightened as he moved along her soaked skin. "It's time we start discussing the rules, Madeleine ... the first being that you are to bathe at least once a day. I do not tolerate lack of hygiene in my home."

She could only nod her head in response. His voice was unsettling; smooth and deep, wrapping itself around her, providing comfort for reasons she could not understand. However, that voice ... no ... it didn't match the viciousness of his words, the cruelty of his intent, and his complete lack of compassion toward her.

Reaching over her, he grabbed a bottle of shampoo as his other hand moved deeper into the hair at the base of her scalp. She winced, her scalp still sensitive and sore from having been dragged down the hall by her hair. Slowly he poured and then massaged the contents of the bottle into her hair. Sensual musk, the smell of a product intended for a man, a smell most women would find inviting, would want to bring close to them. She wanted it nowhere near her, much less rubbed onto her head and her skin. Small iridescent spheres sliding over her, the suds picking up light and throwing it back to her eyes in all colors of the spectrum; beauty once again masking the abhorrence of the act, abuse wrapped in feigned care.

"Lean back."

When she didn't move fast enough, his hands gripped into her hair, pulling her lightly to encourage her compliance. Resisting only met with pain. Swallowing her pride, her modesty, she uncurled from herself, displaying her body to him as she moved backwards against his hand. He held her in that position, not moving to touch her, simply looking at her, studying her skin, her breasts, those parts of her that no other person had seen until she'd been brought to this place.

"Another rule you must obey is that when I tell you to do something, you do it without hesitation. If you can do that, you'll save yourself from the unpleasant events of this morning."

Without another word, he reached up to retrieve the showerhead, using it to rinse the shampoo from her hair. He moved her into an upright position, letting her go briefly to grab a washcloth and soap. Her body flinched involuntarily, occurring before she could consciously hide the reaction. Aaron reached down, holding the washcloth and soap out to her.

"I certainly hope you didn't flinch in reaction to the threat of MY touch. If that were to happen again, I might take offense .... " Aaron's pregnant pause made Maddy feel that much more helpless. "Take the soap and wash yourself while I watch you. Make sure certain parts receive more attention than others. I'm sure you're smart enough to figure out which ones."

Heat filled her cheeks, embarrassment openly displayed to her captor. Shaking, her hands hesitantly reached up to take the soap, to act as he'd demanded. A whimper escaped her lips, but she obediently lathered the washcloth with the soap, scrubbed it against the skin of her arms, her legs, her stomach ... anywhere but those areas she'd known he been referring to previously.

His hand moved down to grasp her, to lead her hands to her breasts. Tears streamed down her face as he cupped his hand over hers; forcing her to touch herself — squeeze herself — beneath his hold. She feared this was the beginning of the worst violence of all, the violation of her in ways she'd never before allowed. Her face twisted at his touch, his hold, at the invasion she knew was to come.

86

Chapter Nine

Pain, both physical and psychological; Aaron could tell both consumed her as she washed herself in the shower. For him, her pain was suffocating, making him want to scream at the injustice of the events in this young woman's life. However, he couldn't show her mercy if she was to survive this fate. Shame enveloped him. His body had responded to touching her, running his fingers along the silk of her flawless skin. Arousal, a nagging sensation rubbed itself along his thoughts as he bathed her, demanded that she display herself. Fear hit, hard and solid; fear that he'd started to lose his resolve; that his father had succeeded in his attempt at corruption.

"Now the other area, Madeleine. Wash yourself there."

She hesitated, her tear streaked face poorly hiding her distress at being displayed so openly to a man he was sure she despised. Reaching down slowly, he reminded her that if not done willingly, he would force her to act. Resignation flowed in the release of air forcing itself across her lips. Trembling, her hand reached down to the apex of her thighs, her eyes tightening as she rubbed at herself with the cloth. The tightening of his pants infuriated him, but this woman was a sight to behold. Small, so small, but built more perfectly than any of the women he'd had the pleasure to touch. The healthy weight of her breasts perfectly accentuated the pinch of her waist, the sensuous curve of her hip. It was becoming too much, he needed relief and he wouldn't find it in her company; at least, not like this.

"Enough ... " He cleared his throat of the constricting desire. " ... Enough. Stand so that you can be dried off." He turned to grab a towel, shaking himself from the erotic heat slowly creeping through his blood. When his eyes returned to hers, her stare struck him physically. Closing his eyes quickly, he regained his composure, once again, donning a mask of indifference. Regaining control, he brushed the back of his hand down her cheek, noting her attempt at concealing her body's reaction. Surprised by her ability to remain still, to allow him to touch her, he brought his hand down further, testing his restraint while testing hers. His hand traveled slowly down her neck. He could feel her body twitch, her disgust and fear overpowering her. Lips parting slightly, he watched his hand as it reached her neck, her shoulder, eventually running down along the side of her body before he pulled away.

He had to stop.

Shoving the towel toward her, he ordered, "Dry yourself and meet me in the hallway when you are done." Not waiting for an answer, he turned, stormed out of the room and beat his hands against the walls of the hallway when he'd crossed it. Resting his forehead against the wall, he resented his father ... himself. His weakness in her presence was stifling, a thing so unnatural, he wasn't sure he could stand it. Not wanting her to see his struggle, he forced himself upright, turning to lean casually, appear unaffected. The pads of her bare feet could be heard approaching before her small form occupied the doorway. Naked, the silk of her skin called to him, the palms of his hands itching to touch her in ways she would never approve.

"You will eat." Not saying another word, distancing himself by refusing more than what was necessary, he simply indicated for her to walk down the corridor in front of him. She complied immediately, not wanting a repeat of the events of that morning. Emerging from the hallway, Aaron's eyes met Xander's. Concerned etched itself within Xander's gaze, a silent question that would be saved to be asked at another time. Aaron moved to pull out a chair at the large table. Turning to Maddy, he indicated for her to sit. Instantly, she complied. Neither one spoke to the other, as Xander eyed them both, wondering what had occurred in the bathroom.

Aaron stepped away. Directing his attention to Xander, he commanded, "Feed her. Return her to the room when she is done." Having missed enough time from business as it was, Aaron moved across the room to enter his office. He let go of his held breath once he heard the soft click of the door locking behind him. Defeated, he dropped into the large leather chair behind his desk. Work would distract him, would help take his mind off Madeleine. But it proved useless; his focus was locked on the woman currently sitting at his dining table. Papers flew from his desk from the force of his fist coming down on the surface of the wood. Rage boiling within him, igniting every nerve, eliciting physical pain from its intensity. His head dropped into his hands as he contemplated how he would train her without losing himself in the process.

A brisk knock sounded on the door, followed by the metal against metal sound of a key releasing the lock. As Xander strode through, Aaron sighed loudly, leaning back into the plush leather of his chair. Xander closed the door behind him as his eyes surveyed the paperwork strewn across the floor. One eyebrow raised, he looked up at Aaron, an unasked question hanging between the two men.

"Just spit it out, Xander. I don't have time to decipher your facial expressions this morning."

Xander approached Aaron's desk, unbuttoned the jacket of his pinstripe suit jacket and sat down in one of the chairs facing his friend. "Do you care to explain what that was this morning? Should I be concerned that your father has succeeded?"

More papers fluttered through the air as Aaron's hands came down hard on the desk again. Xander remained stoic, not even flinching at the show of anger.

"Where is Madeleine?" Wanting to forget her, Aaron surprised himself with his instant question about the woman who could destroy him just by her presence in his home.

"In her room, as you instructed. She ate ... somewhat ... more like a bird. However, I'm not sure she can be blamed, considering the morning she's had." The condemnation in his tone shook Aaron, made what happened between him and Madeleine even more real by the acknowledgment.

"Fuck!" Aaron stood up suddenly, damn near knocking over his chair as he rose. Running his hand through his hair, he began pacing back and forth along the bookshelves that lined his walls. "She needs to be trained, Xander. I have only so much time before the old man will ask that she be presented. She can't go in there without being absolute in her submission. What good would mercy do for her? If nothing else, it will only cost her more than what's already been taken from her."

A curt nod as Xander considered Aaron's words. "Are you able to do this? You seemed ... overtaken ... when I saw you with her in the bathroom. I feared you would take it too far, lose yourself to the task." Framed as a simple question, Aaron knew Xander's words also held warning. They'd known each other since childhood; there was nothing Aaron could do that would fool his friend.

Relenting, Aaron admitted, "I almost did lose myself." Snorting, Aaron continued moving, releasing emotional energy through physical movement. "The old man has really outdone himself this time, found the chink in my armor, so to say. This girl ... "

"What exactly is it about her, Aaron? Yes, her body is something that would drive any man to insanity, but you've had so many, you are not some

91

post pubescent teen whose dick swells at the sight of a naked woman, I don't understand your lack of control." Harsh words, but necessary; Xander often took risks speaking aloud the thoughts that he knew were already running rampant through Aaron's head.

No answer was given to Xander's inquiry. Aaron didn't want to face what demons drove him when faced with Madeleine. Pushing his fascination to the side, he aligned himself back with the business aspects, the plots and conspiracies already in play within The Estate. "Have you spoken with Jason?"

Xander rolled his eyes at Aaron's deflection, but answered, "I spoke with him this morning. He's on our side and will align his men to our needs. Your father's strength fails within the network; most of the men are concerned with his dip into insanity. Your exchange last night helped seal Jason's allegiance."

"How so?"

Clearing his throat, Xander prepared himself for the lengthy explanation. Settling himself even farther into his chair, he leaned on the armrest, his pause obviously annoying Aaron. "Your father is so focused on you, on corrupting his own men, that he's lost sight of the needs of the network. Every man in that room knows who runs The Estate. Your father has become nothing more than a figurehead, one who takes advantage of every man at his service. His mind, Aaron, is slipping so deep, that he never noticed your intention last night; his only desire is to succeed in

92

his games against you. He is losing his hold on so many men. Jason understands that you are the only man within this *family* that will be able to maintain control over the entire house. You haven't been lost to the power of your position ... not like your father."

Finally, having calmed himself, Aaron leaned back against the bookcase while considering Xander's words. "How do we know that Jason speaks truthfully, that he isn't whispering in the old man's ear as we speak?"

"I told him that those who assist will be given higher ranking once The Estate falls within your hands. He's not a dumb man, Aaron; he knows that while your father reigns, he'll remain on the lower end of the food chain, so to speak. Emory and Vincent will never promote him, they're too nervous that he would overtake them if given the chance. Plus, this is house full of murderers, thieves and liars. Loyalty is only given to those that benefit the entire house ... your father has not been that man since he allowed his lead guards to make his decisions."

Aaron nodded at the truth of what Xander was saying. Twenty years ago, it would have been a different story. No man would have dared speak against his father, much less act against him. To do so would have been an immediate death sentence. However, twenty years ago, his father had not yet started his gradual slide into madness and he'd been careful to ensure that all men benefited from the network, kept them rolling in cash so deep, that their loyalty was assured. Slowly, however, whether from boredom or extreme hubris, his

93

father stopped concerning himself with the needs of the many and focused instead on the needs of those within his innermost circle. While he fed his depravity with whores and drugs, his two top men, Emory and Vincent, made decisions that would eventually give the members of The Estate two choices ... loyalty or death ... despite whether they benefited or not. Whereas his father had gone mad, his men had become pure evil.

"Regardless ... " Xander continued. " ... It will take time, another year perhaps until we have the backing to overthrow the men who benefit by remaining loyal to your father. We must be cautious, Aaron. Losing yourself to that girl ... "

"I'd hold that thought if you wish to keep your tongue."

A threat, yes; but Xander was not one to take threats idly, not even from Aaron. Knowing his friend would not remain silent, Aaron answered the unspoken question, "I have not lost myself to her. Our mouse has more spirit in her than I previously thought. She surprised me this morning by approaching me and putting her hands on me. I cannot show her kindness, Xander, a fact you know full well. Her behavior, her submission, is the only thing that will ensure her survival. If she were to misspeak once presented, act in any way not deemed appropriate for a whore, her death will not be a pleasant one. She has not been broken as easily as we thought."

Xander chuckled. "No, that she has not. Although, she was very well behaved once you handed her to me. Perhaps you should continue the training yourself. Whereas she has a healthy fear of me, her abhorrence of you is far more certain."

Razor sharp and laced with acid, Xander's words tore into Aaron's chest, a physical strike that left nothing but pain and rotting flesh. "No, I'll continue the training. You're correct about her hatred, she knows I'm to blame for what's been done to her. It was my face she saw that night at the concert, and it was my face she was met with when she was disgraced before a group of obnoxious drunks." His heart sank further as he thought of Madeleine, of her torment, of the torment yet to come. Even still, he knew he was not impervious to his desire for her. Fearing he would, in fact, lose himself to the temptation she presented, he needed to break rules in her training.

"She'll need clothing while we train her ... "

Xander opened his mouth to protest, but swallowed his remark when Aaron raised his hand to silence him.

"If I am to remain free of the forced corruption, I must be careful in my approach. Yes, she will have to tolerate nudity when she is within view of the members of The Estate, but I believe our mouse will better accept training if she's given some concessions while in our presence alone. She welcomes the threat of death too easily. Her spirit has not been broken Xander, not when she prefers the unknown release from life to the prison she finds herself in now."

"How can you be so sure?" Xander's

question rang between them as Aaron pondered the absolute truth to his statement. It was nothing she said, it was not in the way she weakly fought, or the small glimpses of rebellion in her reactions. It was what he saw in her eyes ... the same look, the same plea for release from the nightmare of The Estate that he saw when he looked in the mirror each morning.

"I just am, the reasons aren't important." Aaron pushed himself to a full stand and walked briskly to his desk. While sitting down, his hand flicked out to open the laptop on the center of the desk, effectively dismissing Xander.

Knowing he'd been excused, Xander stood to leave. He paused while crossing the room. Looking back at Aaron over his shoulder, he asked, "What would you like me to buy her? I've never been shopping for women's clothes."

"Nothing fancy. Just something she can wear that isn't five sizes too big. See if she'll give you her sizes; if not, just guess."

"Aye, aye, Captain." After a mock salute, Xander turned to exit the room. Shutting the door behind him, he left Aaron to his work.

As soon as he was alone, Aaron attempted to keep his mind focused on business, but eventually found himself online researching his unintended guest. Other than pages and pages of news reports regarding her disappearance, there wasn't much beyond praise regarding what some termed a 'musical savant.' It was obvious Madeleine had been sheltered. Even in her adult life, she'd not

96

agreed to many photos, and those that were taken always had her placed behind an instrument large enough to hide her from the world; an instrument that she'd mastered in a way that no other person could dare compete.

Aaron growled at the thought of what he would have to do to her, what he would have to allow others to do. But he'd protected her from the worst. She would not be a toy to be passed around. No. As long as she was Aaron's, Madeleine would not be assaulted in the worst possible of ways. Her embarrassment was certain, her privacy would be shredded to tattered rags, but her body would remain whole. Of that, Aaron would make sure.

Slamming the laptop closed, he stood up from his chair. Crossing the large room with wide steps, he set out to take care of the various business meetings he needed to attend that day. Before leaving, he couldn't help but walk back to Maddy's room. Quietly, he unlocked the door and pushed it open just enough to find that she'd fallen back to sleep on the large king sized bed. Her body lay soft and luscious atop the silken, goose down comforter, her nakedness exposing curves so feminine that the maleness in him couldn't help but react. His breath caught as his eyes moved over her still form. She would be a practice in self-restraint, the toughest challenge he had yet faced, but he silently promised her that no harm would befall her while in his care. She stirred suddenly, a soft, yet frightened cry escaping her full lips. He winced as he watched the skin between her sleeping eyes furrow.

97

His heart tearing itself from his chest, he regretted the fact that he was her nightmare.

Chapter Ten

A door softly sliding against the carpet wrestled Maddy from her slumber. Jumping up from the bed, her arms immediately went to cover her naked breasts as her eyes locked with the deep, sea blue of Xander's. His eyebrow arched as he observed her attempt at modesty.

"Normally, Cricket, I'd reprimand you for your attempt to cover yourself, but it seems your Master is allowing it while in his quarters."

His hand moved from behind his body and Madeleine could see that he was carrying two brown paper bags. Moving quickly to the side of her bed, he noted her hurried movement to place as much distance between them as possible. Placing the packages down, he opened the bags and pulled out clothing for her to wear.

"You were asleep when I left, I had to guess at your size. The clothes may be a little big, but nothing like what you wore last night."

"Why give them to me at all?"

Xander was surprised at the sound of her voice. Slowly he turned his attention away from the clothes and to a small face that held defiance behind the blue of her eyes.

"Now, now, Cricket. It's best you hold your tongue. I wouldn't want to see you thrown in a cold shower again."

99

Raising his eyebrow at the seemingly defiant, small woman, he decided to let the transgression pass as he pulled out a pair of blue pajama pants and a matching camisole.

Turning, he placed the clothes by her still body as she watched him. "Aaron will be back shortly, you should get dressed to await him."

Xander was surprised again to see a sudden depth to her gaze, one that concerned him; made him believe that Aaron had underestimated his mouse and that she wouldn't be ready for presentation once the week had ended. It would be to Aaron's dismay should she fail to prove she'd submitted, been trained to live within the rules set for the lowest member of the Estate.

"Why do you call me that? I'm not someone you care for, why use an endearing term?" Although, her voice was soft, it carried an air of authority, a challenge that should not be included in the tone of a slave.

Xander shrugged and moved away from the bed to lean against the adjacent wall. He indicated to the clothing with his hand. "What have I told you about questions?" When she did not answer, Xander simply commanded, "Get dressed."

Madeleine eyed Xander, inwardly contemplating the beautiful man who operated without concern, without a heart with which he could discern the cruelty that he was inflicting on her by his mere presence. It was unnerving to be confronted with the type of face that would make any normal woman crawl just to be near him while

100

knowing that inside, there was only brutality and disregard.

"Will you watch as I dress myself?" Her voice dripped with contempt as she crawled backwards off the bed, intentionally putting even more distance between herself and the man she considered her captor.

"Such brave words for a woman who is obviously scared out of her mind." Xander's hands fisted as he struggled against correcting her behavior. But this was Aaron's fight, his mouse to bring under control.

"I'll ignore your mouth this one time, but understand, it would be best you get your bursts of temper under control before you face Aaron again. He won't be as kind." Xander's mouth twisted into a sardonic and mocking grin. "But, I guess, you already know that, don't you?"

Madeleine shivered at the forced memory of her encounter with Aaron that morning. The salt of a single tear seeped into her mouth as it trailed along the crease of her lips. She was sick of crying, of tasting the evidence of her hopeless state. Locking her eyes with Xander, Maddy pulled the camisole over her head before gripping the material of the pants and pulling them up her legs to cover her body.

Moving to the window, she glanced outside, turning her back to the monster behind her. She watched as men raked up fallen leaves, grabbing large armfuls and placing them in hefty black bags. She wanted Xander to leave, his presence only

101

further infuriating her. The silence between the two was uncomfortable. Finally after several moments, Xander cleared his throat and began to speak.

"You know, now that you are here, there truly is no return to the life you had before. If you accept it, things will go more smoothly for you. I didn't like what I witnessed this morning." His voice carried a hint of remorse, however, even that was not enough to extinguish the small flame of anger that'd begun to burn within Maddy's soul.

She turned to him suddenly. Realizing that death could only be an escape from this life she'd been forced to now live, that small flame burst forth, raging within her blood, through her cells, through every part of her body. What did she have to lose? Her life? That'd already been taken from her the night of the concert.

"I will never accept what you've done to me. I will get free, if it's through my death than so be it, but I will never comply."

Xander grinned at the sudden fire in her eyes. It was unexpected, but glorious at the same time; this little woman, beautiful and talented, but also harboring the spirit of a fighter. Aaron would have one hell of a surprise on his hands when she finally let loose.

"You will comply, Cricket. There is no other choice."

Without another word, Xander strode to the door, letting himself out of the room and locking her in with only her thoughts for company. Maddy never turned; she simply watched his reflection in the glass as it disappeared out the door. When he was gone, his words rang in her mind. She knew he was wrong, knew that there was always a choice.

Futility, a suffocating weight on her chest, she held back the tears that burned behind her eyes. Crying wouldn't save her; she knew that. Escape was her only true hope and the choice she would make. Suddenly driven by a fight for her life, Maddy searched the room for anything with which she could break the glass. There was nothing. She panicked, thought that maybe if she could get the attention of the men who worked just a few feet from where she was held, they might call the police, might recognize her as the woman who'd gone missing just a few days before.

In a moment of desperation, Maddy banged on the windows with her fists, screaming for help as loud as she possibly could. She didn't fear the cuts she knew would occur if she were to break the glass. She didn't care if she shed her own blood, if it would help her escape. The workers turned to look and she screamed louder, feeling that, maybe, this would be the moment she was pulled from her unending nightmare.

The bedroom door slammed open. Maddy didn't bother to turn to see who entered, she just kept screaming, kept banging against the glass so hard that the shock against the glass hurt the fine bones in her hands. Two large arms came around her, pulling her from the window just as the men outside began to talk, began pointing back in her

103

direction.

Tossed to the floor, the impact reverberated through her hips and shoulders as they forcefully met the ground, even the plush carpeting not enough to absorb the shock. A large hand came over her mouth, her lip splitting where it met with her teeth. Having lost complete control, she thrashed against her assailant, the tears in her eyes obscuring the identity of the person fighting above her.

"What the fuck are you doing?!" Xander's voice bellowed out, echoed through the ringing in her ears. A hard slap, the sound of skin against skin, and a sharp pain across her cheek followed. Continuing her struggle, Maddy didn't care if he hit her a thousand more times, she couldn't exist in this life they'd chosen for her. Escape had to come.

Xander's hands found Maddy's and wrapped tightly around her wrists before pinning them above her head. His legs came down on hers, the weight of his body securing her in place. She continued screaming, refusing to submit to the monster above her.

"Cricket! Stop right fucking now before I have to chain and gag you!"

Barely concerned with the threat, Maddy kept fighting, the animal instinct for survival taking over her logical thought. Releasing her wrists, Xander moved his hands to her head before saying, "forgive me." The impact of her head with the floor jarred her thoughts, sent shooting pains through her skull and down her spine. The next blow left her again in darkness, the tunnel wrapping around her, wrenching her from the present.

~ ~ ~

Maddy's body went limp beneath Xander. Her eyes rolled back as her eyelids fluttered closed. He winced when she finally lost consciousness, but his violence toward her could not be avoided. Turning her head to the side he watched as the evidence of his slap grew across her cheek, red and angry. Letting out a slow breath he removed himself from her, left her lying on the carpeted floor as he moved across the room. Walking out into the hall, he quickly traversed the long corridor to retrieve the chains he'd brought into the apartment the night before.

He knew Aaron would be furious, would become enraged to know that not only had he struck the woman, but bound her like an animal while awaiting his return. But Xander had no choice. Those men outside Maddy's window would undoubtedly talk, would spread the rumored truth that Aaron was allowing a slave to wear clothes, to move about a room unrestrained. Grabbing the chains, he walked back to find Maddy still unconscious where he'd left her. Quickly, he moved her small body to the bed, binding her hands above her, only to bring the chains down below the bed so that he could also bind her feet at the base.

Once her body was stretched taut across the mattress, immobilized by unconsciousness and chains, Xander grabbed another camisole from the bags now lying on the ground from where he'd knocked them off placing Maddy on the bed. Ripping one of the thin shirts into shreds, he fashioned a quick gag to tie around her mouth, to keep her silent until Aaron could return to decide how they would handle this less delicate side to their captive.

Satisfied that she could no longer make a spectacle of herself, Xander closed the curtains, blanketing the room in a hazy gray, not quite dark, but not quite light. His eyes traveled over Maddy's still form once more as he noted how her chest rhythmically moved with her shallow breath. She'd wake eventually, probably injure herself trying to free herself of her binds, but until she understood her place, there could be no mercy for this small woman who had the hidden spirit of a survivor. Closing the door, Xander moved quickly to the living room and sat back into the leather sofa. A sigh escaped him as he enjoyed a moment of peace.

Within the hour, Aaron walked through the front door. The hem of his shirt hung partially out at his waist, the top buttons were undone and the splattered stain on the crisp white of the material was unmistakably blood. Instantly, Xander was on his feet, an unspoken question in his expression.

Aaron turned and walked to the bar, picked up a decanter of dark liquid and poured its contents into a crystal tumbler. Slamming down the first drink, his eyes never left the decanter as he quickly poured another. Finally, Aaron turned to look at Xander. Death haunted Aaron's eyes, the cold and empty shadow of another life ended, absent of regret for having been the one who sent that poor soul into the bowels of Hell.

"I take it the business meetings didn't go well." Xander spoke without emotion. It wasn't unusual for Aaron to return home covered in the evidence of someone else's violent demise.

Aaron slammed back his second drink, the muscles of his throat moving to push the alcohol down. The sound of the glass hitting the surface of the bar top broke up the resonating silence between the two men as Xander patiently waited for an explanation.

"Theo Hollis regretfully met his maker this afternoon. He thought it was wise to steal from the business over the past year. The accountants finally discovered how he'd been pinching off small amounts here and there, until there was no doubt he'd acquired a small fortune by his efforts."

Xander nodded, not in the least surprised. "Theo was never a smart man." He paused, reluctant to inform Aaron of the incident with Madeleine. Breathing out a deep breath, he confessed. "Your mouse caused quite the scene while you were absent. You'll undoubtedly be pissed once you see what I had to do to contain her."

Aaron's shoulder straightened, the muscles of his chest going rigid underneath his shirt and the tendons of his neck becoming clearly defined. "Explain."

"She's found her voice again, this time screaming for help while banging on the windows

107

of her room. I knocked her out, chained her to the bed to await your return."

"Did anybody see her?"

"The maintenance crew was working outside. It is without doubt that she was seen. She was clothed at the time, Aaron."

Nodding his head, Aaron swiftly moved to the doors leading to the back rooms. "I'll change before checking on her. If any people come to inspect my progress with our guest, tell them I do not wish to be disturbed. Rumors spread quickly in this place. I expect to be hearing from my father before long."

"What will you do with her?"

Aaron stopped, his shoulders dropping in defeat. "I'll ensure that she appears as she should, at least until such time that I no longer have to be concerned that visitors will be arriving."

Taking large steps down the corridor, Aaron began to strip off his shirt, but then stopped. He thought of how Madeleine welcomed death and wondered how she would react to the unquestionable evidence of such a fate. Unlocking her door, he pushed into her room, anger boiling within his gut to find her chained, forcefully exposed atop the bed. Shaking himself free of pity, he set out to become her waking nightmare, knowing his cruelty may be the only thing capable of saving her from the unimaginable horror her rebellion could bring about.

Crossing the room, he allowed his eyes to

rake across her body as he approached the bed. Small hints of dove white skin peeked out from underneath the light blue material of her clothes, the contrast startling in its temptation.

Reaching out, he ran his fingertips across that small area of skin, watched as her muscles twitched in response to his touch. Lust was a fire within his mind, the smoke from which clouded the restraint he'd wanted to maintain. But his little mouse had made a spectacle of herself, had revealed his kindness, his weakness in this game. She couldn't be allowed to seal her own fate, to unknowingly cast herself to the wolves that awaited her. Aaron would have to be her monster, one that by his own cruelty would shield her from the true madness of The Estate. Resigning himself to the task, he ran his hands up under the thin camisole that covered her, over the softness of her skin, cupping the heavy weight of her breast. A shudder ran over his skin as he fought back his desire to take this woman while she was bound, at his mercy alone. His fingers grazed over the peak of her breast before taking it roughly, pinching it, enticing it into a taut point that his tongue ached to run across. Her lips parted, a moan rolling out from behind her gag before she'd found consciousness. That pleasure would become terror soon enough as Aaron took from her the dignity he'd attempted to give her before.

Moving his hand over her, he shaped and molded her other breast until both pointed up at him, teasing him with the display of feminine beauty and form. Madeleine began to writhe under his touch, his cock jumping in response, begging for

109

release, begging to be buried within the warm heat of her body. He couldn't help himself as he watched her hips roll in response to his touch. Reaching down, his hand slowly disappeared beneath the material of her pants, along the delicate trail of hair, stopping just short of the place he knew would elicit sensation that would turn her body into a traitor against her soul. Her eyelids fluttered, her body slowly moving, inviting his touch. He watched as realization dawned within her, a light coming into her eyes, with terror following shortly behind it. Within seconds the movement of her body changed from invitation to defense.

"Good morning, beautiful. It's about time you joined me." He spoke in the softest tone he could manage, attempting to hide the lust winding itself through every cell of his body.

She started to cry out, her attempts only infuriating him, causing him to shove his hand further down. Applying pressure to the point of her body he knew would cause unwanted pleasure, he shook his head. "Tsk, tsk, Ms. Clark. Continue fighting and I'll turn your own body against you."

She stilled suddenly, but couldn't stop the flow of tears from her eyes. No mercy ... he fought against the impulse to pull his hand away, to dry the tears running trails down her face. Slowly he rubbed circles over her, felt as her body betrayed her by readying itself for his intrusion.

"I heard about your spat with Xander this afternoon. You do realize punishment is the only alternative I have for your behavior?"

110

Her eyes widened, fear dampening the earlier defiance that had beamed from those brilliant blues.

He leaned down, until his lips trailed along the rim of her ear. "I can make you feel things that would go against the hatred you have for me. I can make you scream out in pleasure while causing you to die inside." To prove his point, he moved one finger along the soft skin between her legs. Her hips bucked up against his hand while her eyes narrowed in disgust.

"Such hatred from a little scared girl. I'll enjoy myself thoroughly, you know." His lie, an acrid film on his tongue, but her life was on the line. Pushing forward with his torment, he bit down on her ear, hard enough to cause pain, but light enough as to not leave a mark on the perfection of her skin. She attempted to turn, to break free of the teeth wrapped around the sensitive rim of her ear.

Pulling his hand from her pants, he grasped at the material of her shirt, ripping it apart easily to reveal her supple chest. "I give you clothes, and how do you repay me? By bringing attention to yourself? To my kindness?" His fingers quickly found her nipples again, pinching them, stimulating them into tight pebbles. "Look how you respond, you like my touch, don't you?"

A whimpered protest snuck out from beneath the material tied to her mouth. His cock pressed harder against the abrasive material of his pants. Pushing himself back up to stand above her, he looked down at the perfection of her breasts, licked his lips so slowly as to ensure that she saw his desire. His guilt warred against his lust. Her eyes closed and opened again as she turned her head back to him, widening impossibly more as she recognized the blood adorning his shirt.

Looking down, he let out a humorless laugh while pulling the material out from his body. "What are you looking at? The evidence of what happened to the other mouse that dared deny my will?" Another lie, but one that might instill in her the knowledge that death was, in fact, a viable consequence to derision.

Reaching out, he grasped her face in his hand, turning her head to examine the red stain left from Xander's hand. "I see you've been marked again." A pause as he gathered his resolve to continue his taunts rather than sooth her as he wished he could.

"Would you like for me to spill your blood, Mouse? Or can I trust you to behave when I release you from your binds?"

Aaron started to remove his shirt, slowly undoing each button. When Maddy moved to turn her head away, he reached over to correct her behavior. "Keep your eyes open, Ms. Clark, I like my slaves to watch me as I undress."

Maddy opened her eyes as instructed, watched as his muscular chest, his skin kissed by the sun, was revealed with each button released. Aaron noticed how her obvious fear mixed with the unusual taste of seduction, how her mind fought against attraction toward a man built to

112

make women want the sin he could bestow. Grinning down at her, he took pleasure in making her witness each step toward his violation of her body. His muscles flexed as he slowly pulled one sleeve off, then the other. When his hands moved to the button of the slate grey dress slacks, Maddy pulled at her chains, winced as the metal cut into the tender skin of her wrists and ankles. Aaron stopped suddenly, watched as she fought for escape.

"Do you fight me even now? After seeing what will happen to a woman who refuses my touch?" Aaron leaned down again, placed his hand spread wide over the expanse of her stomach. His voice no more than a whisper, he warned, "Do not mistake death as your escape. I will grant you pain, I will spill your blood, but I will not release you as you hope."

She stilled. Aaron laughed; a wicked chuckle that he knew would elicit dread from the woman he teased. He felt sick for what he was about to do. Knowing full well that if he didn't bring her under control, she would ultimately suffer even harsher consequences at the hands of the members of The Estate, he pressed on with his assault.

Bringing his lips back to the shell of her ear, he whispered, "Have you ever known the touch of a man, Madeleine?" Standing back to gaze down upon her, he noticed her erratic breathing, imagined he could hear the staccato of her beating heart. "I've researched you, and from what I've found, I don't think you've experienced much in your young life."

He looked down at the beautiful woman, bound and gagged, completely at his mercy. Guilt reared its ugly head but he allowed the fire of lust to reduce it to ashes. He would not lose total control, but he would enjoy touching the woman who'd captured his attention so many months before. Her body shook and quivered before him, her glorious tits bouncing with the small movements of her body.

"I intend to introduce you to the darker side of life, to teach you what a man can do for you, to make you beg for more."

The light of defiance shown forth from her eyes, he wanted nothing more than to replace that defiance with the sated satisfaction of pleasure.

Maddy watched as Aaron sat down on the bed, his hand still splayed over her stomach, the warmth of his skin seeping into hers. Hatred, an ugly beast roaring loudly within her, she held still, refusing to clue him in to his effect on her. His hands, rough and calloused, began to travel down, pushing her pants from around her waist, down further, until completely exposing her to him. She could feel the wetness induced by his earlier touch, felt angry and confused that she'd reacted, wanted more. His finger found her clit, rubbed at it in slow circles until she was assaulted by a litany of electric pulses. Her body truly did betray her in that moment. Starting as a slow burn, the foreign sensation rolled up her core. She found herself pressing into his touch, her hips moving in such a way as to increase the pressure. Tears streamed from her eyes as the tips of her breasts tightened, the weight of them swelling, aching to be touched.

The deep green of his eyes held hers as he continued the grueling rhythm, never speeding or slowing, simply enticing her body to feel something completely alien to her mind.

A toy being wound up, her body hummed from his touch. She wanted him to stop, her mind bathed in revulsion at the moisture she could feel between her legs, at the way her body wanted to push up into his touch, while her mind screamed to put distance between them. The rattling of the chains grew louder as she uselessly pulled at the bindings. The deep, endless green of Aaron's eyes burned into her, a wild glint in each, telling her that he enjoyed what he was doing to her.

Her body continued building in fervent intensity, traitorous jolts of mind numbing gratification. Tears flowed freely as her breathing became more erratic and her heart hammered against the walls of her chest. Her eyes rolled back and when she finally released, the confusion of what had just happened to her body, mixed with her shame for having experienced it, tore her into pieces, leaving her pooled in guilt and hatred toward Aaron and toward herself.

Feeling the slick warmth between her legs, she began to sob, the physical evidence of her arousal and orgasm a humiliation for Aaron to witness. Though liquid and distorted by her tears, she could see that his sculpted lips curved in amusement and triumph.

"How did that make you feel, Madeleine?" His voice rubbed over her, rough and gritty from his arousal. His fingertips trailed down, through her slick skin, causing another jolt to shoot through her body. "I'll make you moan even louder when I finally kiss you there ... but that's for when you are a good girl. And, trust me, Ms. Clark, you will WANT to be a good girl after you feel my kiss."

Aaron stood up and walked to the door, leaving Madeleine damp and exposed. "I'm going to shower and get dressed. I expect that when I return, you will be more willing to work with my instructions and appreciate my kindness. If you do not, then I will leave you soaked in your shame once more, but this time, I won't give you the pleasure of a release. I'll leave you in the madness that comes just before it."

Chapter Eleven

Locking the door of her room behind him, Aaron leaned back against it, letting the cool temperature of the wood seep into his overheated skin. With each loud sob he heard from behind the door, his heart broke apart into pieces, each sliver falling away at the sound of her pain. Yet, even with the sound of her pain, he could not forget the small sounds, the moans she made while he worked her toward orgasm. Judging by the look on her face, the confusion and surprise, he suspected it could have been her first, and it left him feeling like an even bigger bastard than he knew he already was.

Pushing upright from the door, he turned, and the heavy weight of his steps echoed against the wood floor as he moved back, deeper into the corridor to his room. Shutting the door behind him, he moved across the room, his hand reaching over to flick on the stereo. Releasing the sound of Madeleine's instrument, he let her torment envelope him as he listened to the sad song. She was a slave to his lust, while he was a slave to her pain.

His cock still rigid against his pants, he moved into his bathroom and turned on the shower. Stripping himself of the offensive material, he stepped into water so hot it would strip him of the film of shame on his skin. His hand found his shaft, so full of blood it felt as if the skin would split from his urgings. Slick from water, he gripped himself hard, sliding his hand up and down to the same rhythm he used on that beautiful woman only moments before. His other hand braced against the tiled wall, his eyes closed and he imagined that the pain of his grip was, instead, the pain of sliding inside the tightness of Madeleine. A virgin, no doubt, the conquest would be sweet for the taking. But the rhythm was such a tease, Aaron worked himself faster, harder, until he felt his balls swell with his future release. His lips parted, the water dripping as it ran down his cheeks to his mouth. A hiccupped moan burst from his chest, the salt of his seed spilled out onto the tiled floor. Shame, a warm blanket suffocating him, he lowered his head into the spray of the water, opened his eyes to watch the evidence of his lust as it rinsed down the drain.

"FUCK!" His voice tore against his throat as he screamed out his frustration. He wanted this woman, there was no fucking doubt that he itched to bury himself deep in her soft heat; would work her into a frenzy that gripped at him, milking him of everything he had to give her. The temptation was so strong. How easily he could slip into the corruption dangled before him by the man whose blood he shared.

A shock shot down the bones of his arm as he slammed his fist against the tiled wall. The skin of his hand tightened, white peeking out where the blood had been squeezed aside. Stepping out of the shower, he toweled off, before moving into his closet to get dressed. After slipping a simple black t-shirt over his chest, he pulled on black slacks and buckled a leather belt around his waist.

Her song played throughout the room, the

deep resonance of the cello haunting him with loneliness and the depth of misery. Had she somehow known her future would be so bleak? Was her soul aware of the circumstances that would follow from her public performance on that fated night? If her music was any indication, then yes; Madeleine knew that the outside world would eventually steal her away, toss her into a nightmare from which there was no imaginable end. That's why she'd hidden herself away behind an instrument so large, behind the safety of the studio walls.

Throwing his door open, he stomped down the hall, pausing just outside Madeleine's door. His head dropped to his hands, he needed her ready in case company arrived. Unlocking the door, he stepped in the room, stopped suddenly when her head turned to him, her eyes the color of an angry sea burned into his. She was livid, rage pouring from her razor sharp stare.

"Did you need to be fucked into compliance, Ms. Clark?" His hand reached to his crotch, her eyes following, widening at the reminder of how he could take her anytime he pleased. His steps were purposeful, almost feline in their quality. He stalked his little mouse, his breathing becoming ragged at the temptation of her skin laid out like a sinful buffet, begging for his indulgence. Running just the pads of his fingertips along her stomach, his mouth filled with desire, his cock reawakened at the goose bumps that formed beneath his touch.

Eyes the color of forbidden forests gazed down upon her, desire and lust burning behind the

119

swirl of multi-hued leaves. Maddy stared up at Aaron, her chest heaving as his hands moved up her abdomen, stopping short of her breast before he removed his touch from her skin.

He cleared his throat. "If I remove your gag, will you promise not to scream?" His finger slid along her bottom lip that was pressed outward by the cloth tied to her head. His hands reached behind her, loosening the material, pulling it away from her face and leaving the skin at the corners of her mouth burning from their collision with the cool air of the room. Her instincts told her to scream, to use her voice to chase away the demons that held her. But it was useless while bound by her metal shackles, stretched out taut across the length of the bed.

Dropping the cloth silently to the ground, he reached up to brush his finger across the marks it had left on her mouth. His finger slid along her lips, dipped down into the warm moisture of her mouth. The invasion angered her, her teeth locking themselves against his skin. Aaron hissed above her, his eyes closed and his head falling back from the pain she returned to him. He pulled his finger free, brought it up to his face to inspect the blood, the color of scarlet rubies, as it dripped from where her teeth had broken through.

Anger should have been returned to her, the sting of his fist as it met with her face; but instead, Aaron gave her a wicked grin, and lust was now a raging inferno behind his eyes. His voice rasped out from between his full lips. "Oh, the things you do to me, Madeleine." Her body clenched at the depth of his voice, the sound of raw desire pouring from each word, fur and razors, satisfaction and pain.

He reached down to rub his finger around the peaks of her breast; the angry color of blood staining the milk of her skin. His head lowered suddenly, taking her nipple into his mouth, his tongue laved against the peak, the warmth and suction working the tip into a tight pebble. Intense pain followed, the feel of his teeth as they bit into her sensitized flesh. She cried out, her body bucking against the warring sensations, her breast swelling with pleasure and the sting of his teeth. Continuing to work at her breasts with a mouth skilled in sinful decadence, his hand moved down her stomach, down farther until his fingers rested atop the opening of her body. She stilled, her breath catching, forcing her breast against his face while fear soaked every inch of her skin. With one final stroke of his tongue against her taut peak, he stood up, his lips swollen from his torment of her breasts. His hand remained against her, his eyebrow arched in question. "Do you want me here, Madeleine? Inside you?"

Shaking her head, her eyes begged him to stop, to not take from her something she'd never offered. He smiled at her response. "I like pain, but you must understand, that I also like to return it to the giver. You can bite me as much as you please, but know that the sting of my teeth will follow."

Madeleine shuddered at the venom in his words. There was no doubt that this soulless creature was made more beautiful in order to entice even the most virtuous of women. Pure mockery was his tone; conquest and spite, the

121

meaning of his words.

"I'll not fuck you now … " A finger slowly slid along the crease of her silky slickened skin. " … but I will have you — and when I do, you'll be dripping wet, crawling towards me. You'll be *begging* for me to take you." Quickly, his hands reached up, ripping away the remaining material from her body. Once her pants and shirt had been removed, he moved to pick up the other clothes spread at the base of the bed. "Modesty was a gift I attempted to give you, but your behavior shows me you cannot be rewarded as of yet." Moving to the door he cradled the pile of clothes in his arms, turned to look back at her naked form once more. "You've undoubtedly attracted some unwanted attention today, Madeleine. As a result, I'm expecting guests. I'll leave you, naked and bound for their inspection, but I'll not let them touch you … *if* you behave when they visit." He allowed her a moment to let his words sink in before delivering the final threat. "If you misbehave, Mouse, I'll leave them alone with you, to play with you as they see fit."

He closed the door, but didn't bother to lock it. His mouse was chained to the bed, locked into a position meant to seduce and satisfy the feral side of a man. The slick of blood on her skin coupled with the indignity of her nakedness and position would suffice to make any man believe Aaron was doing as he was told. Moving quickly to his room, he dumped the evidence of his kindness where they would not be found, before he walked back out into the living room, into the concerned glare of his friend.

122

Brushing aside Xander's silent question, Aaron moved to the bar, picking up the scotch and filled his glass to the rim. He slammed back the strong bite of the liquor, replaced the glass on the surface of the bar and turned toward the man standing faithfully behind him. "She's been prepared. There will be no question that I've succumbed to cruelty and lust."

"Have you?" Xander took a few steps back, leaned casually against the wall as he scrutinized Aaron. "I heard her cries. Do I even want to know what caused them?"

Aaron's lips turned up into a savage grin. "She's been left dripping wet and displayed for any man that arrives. The smell of sex has been left as a fine sheen on her skin ... " He eyes glared back, daring Xander to protest his actions. " ... That is all you need to know." As Aaron turned to walk toward his office, he heard Xander push himself upright, his footsteps following closely behind. Aaron turned back, met eyes with the raging blue orbs that glared back in his direction.

"I worry about you, Aaron. Do you slip as your father did? Have you lost yourself to the temptation of flesh that has been gifted by a madman?" Carefully spoken words, questions that could easily result in violence. Xander stood strong against Aaron, a beacon anchoring him to sanity, to remaining true to his task.

Aaron sighed, his shoulders dropping with defeat and regret. "I didn't fuck her if that's what you are wondering. I did enough to make it appear that I have, but she remains whole, untouched inside."

Xander winced, instantly understanding what Aaron must have done. His eyes softened as pity coursed through his veins. Wishing to free Aaron of his guilt, he nodded his head, spoke lies intended to soothe. "It is understandable Aaron. Your mouse would forgive you if she knew how your actions are designed only to save her life. You had no other option."

"And if they don't come ... if the maintenance crew somehow kept to themselves the sight of a clothed slave?"

Xander considered Aaron's question, knew better than to believe that any person within The Estate could keep such a sight a secret. "They'll come. How long have we lived here that you can possibly doubt that the rumor isn't spreading like flames within the network? You did what you had to do." A meaningful look occurred between the two men, prisoners, themselves, to a world of brutality and madness. "The regret you wear is enough to tell me you haven't been lost, Aaron. He will not win in this game. We are too close to ending it." Xander was resolute in his words, sure that they would pull enough men to their side, that, eventually, they could overpower even the most evil of the devil's creatures.

"If they don't, I'll be nothing more than an animal. A man who took pleasure in a woman's torment." It was a confession; one he knew his lifelong friend would hear. Turning again, he took long strides toward the doors of his office, throwing them open, he walked to his desk, sat down the full weight of his guilt into the leather chair, picked up papers that would lead him to the next man that dared to steal from The Estate. His hands itched to take a life, the satisfaction of watching another traitorous creature go blank underneath the slice of his blade. It was a cruelty built from years of being the executioner for The Estate; the lethal force hidden behind the cloak of a suit and tie. He wondered if it was any different, the amount of lives he'd extinguished surely made him nothing more than a man who deserved to end up on the receiving end of that same blade. Before, he'd been able to soften the brutality, been able to mask it under the belief that those he killed deserved their fate. In a sense, he'd rid the world of thieves and murderers; he'd helped eradicate a filth that poisoned other innocent lives. But there was no such excuse for his actions against Madeleine. Only that he would save her from a more brutal form of rape, of the pain that would be inflicted on her by men with no morality left within their conscience.

Having become lost to his work, he didn't hear when a knock sounded at the doors of his apartment. It was only when Xander moved to answer that Aaron looked up from his desk, gazing across his office and the room beyond to watch and see who stood on the other side of those large, wooden doors.

When Xander's spine straightened and the muscles beneath his shirt tensed, Aaron understood who'd arrived. He pushed back from the desk, stood swiftly and moved to receive the visitors that darkened his door. Xander stepped

125

aside, revealing Emory and Vincent standing in the hall.

"Come in. I'd like to say I'm surprised to see you, however I suspect you've been sent for a particular purpose." Aaron stopped and stood in the center of his living room, watched as his father's men moved into the interior of the apartment. Both men were large, their height and brawn matching that of Aaron and Xander. But their eyes held a different light, a deep-seated insanity that spoke of violence and decay.

The men stood, both with brown hair slicked back, revealing brown eyes so dark they mimicked the darkest of night. They could have been twins, had their facial features not been so drastically altered. The tan skin of Emory's face was shadowed by stubble, the only break in the hair being a large scar that ran down the side of his cheek. Vincent also had the coloring of a person who'd spent hours in the sun, but his face was clean shaven, his cheekbones sharp points that made his face appear sunken and hollow. Silence hung heavy between the four men, the threat of violence scenting the air, creating a heaviness that seemingly absorbed the oxygen in the room, made it difficult to breathe. Emory spoke first, his voice grating against Aaron's nerves.

"There's a rumor circulating the house; one that's peaked your father's curiosity. The maintenance crew could swear they saw your slave beating against one of the windows of your quarters. They weren't sure, Aaron, but they believe she was clothed as she attempted to gain their attention." Emory moved forward, a slight

126

curve to his mouth, the only indication of his amusement. "You must know better than to provide clothing to a slave."

Aaron stood strong, his shoulder's pulled back, his spine locked into place. "Of course. I'm sure it was only a reflection that they saw. The slave is as she should be; she had a moment of insanity that has been curbed. It's to be expected while she is being trained."

Emory glanced back at Vincent, both men wearing expressions of ill intent. Vincent spoke next, thoroughly enjoying his next words. "We will need to see her, Aaron, so that we can report back to your father as to how she was found."

Xander stepped forward, anger raging red across his face. Aaron held up a hand, reminding Xander to hold his temper. Stepping toward the doors of the corridor, Aaron spoke back to the men from over his shoulder. "Then come take your look. But in the future, I do not appreciate being disturbed while in my quarters. I've been given a week, I'll use it without interruption after this visit." His words a razor edged warning, Aaron led the men to Maddy's room, cursed under his breath about what he must do. Opening the door, he stepped into the room, held the raging blue of Maddy's eyes as the three other men entered behind him. Her skin blushed red when she noticed his guests, her arms and legs uselessly pulling at the chains keeping her bound and displayed.

Turning to the men, Aaron motioned to the naked woman. "As you can see, she wears no clothes. She's been used to my satisfaction. You

127

can report back to my father that there is no need for concern." Shifting back to the door, Emory stepped close to Maddy, moved as if to touch her when Aaron quickly moved to block her from Emory's hand.

His words dripping with menace, he spoke a reminder. "Is it your hand you wish to lose today? You heard my father, it was you that he requested spread the word of his directive." Emory's dark eyes met Aaron's as he pulled back from his attempt. Through clenched teeth, Aaron continued. "Do not think you stand in his place just yet, Emory. He has not been so completely lost that he's placed you on his throne."

Emory smiled, a veiled threat hidden behind the face of a man not unknown to violence and death. "Then you will touch her for me. Give us something to take back to your father, so that he can feel satisfied to know that you are well aware of how to appreciate his gift."

Maddy tensed at Emory's words, looked to Aaron with eyes filled with panic and disgust. Letting out a slow breath Aaron turned to glance at his mouse, his eyes begging her to understand that, in this moment, she must behave appropriately. Blinking once, Aaron moved to demonstrate his dominance over the small creature that lay helpless before him.

Chapter Twelve

Maddy's breath caught as Aaron moved closer to her, saw something in his eyes that she thought she'd mistaken for remorse. He slowly reached toward her, rubbed the tips of his fingers along her legs as he held her stare. Leaning down he brought his mouth to her ear, whispering so that only she would hear the words he spoke. "Behave for me, Mouse, and I'll keep the wolves behind me from touching you. Struggle against me, and I'll have no choice but to leave you to their mercy."

Raising his head slightly, she could feel the warmth of his breath brushing down across her cheek. His lips, so close to hers, she wondered if it was his intent to kiss her like a man would a lover. Such an invasion would be an insult, but then again, every touch, every brush of his fingers against her skin had been taken against her will; the ultimate insult being her continued display to the multiple men in the room. Her eyes moved to look over his shoulder, to the two men with whom she'd not yet had contact. One man, the one with a jagged, wide scar that ran from his ear, down his cheek, to the tip of his chin ... his was the face of a monster. His cruelty was openly displayed in the violent black of his eyes and the threatening leer on his face, the wicked curl to his mouth. Her eyes went to the second man, his expression no different than the first. She shivered at the sight of the men, knew that they would be more cruel than the ones

129

who'd held her until this point. Looking back into Aaron's eyes, she saw a small glimmer in the deep shades of green, a plea that she wouldn't have noticed if her fear hadn't been mirrored back in his gaze. He was nervous, afraid of some unknown threat; one that Maddy felt must have something to do with their newfound audience.

Aaron's eyes never left hers as his hands traveled back down her body, along the length of her torso, winding it's way back to the apex of her thighs. Standing up straighter, Aaron kept his gaze locked to hers; his eyes, the color of a forest blanketed in the shadow of a violent storm. They were so green, set against the thick black of his lashes, the sun-kissed tan of his skin. His finger found the same spot as before and he started moving it against her, causing her breath to hitch, her body to tremble. His eyes were still and resolute on hers, never moving even when he finally opened his mouth to speak again.

"Show me how much you want me, slave. Thank your Master for granting you pleasure before his own." The bitter film of disgust covered her tongue, she bit down to stifle the embarrassment and anger building up inside her. But he still worked at the bundle of nerves, her body's natural reaction a thing so far outside her control, that it slickened even in her repulsion. His other hand came to her breast, his fingertips trailing along the side of it, the chills causing it to peak on its own. She swelled under his touch, kept her eyes trained on his, tried to forget the more frightening men that stood behind him. A now familiar fire began to simmer within her, a tingle along her skin and deep within her body at the same time. Her breathing grew impossibly faster, her eyes daring to break his gaze to roll back in response to what his hands were doing to her body. His fingers pinched down on the sensitive skin of her breast, a sudden flash of pain shooting through her, causing her to cry out from the sensation. Opening her eyes she found mock rage burning behind his, he pinched her again, this time hard enough to induce tears from her eyes.

Aaron's next words sounded like both a command and a plea at the same time, "I told you to thank your Master, slave. Do so, now." His voice was saturated in anger while his eyes begged her to respond. He was worried. Only she could tell, the other men at his back not able to see the expression on his face. She opened her mouth, not understanding why she felt compelled to respond.

"Thank you." Her lips cracked from her breath brushing across them. Her voice, so low, that she wasn't sure he had heard her speak.

Silence as they stared at one another, relief seeming to flood his body, his eyes lit for a split second by her compliance. His brow furrowed again and he bit out another command so condescendingly, that she imagined she'd been hallucinating to think he could have, for a second, been concerned for her. "Say 'thank you, *Master.*' Another pinch to the side of her breast, the sensitive flesh shooting out sparks of radiating pain. The men behind Aaron laughed, took pleasure in the violence and insult used against her.

One tear finally fell down her cheek. Biting

131

back her instinct to rebel, she decided to play along, somehow understanding that she faced far worse torment if she refused to obey. Her lips ached as she spoke, her voice cracking from the unending friction of his hand against her sensitized flesh.

"Thank you ... Master." Breathy and shallow, her voice caused Aaron's breathing to become irregular. He felt sickened by the erotic rub of her words against his skin, the odd satisfaction he felt when he should have been enraged. He was the worst kind of bastard, his pants tightening in response to her forced submission. When her eyes began to roll back again, he quickened his movements, added more pressure against her swollen skin. Her lips parted, her head fell back. He felt her muscles quiver against the tips of his fingers as he slid one down to rest atop the opening of her core. The sound of her moans excited him; having become so lost in the expression on her face, he'd forgotten about the men standing behind him. Wrenching himself back to the situation, he brought himself under control, straightened his shoulders and settled a mask of indifference back on his face.

When she stilled and had seemingly recovered from the violent quakes tearing through her body, Aaron pulled his hand up, trailing her own moisture up along her stomach, between her breasts, stopping at the base of her neck. She looked up into his eyes, an odd emotion racing across his face before being replaced with a distant and emotionless expression.

Aaron cleared his throat, lifted his hand to

tap a single finger against her lips. "Good girl." He turned suddenly and took a few steps in the direction of the other men in the room. Indicating the door with his hand, he stood blocking Madeleine from their eyes. After several moments, she heard footsteps as the men left the room. Her eyes followed Aaron as he moved to the door, glancing back at her one more time, before stepping out into the hallway.

Shutting the door, Aaron followed the men as they moved into the living room. Once freed from the confined space of the hall, he watched as Xander broke off from the group, immediately moving to open the front doors in invitation for Emory and Vincent to leave. His father's men began to step through the door when Emory stopped, turned back to look at Aaron.

"I find it *interesting* that you chose to get the bitch off instead of taking your fill of her and tossing her aside. Perhaps your father never taught you what he meant about how to use the whore."

Aaron attempted to stifle a grin, but its force was so strong that one side of his mouth curved up as the grin broke free. "I'm flattered you were hoping for an opportunity to stare at the movement of my bare ass, but unlike some … " His eyebrow arched to indicate the man to whom he was speaking. " … I don't display my cock in public. I prefer a much more, private, location." A humorless laugh escaped him. "Now scurry on back to my father. Perhaps he can give you more lessons on what it means to use a whore."

Emory scowled at Aaron's implication.

133

Nodding once, Emory turned and walked out through the doorway, followed closely behind by Vincent. Once Vincent's foot had cleared the doorway, Xander slammed the door so hard, the walls shook from the impact. Eyes the color of a raging sea met eyes the color of a dark forest when Xander finally turned back to face Aaron.

"Give me the keys to her chains." Aaron's hand came up immediately, taking the keys from Xander.

Maddy could hear the sound of weighted footsteps approaching the room. Since having been left alone, she hadn't stopped crying. Her shame, the grueling pain of her bindings, and the orgasms she'd been forced to experience, wept from her in the form of tears produced from a body in need of water. The salt of her tears burned her eyes as they fell, trailed hot along her cheeks before pooling at the corner of her mouth and the dip between her lower lip and her chin.

Anger a building volcano within her, she cursed herself for having given in to his commands. However, in the back of her mind, she somehow knew her fate would have been much worse in the hands of the men at Aaron's back. She found it odd that, even though Aaron had been the one to violate her the most, she somehow trusted him more than the pure evil that'd stood just behind him.

She heard the sound of key being turned in a lock, the door being pushed open, and Aaron walking through swiftly before closing it behind him. A few large steps and he was by the bed, immediately moving to unlock the chains at her feet. Maddy silently watched him, wondered what horrors she would endure once freed. After Aaron removed the first shackle from her ankle, Maddy hissed as air met the cuts made by the metal against her skin. Aaron's face twisted momentarily before he set out to release her other ankle. Once her legs were freed, he moved up to her wrists. Before removing the shackles from around her wrists he quietly instructed, "You're not going to want to pull your arms down immediately when I release you, your shoulders are going to hurt. Once you are freed, I will help you lower them." Maddy listened to the sound of the metal key being inserted into the first lock. As soon as she felt air in place of where the metal had circled her wrist, she pulled her arm down in an attempt to cover her body. The pain that shot through her shoulder and arm caused her to cry out. A low sigh sounded above her.

"When are you going to start listening to me, Ms. Clark?" Aaron shook his head, an amused grin peeking out from the corners of his mouth. Maddy scowled at him before looking back to inspect the damage to the skin on her wrist. He released the second hand, reached down to massage the sore muscles at her shoulder. She wanted to pull away, to resist his touch, but the firm grip felt good as he slowly lowered her other arm from above her head.

The bed lowered underneath, taking Aaron's weight as he sat down beside her. His eyes watched her hands as she rubbed at the red and torn skin at her wrists. They sat silently for a while;

135

she refused to look up at him, to acknowledge his presence beside her. Having grown accustomed to the lack of sound, she jumped when he finally spoke again.

"I need you to understand something about where you're being held." His voice was soft, regretful, as if confessing. "There is no person on these grounds that does not belong to The Estate. Maintenance men, maids, cooks ... they all are loyal to the family. What you did this afternoon, when you banged on the glass, it endangered you more than you realize."

His hand came up to softly grasp her chin, move her head so that he could lock his eyes with hers. Concern etched his gaze as he spoke again. "I am your Master, Madeleine, but I am not the worst nightmare you will have to face in this house. Those men ... " His eyes narrowed at his inner thoughts. " ... they will hurt you, make you feel pain that you never imagined possible. Death would not be granted quickly. The torment they would inflict, it would be endless; hours, days, weeks, that is the amount of time you would suffer at their hands."

A chill brushed across her body, the truth of his words a stream of ice weaving through the blood in her veins.

After staring down at her for a few minutes more, he released her chin, and spoke to her in words meant to be obeyed: "You will get cleaned up and eat something. It can be different this time, not as violent as our encounter this morning." He couldn't help himself, even chapped, her lips called

136

to him with the lush fullness of her pout. Leaning down he brushed his mouth across hers, reveled in the feel of the stolen kiss. He was not surprised when she pulled away suddenly, detesting the feel of his lips against hers. A warning in his eyes, he stood up, reached his hand down to her. "Follow me to the bathroom, Mouse. We need to get you cleaned and I need to tend to your wounds."

Painfully, her arms came down beside her as she attempted to push herself up into a sitting position. The jolts of shocking pain traveled down her arms, causing her to fall back against the mattress. Aaron reached down as she tried to move away from his touch. "I'm going to pick you up, Madeleine, carry you to the bathroom due to your weak state. Do not fight against me. I'd hate to have to correct your behavior while you're already so injured."

His arms slid underneath her, the tips of his fingers trailing along her back and underneath her bottom. A slight thrill of remembered pleasure ran through her body at his touch, and Maddy winced in shame at the feeling. Aaron's eyebrow arched, his knowledge of her reaction an unhidden thing. His mouth came to her ear, the warmth of his breath tickling the skin, trailing down her neck. "I hope there comes a day when my touch does not disgust you; that, rather, you can smile when my hands rub along your body."

Lifting her easily, he removed her from the bed, carried her naked body out of the room, but turned right instead of left; taking her to a different room than the bathroom he'd taken her to that morning. He balanced her weight while using his

137

hand to open the large double doors at the end of the hall, passing quickly through a bedroom dressed in decadence and excess, into a bathroom just as beautiful and stunning to the eye. Placing her down on a chair near a marble counter, he moved to the large, claw-foot tub in the center of the room. While his attention was turned to filling the tub, Maddy looked around the large expanse, noted the dark marbles and stone surfaces, a place dripping with masculine colors and materials. Even the tub in the center was colored a deep black; veins of gold and silver wrapping their ways through the stone from which the tub had been fashioned. Behind the tub, stood a glass-encased shower with steps leading down into a sunken floor below. The walls of the bathroom were painted a stunning red, broken up only by the dark countertops and floors, the brilliant whites of the linens spread throughout the room.

Aaron turned back to her, but quickly moved to a closet behind her, taking out a large white box before approaching her again. Placing the box on the counter, he moved to pick her up. Her body went to flinch, but she remembered his words from earlier, how she needed to learn to accept him so that she wasn't thrown to the wolves. Resigning to her fate, Maddy reached up, wrapped her arms around his shoulders and allowed herself to be carried and placed in the warm waters of the bath.

Maddy hissed when the water met with the open skin on her ankles and wrists. Immediately pulling her legs and arms from the water, she draped the injured appendages over the sides,

138

allowing the cool air to soothe the burn inflicted by contact with the water. Aaron stood up, walked to retrieve the white box from the counter before moving the chair over to sit next to the bath. Placing the box on the floor, Maddy watched as his eyes heated while he looked over her body, his chest moving quicker in time with his hurried breath. Forcefully wrenching himself from his perusal of her skin, Aaron reached down to open the box, pulling out an antibiotic salve to use on her broken skin.

"This ointment will clean your wounds, keep infection from settling into the cuts." Quickly his hands moved to unscrew the lid, his fingers dipping down into the colorless contents of the container. Spreading the cool gel along her right ankle, she hissed out again, her head falling back from the pain. Aaron's eyes raked over the subtle bounce to her breasts as she moved, his teeth coming down on his bottom lip as he fought to not take what could so easily be his. He continued massaging the salve into her skin, moving from one leg to the next, then up to her wrists.

Maddy watched him as he worked to smooth the medicine over her injuries. She noticed how the light shone onto his hair, making the black color appear like it had hints of blue in its depths. The angle of his jaw was sharp, deadly, but so beautiful in its shape that she could imagine the feel of running her hand along the skin. When he looked up, she looked away quickly, a blush racing across her cheeks from having been caught staring. A grin formed over Aaron's lips as he watched that blush turn into a heat that traveled along the silken

139

white of her skin, over her breasts and across the flat expanse of her stomach. Her curves were so intimately feminine that he longed to sink his teeth into the fleshy parts of her chest, her hips, and the heart shaped perfection of her ass. Shaking himself of his desire, he dipped his fingers into the water of her bath, cleaning them of the remaining gel before screwing the lid of the container back in place.

Packing the box of medical supplies back together, he moved to the closet to replace the box. Grabbing out a large, soft white towel he moved back to Maddy, placing the towel on the chair before picking up a washcloth and soap she'd not noticed before. He glanced over to her, the light sparkling off the emerald color of his eyes. "I'm going to clean you, Madeleine and you will allow it this time, understand?"

She did understand, knew that there was no place on her body safe from this man's touch. Disgrace washed over her mind as she recognized a small bit of longing for the feel of his hands, the return of the sensations he forced upon her while she'd been chained. Her heart sped in its beat, her breathing becoming quick and shallow as he used the soap to build a thick lather on the cloth. Reaching over her, his arm brushed across the tip of her breasts as he massaged the soap into her neck, along the soreness of her shoulders and down along her arms. She watched as his lips parted, became impossibly more full as he worked his hands across her skin, the silence between them deafening and weighted.

The rough feel of the cloth rubbed down over the tops of her breasts, finally rubbing across where Aaron's teeth had left their mark when he'd corrected her earlier behavior. Sucking in a jagged breath, Maddy noticed how her body pushed upwards into his touch, a sleeping demon aching for the sin his hands had forced through her body when she'd been bared to his mercy before.

Chapter Thirteen

Aaron watched as the tips of Madeleine's breasts pebbled under the rough texture of the washcloth. His tongue felt full and rough in his mouth as he moved the cloth lower, along her stomach to the juncture of her thighs. A small moan escaped her perfectly shaped lips, her hips thrusting forward begging for his touch. Pulling himself back from the intensity of his desire, he rubbed the cloth along the sensitive skin, noticing how it swelled at his touch. Instantly confused, he looked up into her blue eyes, the swirling colors muddled by the haze of desire, her lids fluttering closed as he washed her.

Confusion clouding all logical thought, he watched as her body writhed before him, her legs barely spreading, inviting his continued touch. He stopped momentarily, but then started to move the cloth down the interior of one thigh when she whimpered, her eyes fluttering open again, the force of the churning blues burning into him. His hand stilled, her full lips parting, the begged whisper barely loud enough for him to hear.

"Please ... "

Slowly, Maddy's hand smoothed down the skin of her own body, her fingers lightly brushing over his as she pulled his hand back to a spot she'd never explored, but one where he'd shown true mastery over her spirit. Aaron's mouth parted, his breaths forcing their way over his trembling lips, his pants tightening impossibly full as he dropped the washcloth into the water and ran his fingers between her slickened and swollen flesh. Was it possible that his slave already craved his touch, the sensations no longer forced, but welcomed? When he pressed down on the swollen bundle, a higher pitched, yet soft cry escaped her lips, her back arched, pushing the bountiful weight of her breasts upwards, the tight peak of her nipples poking out just above the water.

His neck moved as he swallowed the lump stuck in his throat. His heart pounded against his chest, feeling like it would push through as he watched her respond to the pleasure he gave her. Remembering his place and hers, he pressed on, knowing full well, her compliance would push him toward a dangerous edge, one he was not sure he could back away from if too closely approached. "Please … what?" His words were slow, the low baritone adding strength to the rasp of his voice.

Opening her eyes, she pulled up her head, the corner of her mouth curling up at one end. Only the sound of their breath and the light swirl of the water, before she opened her mouth and breathed out, "Please … Master."

Losing his control, a shudder ran through his body. He bit his lip, forcing back the desire to drive his hand deeper, taking a piece of her that could not belong to him, not while she was his captive, an unwilling participant to his desire. Speeding up the motion of his hand, his breath caught when he saw the shudder of gratification vibrate along her body, saw her cheeks fill with a sinful glow, her eyes roll under the thin lids above

143

them. Her body tensed suddenly, her chest stopped moving as she held her breath, was delivered to a place of pure hedonistic pleasure and pain.

When she relaxed, he pulled his hand away, closed his eyes, and attempted to distance himself from her display. The friction of his pants against his hardened length pained him; it begged to be released, to be wrapped within the soft heat he knew existed inside this glorious beauty, which sat sated and satisfied before him.

"I believe you're finished. Stand up, I'll dry you." Aaron pushed himself forcefully out of the chair, needing to put distance between him and the temptation of her body as quickly as possible. Maddy's brows furrowed momentarily before she pulled her legs into the water; she pushed herself into a standing position before him. He wouldn't let his eyes meet hers, couldn't let her see the desire dominating his thoughts. After wrapping a large towel around her, he held out his hand to help her as she stepped over the lip of the tub onto the stone floor below.

Once she secured her footing, he dropped her hand, the friction of her skin against his was too much contact. "Follow me." Taking large steps out into his bedroom, he led her to the large closet, and pulled her clothes from the chest where he'd hidden them. Separating out the clothes that had been destroyed earlier in the day, he handed her the untorn set and motioned for her to get dressed. When Maddy complied, Aaron's eyes perked up at the movement of her body, his breath was so hot over his lips it burned. He shook his head, replaced an indifferent mask over his expression as he stood over her, shadowing her small form by his size.

"If I allow you modesty, you must obey me in all other areas. Do not flinch from my touch, when I ask you to speak, you'll do so." Staring down at her, he smiled shyly as she nodded her head in understanding of his orders. Satisfied that they reached this point, Aaron placed his hand against her back, led her from his room and down the long corridor to the dining room. Xander sat up from the couch as they entered, his eyes widening to see Madeleine easily complying with the commands barked out by Aaron.

Aaron indicated for Maddy to sit in a chair he pulled out from the table before he moved to the bar and poured himself a glass of scotch. He lifted the glass to his lips, worked the bite of the liquor down his throat with one forced motion and slammed the crystal tumbler back down on the dark wood surface of the bar. Taking care not to look back down at Maddy, he turned to Xander, barked out an order that Madeleine be fed, then in several large strides, he crossed the room, threw open the doors of his office, slamming the doors behind him as he disappeared into the dimly lit room.

Xander turned back to look at Maddy. Her eyes were locked on the wooden doors through which Aaron had just passed. A hint of sadness furrowed her brow, and Xander was left wondering what the hell had just changed between the Master and his slave. Looking between Madeleine and the door one last time, Xander

145

shrugged his shoulders and crossed through the kitchen to pull her dinner out of the large refrigerator. He poured the contents of the dish that had been delivered earlier onto a plate and placed it in the oven to heat.

"Does he ever eat?"

Shock tore through his body at the soft sound of her voice, the innocent question that revealed so much more than she'd understood. Stunned silent for a split second, a single laugh barked out from his chest, his lips turning up at the appearance of a woman, completely opposite of the wild beast he'd just earlier left chained to a bed.

"He eats." A quick glance between them before, once again, looking away. Xander kept his eyes trained on the oven as he heated her food. "I'm a little surprised, Cricket. Was that concern I heard in your question?" He chuckled. "Has your Master drugged you?"

She sat so quiet for so long that Xander thought her speech just moments ago had been a rare moment now lost. But when her rose colored lips moved again, she gave him an answer so weighted with hidden meaning, he almost lost his hold on the plate as he lifted it from the oven.

"Something like that ... "

Steamed billowed up as Xander used a fork to release the trapped heat in the food. Picking up the plate, he turned and placed it on the table in front of Maddy. He handed her the fork, his mouth once again curling into an amused grin. "Can I trust you with this, or should I be concerned about suddenly having an eating utensil shoved in my back?" He handed her the fork and returned to the kitchen to pour her a glass of cold water.

Placing the glass in front of her, he stepped back, waiting behind her as she ate. She took a few bites then grabbed the glass, damn near polishing off the entirety of its contents. When she replaced it on the table, Xander picked it up, moved into the kitchen and began to fill it again. He turned to look at her over his shoulder. "Apparently, you're thirsty." He walked over, placed it in front of her and took his place standing behind her.

Maddy picked up her fork, began to scoop of a portion of the rice and chicken on her plate, but placed it down again, turning in her seat to look at Xander. "You don't have to stand there, lording over me. I won't run. After the events of the afternoon, I have a feeling there are far more evil men on the other side of those doors."

Xander's amused expression darkened at her words. Thoughtfully, he gazed at her for several moments before responding. "Don't mistake your Master's kindness for a weak spirit. He has killed more men than you've probably ever known in your young life. There are different types of evil in this world, Cricket. Some, more openly displayed than others."

Her eyes widened at his statement; wordlessly, she turned back into her seat, kept her eyes trained on the food before her. He didn't like scaring her, but she couldn't be allowed to believe weakness existed within the man to whom she now belonged. Weighted silence hovered over them as Xander maintained his position of sentinel behind her, waiting until she'd had her fill of the food and drink on the table. When she pushed the plate aside, he stepped forward, took it from her and moved to place it in the sink. Moving back beside her, he motioned for her to go to the living room to sit quietly on the couch.

Maddy complied without hesitation. Finding comfort in the clothes that covered her body, she worried that any hint of rebellion would leave her naked and cold without the luxury of cloth covering her skin. Her eyes followed the broad and heavily muscled expanse of Xander's back as he rinsed the dishes in the sink, before bending down to place them in the dishwasher. When he'd completed his task, he crossed through the dining room into the living room, sat down on a chair positioned next to the couch.

Picking up his phone from a side table, Xander read through the many texts he'd received in the short time since Maddy had been in his presence. Reading a message from Jason, Xander stood immediately, strode quickly across the living room to knock on the door of Aaron's office.

The door opened and Xander glanced back at Maddy, mouthed 'stay' and then disappeared behind the doors with Aaron.

Aaron looked up from his desk. Xander crossed the room and stood above him looking down at the anger-ridden expression on his face.

"Did she eat? Where is she now?" Aaron's

148

voice was concerned.

Understanding flooded Xander, unease suddenly touching upon his thoughts as to what, exactly, had happened between Aaron and his slave. "Is there something that's happened, something you regret?"

Shaking his head, Aaron settled back into the leather chair. He joined the tips of his fingers — forming a steeple — and pressed his index fingers to his lips before responding. His eyes narrowed just as he pulled his hand through his hair, obviously fighting some demon inside him. "No. I didn't cross any line not previously crossed." He looked up pointedly at Xander. "I came close, though ... " His voice a hushed confession. " ... She asked for it, wanted me to violate her body, to return to her the force of her orgasm." His fingers came up to squeeze the skin between his eyes. "She liked it, Xander. There is something so absolutely wrong about that. I almost threw her down and taught her exactly what it felt like to be a whore."

Xander stood still, his stance one of respect. He didn't dare move until Aaron had finished confessing that which haunted him. Slowly, he responded, "Even if it's wrong because it is done while she's held against her will, if she's finding pleasure in your touch, why not grant her that small bit of satisfaction ... a miniscule trace of light in her darkness?"

The deep hued green of Aaron's eyes looked up, rage burning behind them. "I won't fuck her while she's a captive. That part of her is not

149

mine, not if it isn't freely given. I'm not like the monster who raised me, I'll never let that happen." Aaron stood up, began pacing along the line of bookshelves on the walls. "I need to leave, Xander, I have to clear my head before continuing the training."

Suddenly remembering why he'd disturbed Aaron in the first place, Xander turned to his friend. "I have a good way for you to blow off some of that pent up anger." Smiling, Xander picked up his phone, tossed it to Aaron across the room. "That text is from Jason. It seems, while he was meeting with Patrick and his men discussing their loyalty to you, a spy was discovered in the room. They caught him before he was able to leave. They're holding him so that you can find out exactly why your father would send him."

A feral smile came over Aaron's lips as the promise of violence shown out from his eyes. "You don't say? I'll pay him a visit, hopefully walk away more knowledgeable of exactly how cunning my father continues to be." Moving to the doors, Aaron threw them open, crossed the living room without so much as glancing at Maddy on the couch. Continuing his quick pace to his room, he pulled on the straps of his shoulder harness, checked his guns to ensure they were loaded, before placing them into the harness. Pulling open a drawer, he pulled out his favorite knife, inspected the weapon before placing it back in its sheath and tucking it into the waistband at his back. He reached in the closet and pulled out a leather trench that reached down to his feet. Pulling the sleeves over his arms, he turned and stalked back out toward the living room, gave one final glance at Xander before letting himself out of the apartment.

Death, violence and the feeling of steel slicing across the spy's jugular would be a perfect distraction to the unwilling siren waiting for him in his home.

Chapter Fourteen

Aaron moved quickly through the halls of the large mansion. The entire property did not consist only of the building in which he lived. No, the broad expanse of land had been turned into a compound of sorts. Multiple buildings spread apart to house the members of The Estate; only those most trusted were allowed to live on the property itself.

Pushing out through the double doors that led into a large courtyard, Aaron kept to the shadows as he moved across the grounds. With large, purposeful strides, he ducked out into the woods, away from the cameras he knew surrounded the buildings on the property. Violent anticipation, a chill in the air, as Aaron made his way to Jason's quarters, a large, two-story house that stood on the outskirts of the property. Winter was coming and the air had dipped to such a cool temperature, that Aaron's breath fogged out before him, his lips parting slightly as he allowed the pent up heat to escape his body. The leaves crunching underneath his feet were the only sounds he could hear as he moved quickly along the line of trees. Every once in a while, the branches would split apart just enough to allow moonlight to streak down and illuminate his path.

The heavy steps of his feet fell rhythmically as his boots hit soundly against the dormant ground. When light appeared in the distance, Aaron grabbed the blade at his back, arming himself against ambush or attack. Normally, Xander was at Aaron's back, never allowing him to go into a possible den of vipers alone, but with Madeleine held in the apartment, one man had to stay behind who could be trusted to keep her safe, to not lose himself to her temptation. Aaron would rather know Madeleine was safe from harm than ensure that he had eyes behind him that would see approaching danger before it got too close to feel the sting of his blade.

As he approached the well lit home, his steps slowed, shortened as he peered out over the grounds surrounding the building. Even though Xander was convinced that Jason was loyal, Aaron trusted no man beyond the one he'd chosen as his first guard. The only shadows cast across the grounds were those of the large trees that surrounded the home, no signs of movement or life could be seen as Aaron perused the immediate area. Sure that no man awaited him in ambush, Aaron walked calmly across the exterior courtyard, down the large winding steps, and pushed into the house through a lesser used service door.

Making his way through the kitchen, several cooks jumped in surprise. His leather coat billowed out around his feet creating an eerie shadow as he moved through the dining room and halls. When he approached the front living room, he slowed again, listened as several men spoke quietly nearby. The conversation wasn't anything of use, mindless chatter from men who sounded like they already tied one on early in the evening.

"And how did I know you would not be

knocking on the front door?"

Aaron spun around, immediately moved to grab the other man in the room and knocked him against a wall with the steel of his blade cutting into the first layers of the skin around the man's neck.

Not surprised to have been overtaken by Aaron, Jason wore a blank expression, knowing full well that Aaron is his father's most deadly assassin.

"Remind me not to come up behind you a second time." Jason's voice was tight, his throat moving against the razor-sharp edge of the blade held firmly in Aaron's hand. A bead of ruby liquid trailed from the edge of Aaron's knife, down the stubble scattered along Jason's neck. Slowly, Aaron let go as he pulled his weapon back to place it in the sheath.

Jason hand's came up to wipe away the single drop of blood running along his skin. Looking down at the red stain on his hand, he looked up at Aaron, and smiled before saying, "I would ask you for a shave with that thing, if I wasn't concerned about your blade cutting too close." He chuckled, reaching out to shake Aaron's hand.

Aaron straightened his spine, suspiciously eying the man standing in front of him, before finally relenting and taking Jason's hand in a firm grip. "Jason ... What do you know about the spy?"

Jason nodded, quickly noting Aaron's desire to cut to the chase. "I was meeting with Patrick and some of his men this evening. We were discussing the changes Xander has been pushing regarding the hierarchy of The Estate. I'm behind you one hundred percent, Aaron. Your father has lost himself to a power trip of madness and greed. This network has become far more corrupt in the past few years, being led by those two jackals, Emory and Vincent. You already control the legitimate business, there's no reason you couldn't rule the darker side as well. You're a smart man and the most lethal son of a bitch around here. We want to side with you."

Aaron blinked, but kept an indifferent expression on his face. Never one to chat with men he didn't know well, he wanted to keep words and actions to the task at hand, give it more time before discussing conspiracy and allegiance. "The spy? Tell me about him."

"He's a bottom-feeder, a common crook who got caught trying to record the meeting. He'd tagged along with one of Patrick's men, supposedly applying for entry into his unit. Patrick was the one who caught him, took the recording device and locked the asshole up before contacting Xander. It was surprising to hear that *you* would be coming to talk with him."

Considering the information, Aaron was quiet for a moment before finally responding. "This sounds easy enough. It shouldn't take too long for me to find out for whom he works, if it was my father who'd sent him in. Take me to him." Aaron looked over as Jason nodded his assent and turned to lead Aaron down a corridor to their right and up a set of narrow stairs that must have been intended for easy movement by staff personnel so that they could remain out of sight of any houseguests. Aaron continued following Jason noticing that, although the man was just short of six feet, the width of his shoulders almost equaled the length of space between the walls of the corridor they now traveled. A heavily muscled man, Jason was no stranger to a fight. His features were made even more striking by the pure white of his hair and the light silver of his eyes. The stark beauty of Jason was enough to fool any man who didn't expect the pure rage that Aaron knew existed within the man who could end up his greatest ally.

Stopping suddenly, Jason unlocked a small, interior door, leading Aaron inside a closet-sized chamber where the spy had been kept awaiting his arrival. There was barely enough room for the three men to move around, but Aaron didn't need ample amounts of space for the purpose of his visit.

Aaron's coat blew out around his feet as he swiftly entered the room, noticing how the suspected spy's eyes filled with panic upon his entry. A pathetic excuse for a criminal, he sat bent over a small, square table set in the middle of the room. His thin brown hair was balding at the top, and wire frame glasses circled eyes that belonged more to a rodent than to a man. His thin frame shook from dread and fear and his clothes were torn and stained red from the beating he'd already taken from Patrick. The spy reminded Aaron of Theo Hollis, the man whose blood ran free from his body earlier that day after Aaron discovered his theft from the business.

Pulling a chair from the table, Aaron turned it around, sitting down while resting his muscular arms over the back of the chair. The sound of the chair's feet as they struck the wooden floor echoed through the small room, accenting the vile stink of fear already overpowering the small space. Aaron stared silently at the spy for a few moments, allowed terror to fill the man's entire body before asking his questions. As those quiet moments passed, the only sound breaking the silence was the anxious breath of the man sitting across the table.

With a voice saturated in threat and cruel intent, Aaron finally asked, "Who are you?"

The beady brown of the man's eyes peered up, widening when they saw the scathing grin stretched tight against Aaron's face. Opening his mouth, his breaths became heavier, his heart undoubtedly beating through his chest in anticipation of the death that was sure to come. "M ... My name is Collinsworth ... Mark Collinsworth."

Aaron nodded, amused that the pathetic creature before him was able to speak clearly while fully aware that his last minutes on Earth were stretched out before him. "Do you know who I am ... Mr. Collinsworth?" A simple question, but one laced with the eventuality of pain and death.

The spy looked up, blinked his small eyes a few times before nodding in acknowledgment of the question. "You're Aaron Carmichael; you're Joseph Carmichael's son."

Aaron's heart beat faster at the sound of his father's name. The feel of his blade against this man's throat would be that much sweeter after the

157

filth of his father's name had been allowed to roll so easily off the spy's tongue.

"I am." Leaning back, Aaron moved his arms so that only his hands gripped the backside of the chair in which he sat. "You must know why I'm here speaking with you tonight. Do you mind telling me and my friend, Jason, why, exactly, you thought it a wise idea to record what was intended to be a private meeting?"

The spy fidgeted in his seat, his beady eyes traveling back and forth between Aaron and Jason. Losing his patience, Aaron spoke in an effort to speed Mr. Collinsworth's answer along. "I can begin removing parts of your body, Mark, if you feel that will help you discover the answer to my question." A threat yes, but an act Aaron had been known to commit many times in the years he'd acted as assassin for the network.

The scrawny man's body began to shake violently upon hearing Aaron's threat. Laughter, mocking and cruel, bubbled out from Aaron as he watched the man before him reduced to a fit of absolute horror. "Don't piss yourself, it will only make my job a lot more ... messy ... in the end. I'm actually quite fond of the boots I'm wearing. It would only anger me more if I was forced to dirty them by stepping in your piss."

"I ... it wasn't my initial intention to record the meeting, but when I heard there would be an uprising against Mr. Carmichael, I thought such information would be valuable, might help bring me to a higher position within the network."

Aaron smiled, felt pity for the stupid man sitting before him that was far too honest for his own good. "To whom were you planning on selling that information? You must have had an idea of someone that would find it of interest."

Resignation dampened the man's eyes, the droop of his shoulders a clear indication he knew what was to come. "I believed Mr. Carmichael himself would take notice of me if I were to deliver the information, that he would give me a position above that which could be granted by Patrick's unit."

"So your attempt at espionage was your idea alone, you weren't sent by any man in particular?" Aaron suspected the spy truly did act on his own, thinking he'd stumbled upon information that would make him a higher ranked member of The Estate. Unfortunately, the weak son of a bitch neglected to think that by presenting the information to his father, he'd also be revealing himself to be the rat that he was. Aaron's father did not gain his throne by allowing men known to talk to live for any longer than it took them to deliver their message. Loyalty did not exist among criminals when loose tongues were involved.

The spy shook his head "no", dropped his eyes to the dirty and scarred table positioned between them.

Further questioning wasn't necessary, this man was no more than an unknown leech attempting to feed off the network. With a quickness akin to that of a snake, Aaron jumped across the table, the sound of his chair striking

159

heavy against the floor as he pinned the pathetic shell of a man to the wall, his blade tearing through skin and tendons, the gurgled sound of the man's trachea and esophagus being ripped open by the forceful slice of steel. The arterial spray burst out, bathing Aaron in the evidence of violence and death. Dropping the man like nothing more than a butchered animal, Aaron gazed down at the lifeless body, watched as the head rolled and twisted into an unnatural position, held to the body by nothing more than the bits of spine still attached. Aaron's chest heaved with labored breath, the weight of his demons momentarily lifted by the act of an executioner.

Turning, Aaron noticed how Jason's silver eyes were held wide, lit by a mix of respect and mortal fear. Aaron could imagine the nightmare he must portray, a man skilled in the art of execution, who preferred the steel of a blade to the impersonal use of lead bullets when taking down his kill. Aaron's eyes followed the thick muscles that worked along Jason's neck as he swallowed down his surprise at witnessing the ruthless acts of an assassin as proficient as Aaron.

Looking back at the corpse now bleeding out on Jason's floor, Aaron laughed when noticing that the spy did, in fact, release his bowels upon death. The foul smell slowly filling up the room, he turned to Jason, and with no emotion in his voice, he commented, "You may want to send up any other man you suspect isn't as loyal as they portray themselves to be. Let them see an example of what they will become if discovered."

Jason coughed from the fetid smell of

160

excrement and death wrapping itself within the enclosed space. "This sight is enough for even a man of my status to grow nervous in your presence. I'm awed by the swiftness of your hand, Aaron. Great power obviously resides within a man of so few words."

A simple nod in response, Aaron wiped off what blood he could from his face and blade on the sleeve of his jacket before exiting the room and making his way back through the maze of corridors through the house. Hearing Jason's weighted steps following closely behind, Aaron turned and locked eyes with him. "Although it appears my father's dogs haven't yet sniffed out our plans, we should act more carefully from this point forward. It won't be long before more fools believe they can garner a higher position by reporting back. I want Xander notified of any future meetings. They should be coordinated so that he can attend." Aaron turned to continue his path, but stopped short. Quick words spoken from over his shoulder, he ordered, "No man that hasn't proven his loyalty will attend future discussions. I'm somewhat concerned it has been allowed up to this point."

Aaron didn't allow Jason time to respond. His task complete, he left the large house, his mind drifting back to the small woman held in his quarters.

Chapter Fifteen

Maddy sat back against the soft leather of the couch, watched as Xander paced the floors awaiting Aaron's return. Her mind drifted to Xander's words, his acknowledgment that Aaron had a soul as evil as the men who'd watched her in the room earlier that day. Trepidation coiled its way through her bones until it rested on her skin as a fine sheen of sweat.

When the front door finally slammed open, Maddy watched as Aaron entered, his face covered by the evidence of his activities, the stain of death almost black as it lay smeared across his features. Startled, she curled in on herself. When the deep green of his eyes met hers, a quick flash of light behind the horror that clouded his gaze surprised her.

Sparing her no more than a quick glance, Aaron made his way to the double doors leading to the back bedrooms, threw them open before walking heavily down the corridor, disappearing as quickly as he'd arrived. Xander sighed while standing next to her, rolled his shoulders back to release the tension built from his wait, eventually pushing himself forward to follow Aaron down the corridor. Locking the front doors on his way through the room, Xander glanced back at Maddy as he asked, "Are you intelligent enough to know that escaping this room would be to your detriment?"

162

Maddy nodded, knowing full well that moving from her spot would only lead her into the arms of a far greater form of torture. The flash of white teeth struck her as Xander smiled before turning to follow Aaron down the hall.

Entering his bedroom, Aaron immediately stripped himself of his jacket and weapons, picked up a rag lying near him to better clean the steel of his blade before re-sheathing it and placing it in the top drawer of his bureau. Reaching behind him, he grasped the collar of his shirt, ripping the soaked material from his body before venturing into the bathroom, looking forward to the sharp bite of hot water.

Stepping down into the steam laden enclosure, Aaron bent his head into the water, watched as the blood swirled angrily down the drain, changing from a stark red, to a muted pink, and then clear once the remnants of the spy's death had been washed clean from his body. Only when he felt his skin begin to blister from the heat of the shower's spray did he step out. Grabbing a towel, he wrapped it loosely around his hips before walking back into his room.

With an arched eyebrow and the shrewd understanding of a man who knew Aaron better than he knew himself, Xander lurked in the doorway of the room awaiting Aaron's report. He stood quietly, his hands tucked casually into the pockets of his dress slacks as Aaron disappeared into the closet to get dressed. Seconds later, Aaron emerged in only a pair of black silk, loosely fitted pants that flowed about his legs like water.

"Jason has reported back to me that the spy acted on his own, but I was wanting to know your thoughts on the matter." Xander leaned back against the wall, patiently allowing Aaron time to come down from the peak of rage made apparent by the lethal edge to his expression.

Sitting down on the edge of the king sized bed, Aaron let his head fall forward, watched as the drops of water fell from his damp hair to the floor. Letting out a sigh of exasperation, he looked back up. "Jason's correct. The man's name was Mark Collinsworth, a bottom feeder, I presume, who thought he could make his place in the network by reporting back to my father."

Xander chuckled. "I'm sure your father would have appreciated that information, it's too bad that Mr. Collinsworth didn't understand he would have lost his head either way. Loose tongues are never acceptable in a den of criminals."

Aaron allowed Xander's levity to breach his rage, chuckled in response to the sad truth of Xander's words. The two men remained quiet, both resigned to their thoughts when Aaron finally breached the silence with a question. "What shall we do with the mouse for the evening? Can she be trusted not to make a scene of herself again?"

Considering the situation carefully, Xander choose an answer tailored toward the needs of Aaron over the woman who was, unknowingly, working her way into the cold hearts of her captors. "I could chain her again, ensure that she does not draw attention to herself," Xander said.

"No." Aaron's response was sudden and assured. "Her wounds are still too raw, if they were to grow worse, she'd be denied the medical attention necessary to heal." Sighing loudly, Aaron ran his hand through his hair before resigning to his next command. "Bring her to my room, I'll let her sleep beside me, keep her from becoming a danger to herself."

Biting back his desire to protest Aaron's decision, Xander strode out of the room without another word, leaving Aaron to his thoughts that were overflowing with blood, torment and deceit.

Maddy sat in the tranquil living room, looked around at the luxury that filled the space; the fine linens, statues that she imagined would cost more than the small house she'd called home her entire life. Not daring to move, she was oddly relieved to hear footsteps approaching in the corridor. Although these men would never let her go, had hurt her in ways deemed evil by the world around her, she couldn't shake the feeling that they were protecting her from even greater monsters, men who would feed on her pain, gain pleasure from tearing her mind, body and spirit to shreds.

Xander appeared from the dark recesses of the hall. Standing with his shoulders held back, and his hands folded together in front him, he eyed Maddy before speaking. "Aaron has requested you stay in his room with him tonight."

Her breath hitched and anxiety rolled through her small body in waves as she wondered about the extent of Aaron's plans. Having no other choice, Maddy began to stand, but Xander waved

165

his hand indicating for her to remain seated. A serious look plastered across his face, he stated, "You should know, Cricket, there is nothing more important to me than your Master. If you were to hurt him while he sleeps, or even make so much as an attempt, I will make sure that your death is as slow and agonizing as possible."

A violent shudder tore through her body as she listened to words spoken without apology, so truthful to their depths that just the sound was terrifying. Maddy looked down into her lap, waited for Xander to finish what he had to say, to give her his next command.

"Let's go, Cricket. Your Master awaits you."

Standing on weak legs, Maddy moved slowly across the stone floor of the living room, the broken skin at her ankles sore and burning with each step. The conflicting feelings flooding her heart were unexpected and alarming; desire for a man that held her captive, fear of what the man would do to her next, but also, anticipation for his touch, a feeling of safety when in his presence. She wondered if she was losing her mind, succumbing to psychological abuse at the hands of the people who stole her from her life. Her eyes shadowed as she passed Xander, her steps light as she traversed the hall, her body heavy as she led herself toward the unknown.

When she entered the room, Aaron was sitting on the edge of the large bed in the center of the room. His body bent forward, he held his head in his hands, the muscles of his back and strong shoulders made even more defined by the lights in

166

the room. His black hair was damp but still appeared as fine silk, the color of the onyx colored strands tempting her touch as it contrasted against his sun-kissed skin. Maddy waited in the doorway, not sure if he was aware of her presence, if she was free to enter the room without his command. Standing silently, she waited for him to look up at her, but he stayed in his position, his back and shoulders moving only with his breath.

After several minutes, Maddy finally cleared her throat to gain his attention. His head shot up, the dark emerald of his eyes burning into hers. Her knees faltered slightly, but she stood strong, perfectly still until such time as he asked that she move forward. Darkness and phantoms of some unknown source darkened his expression. His full lips were pulled tight into a fine line, the skin at his brows furrowed in agitation. His eyes remained locked with hers for only a few seconds before they started to travel down the length of her body, stopping only when they'd reached the wounds at her wrists and ankles.

"You need more ointment on your cuts." Standing, Aaron moved toward the adjacent bathroom, looked back over his shoulder when Maddy didn't immediately follow. "Come with me, Mouse, so that I may tend to your wounds."

Finding her voice, Maddy spoke out of turn, not thinking about the repercussions her words could elicit. "I would prefer you call me by my name." She peaked up at him through her lashes. "Maddy, I would prefer that you call me Maddy."

Aaron stopped with his bare back turned to

her, taking several minutes to finally respond, he asked, "What makes you think you are allowed to ask that? If I wanted, I could call you slave ... " He turned to face her, the contours of his chest perfectly shadowed, his strength unquestionable. " ... or whore." His swagger was slow as he approached her, a hunter skilled in pursuit. "Would you prefer those names to 'Mouse'?"

Sucking her bottom lip between her teeth, Maddy fidgeted with her hands, refusing to look Aaron in the eyes. She could feel his gaze touching her skin, his perusal of the woman barely half his size. The heat of his body rolled off of him as he circled her. It was the feeling of a soft blanket and lustful threat wrapped around her at the same time. When the deep resonation of his voice occurred again, she cringed, fearing he would strike out at her for the incorrect answer. "Why do you dislike the name I have given you?"

Continuing to fidget, Maddy trained her eyes on her feet, not daring to look up into the endless green she knew stared down at her. Gripping her under her chin, Aaron pulled her face up to look at him, his eyes searching hers for the answer to his question. "You will speak when I tell you." Dropping his hand from her face, he took a step back placing distance between them. "Now answer me."

Her heart pounded against the walls of her chest, her throat constricted, making it difficult for her to breath. Fear consumed her as she stood in the shadow of the man who'd taken at least two lives that day. Barely a whisper, her voice squeaked out the answer to his question. "Because a mouse

168

is a furry little rodent, something detested."

Aaron stood thoughtful and silent above her. When he didn't respond, Maddy quietly added, "I guess it's better than Xander's name for me."

Laughter bellowed out, causing the toned muscles of Aaron's broad chest to flex and relax before her eyes. The sound of his amusement so real, it caused her to want to smile in response to seeing a piece of his mask falling away, revealing parts of him not witnessed by many people. Containing himself, Aaron's eyes sparkled as he asked, "And what, exactly, is Xander's name for you?"

A scowl creased the fine skin between her eyes, her mouth pulled into the pout of a sulking child. "He calls me 'Cricket' ... an insect. It's odd that you both refer to me as nothing more than a common household pest."

Aaron's smile faltered as he looked down upon the beautiful girl who didn't fully understand her role. "No, Madeleine, you are not a common household pest ... "

Maddy looked up at him, anticipating what he would say next.

For a fleeting second, he looked genuinely amused, but his expression was quickly replaced with indifference and contempt as he stated, "you are lower than even a pest in your role as a slave."

Her heart broke at those words. Any inclination she had that Aaron and Xander had protected her, could be concerned for her, was

169

blown away by the vile truth to his statement.

Turning back in the direction of the bathroom, Aaron snapped his fingers, indicating his command for her to follow. Her feet padded across the cold floor as she submitted to his command. Once they'd entered the room, he motioned for her to sit in the same chair he'd occupied when he'd bathed her only hours before. Retrieving the white box, he moved to kneel in front of her. Her eyes raked down the smooth lines of his back as she took in the way the muscles bulged and stretched under his smooth skin with his movements. The sting of the ointment wrenched her from her perusal of his body. Drawing in a sharp breath, the chill of the air brushed across her teeth, a slightly painful tingle running down the bones of her jaw as a result. Desperately, Maddy tried not to notice how Aaron's strong hands massaged over the skin of her ankles and wrists. He was at least twice her size, the large area of his hand easily wrapping around the width of her arms and legs. So firm, she remembered what those hands had felt like when causing her pain ... or when causing her to lose herself, to float on the wave of a sensation she had never before known. Bumps ran along her skin, betraying the warring emotions currently ravishing her body. She should fear this man, hate him, detest him with all that she was worth; but, yet, she couldn't stop her eyes from closing, her head from lulling back from the feeling of his touch.

"I'm going to wrap gauze around the broken skin at your ankles, ensure that the ointment stays in place as you sleep." Aaron continued tending to her injuries while Maddy looked him over, wondered how a man so lethal, so cruel, could also be as kind as he was in this moment. He had the body of a warrior, hard, bulky muscles that were cut into his back and chest, as if a master sculptor had molded him from clay. His skin was golden brown, a color that contrasted sharply against the pale white of hers. The black silk that adorned his head had almost dried and she couldn't help but reach out to see if it truly was as soft as it appeared. When her hand lightly brushed against the raven-black hair, Aaron looked up, the light behind his eyes a mixture of anger, sympathy and raging desire.

Correcting her behavior, Aaron reached up, grabbed the wrist of the hand she'd extended out to him, placed her hand back in her lap softly while his words wounded her more than the shackles had done that day. "You may not touch me without permission, Mouse; you do not have that right." The tone of his remark was razor sharp, a warning wrapped in luxurious baritone, cutting and soothing at the same time.

Having completed his task, Aaron repacked the box of supplies, stood up and quickly moved to the closet to put it away. Without turning back to her, he strode toward his bedroom, snapping his fingers once, calling her as if she was nothing more than a dog. Standing, Maddy had to balance herself from falling on trembling legs. Following him into the room, she noticed how Aaron seemed to know where she stood without having to look back. She watched as he crossed the room, disappeared into his closet, only to emerge again holding something

171

small and white in the palm of his hand. Briefly, he glanced at her, his words curt and without emotion as he instructed her to sit on the bed. Apprehension and unease filled her body. She'd never slept in a bed with a man, wasn't sure that, tonight, this man wouldn't take her fully, use her as she'd been intended. Staring at her hands, she didn't watch as Aaron moved into the bathroom and back out into the bedroom carrying a glass of water.

Extending his hand out where she could see what he held, Aaron towered above her. Focusing on what he held rather than the proximity of his large body to hers, Maddy realized that he was handing her two small pills and a glass of water with which she could swallow them down.

"Take these. They'll help you sleep."

Staring at the pills, Maddy shook her head in protest. He was drugging her, making it so she could not fight against him. Finding a cache of strength somewhere deep within, somewhere hidden to even her, Maddy glanced up at the man staring back down at her. "I know what you are doing. I'm not stupid. If you are to rape me tonight, use me as nothing more than a method to get off, at least leave me conscious so that I'll remember just how cruel you are."

Green, the color of jade, the color of budding life in spring, burned down into her; backlit and heated by a fire of rage, of need. Aaron's mouth curved at the ends, an unknown thought amusing to him as she attempted to stand up to a man who controlled her completely ... owned her in a way that no man should be allowed.

Like lightning, he moved quickly, so fast and unexpected, that Maddy gasped when the weight of his body came down on her. The pills fell from her hand to the floor as Aaron pushed her back on the bed, held his body above her, his hand roughly traveling up the side of her torso, lifting her shirt to expose her breasts to his gaze. "If I wanted to take you, Madeleine, I wouldn't have to drug you to do so." The heat of his mouth stung as he wrapped his full lips around the peak of her breast. His tongue laved against the sensitive tip, his teeth grazing the same area where he had marked her before. A cry escaped her lips, part fear, part surprise; part lust so subtle, it caused her heart to skip in its rhythm. As he worked her body into a frenzy, his hand traveled down to cup her between her thighs. A single finger tapped against the opening to her body, she cried out again, not understanding the heat that bloomed within her core. He pushed up suddenly, watched as she lay panting beneath him. "Even if your mind did not remember my cruelty, your body certainly would. The pain of being split apart when I bury myself within you cannot be easily forgotten ... even if done while drugged."

Just as quickly as he'd come down on top of her, he stood. His eyes searched the floor and when he found the pills, he bent over to pick them up. This time not an offer, but a demand, his hand reached to wrap around her face, squeezing her cheeks until her mouth fell open. Shoving the pills onto her tongue he grabbed the glass of water, poured the contents down her throat, washing her new form of chains down into her body. "I have no

173

plans to grant you the satisfaction of my cock, I simply want you to sleep. I don't feel like spending the evening jumping up every time I think you are attempting to escape."

Aaron took the glass and as he walked to place it in the bathroom he commanded, "Lie down, *Maddy*, close your eyes and let sleep take you. That will be the only thing having its way with your body tonight."

When Maddy obeyed his instruction, Aaron continued his course into the adjacent room, placing the glass on the counter, he stood back, took in the image reflected back at him by the large mirror over the sink. His pants tented in front of him, a reminder of having touched, having laid his weight upon her just moments before. She was soft in every area where he was hard; her skin, silk against the rough surface of his. Even though her body was masked in the spice and musk smell of his soap, there was still a wisp of something about her, a natural essence that called to him, awakened every nerve ending, everything distinctly male within him.

Resisting the urge to grab himself, to milk himself to relieve the taut skin wanting to tear open from the rush of blood, he turned to lean against the counter. His head lulled back as he waited for his body to calm, his breathing to become regular, his heart to stop forcing blood into the part of his body that desperately craved the moist heat only her body could provide.

Losing track of time, he straightened his shoulders, pushed himself back up onto tired legs and moved back toward the bed where he knew she lay sleeping. Half of one of the pills he gave her would have knocked a grown man on his ass; two would ensure that her tiny body stayed wrapped tightly within the arms of oblivion at least until morning light. His eyes immediately sought her as he entered the room. The soft curves of her body awakening the nerve endings in the palms of his hands, allowing him to imagine the exchange of pleasure ... of pain that could occur in the throes of passion ... of raw and unapologetic lust in those moments when he laid his hands on her skin. Fisting his hands, his finger stung where she had bitten him earlier that day, the stretched feel over the once broken skin causing him to smile in memory of her spirited fight. Even chained, she'd found a way to strike out, her temper more alive than he'd ever imagined.

Silently he stalked to the side of the bed, watched over her as her eyelids fluttered, the induced sleep taking her to some place far away from the nightmare that had become her life. The mattress dipped under his weight as he sat down beside her, studied her ... wanted her.

The true depth of his father's cruelty was laid across his bed, softly breathing, dreaming of beautiful worlds away from his life ... from him. The torture inflicted was so subtle, but brilliant in its execution. He'd never desired a woman for more than a few hours, but this woman, she sang to his soul through the use of metal and wood, an instrument through which she spoke to him without knowledge that he understood the stories she told. Her captivity, the abuse he must inflict, all in an effort to save her life ... he'd been left with no choice but to turn his own angel against him, to treat a treasured jewel as nothing more than filth scraped across the bottom of his boot. Yes, his father was a genius. Even in the madness that claimed him, he was a devil who didn't need to destroy those around them; rather, he led people to destroying themselves.

Leaning down, he breathed her in, his cock swelling again as he lost control of his body, of his mind. Brushing his lips against the shell of her ear, he whispered, "Do you sleep, my angel?" When she didn't stir, the corners of his lips turned up, betraying his feelings for the beautiful woman who lay beneath him. "Dream of me, Maddy. See me as I want to be; not the nightmare who torments you, but the devoted and mystified man who worships at your feet."

Brushing his lips softly across hers, Aaron stood up, walked to the stereo, flicking it on to bathe the room in the sound of Madeleine's soul. She was sleeping, she'd never know it was her music that sang him into slumber each night, would never know how she touched him on a level even he couldn't recognize or understand. The voice of a woman, one that could invade and infect even the most deadly and tortured of souls ... the one that resided within him.

Lying down beside her, he struggled against the urge to pull her small body to him, to cradle her like the precious person that she was. His eyes closed, he lay there searching for sleep, but not finding the sweet oblivion that he sought.

176

Sleep escaped him for so long that the CD he played, the resonate sound filled with memories and dreams, ended; blanketing him in a silence so deep, his heart called out for more. When the music stopped, Maddy cried out in her sleep. Eyes that, when closed, had appeared so peaceful, so deep inside sanctuary, now furrowed, the delicate skin turning pink from the tension that creased her brow. His hand reached out to her, attempted to smooth away the pain that consumed her, but nothing could console her.

Pushing up from the bed, he padded barefoot across the floor, starting the music from the beginning. Once the deep tones again played throughout the room, Aaron noticed how his captive stilled, appearing peaceful once again. His breath caught in that moment. Aaron laughed, finally discovering a method to ease her torment, a gift he could give her that would still fall within his father's rules for a slave.

Swift as a runaway train, Aaron powered down the corridor to Xander's room. Not bothering to knock, he threw open the door so hard the sound of the door as it hit the wall had Xander immediately on his feet; a gun in one hand, a blade in the other.

Ducking quickly to his left, Aaron chuckled as the sound of steel impacted with the wall where his head had just been. Xander blinked sleep from his eyes, bringing the gun up, but immediately lowering it when he noticed it was Aaron that invaded his room.

"What the fuck, Aaron? Are you trying to

lose your fucking head?" Xander placed his gun on the bedside table, leaned back against the wall, as his hands rubbed his eyes back into focus.

"You'd be dead before you could pull the trigger if I truly wished you were no longer breathing." A feral smile beamed from Aaron, a simple reminder of who the actual assassin was in the room.

Xander pulled his hands from his eyes, looked at Aaron with contempt, but then smiled and nodded his head in assent. "You are correct, my old friend. It is only the executioner who so thoroughly enjoys the scent of spilled blood."

Sighing, Aaron ran his hands through his hair. "I need you to do something for me."

Xander balked, still pissed off that Aaron had wrenched him from sleep. "At one in the fucking morning?! Go fuck your slave, Aaron, that's what she's there ... "

Aaron's hand was around Xander's throat instantly; his movement across the room a slight blur as he pulled the knife from the wall, had it pressed tightly against Xander's stomach. With his mouth pressed against Xander's ear, he warned, "I'd hold that thought if you wish to keep your intestines from spilling across the floor." His voice, a venomous tone; poison and blood dripping from the words that he spoke.

Xander stood still, not reacting to the snake when it was coiled to strike. "My apologies, Aaron. I was merely attempting humor."

178

Releasing his guard, Aaron stepped back, flung the knife so that it pierced the wall in the exact spot where it had previously landed. Only the slight arch of Xander's brow gave away his impressed state. Aaron was lethal with a blade and any man who wanted to keep his body intact would be wise to remember that fact.

"What can I do for you at this *convenient* hour?" Plastering a fake smile to his face, Xander finally stepped back from Aaron and strode to his bureau in search of a change of clothes.

Following behind Xander, Aaron asked, "Do you know the details of Maddy's abduction? Did they take her instrument as well?"

Although Xander suspected where this request was going, he couldn't help but focus on another oddity in Aaron's question. *"Maddy?"* Turning to face Aaron, his humor was evident by the curl to his lip. "Since when do you call her 'Maddy'?"

Straightening his spine, Aaron crossed his arms over his large chest and arched his brow in response. "Cricket?"

The two men stood staring at each other before bursting out in coordinated laughter. Gaining control of himself, Xander answered, "What? I thought it would be fitting considering the little creatures rub their legs together to make music."

Stunned momentarily silent, another short burst of laughter broke free of Aaron's mouth.

179

"First off, I believe it's their wings that they rub together … " Xander shrugged at Aaron's correction. " … and second, I need you to find out if they took her instrument. If it's somewhere on the property I want you to retrieve it, bring it back to my quarters and give it to me."

Nodding, Xander knew better than to ask questions. "It'll be done. Just let me get dressed."

Aaron slapped Xander on the back before turning to head back into the corridor. By the time Aaron reentered his room, he could hear Xander enter the hallway, walking in the direction of the living room. Satisfied that his orders would be carried out, he returned to his bed, lay down beside Madeleine, falling asleep quickly, anticipating what was to come.

Chapter Sixteen

Sunlight, garish and proud, spun its slender tendrils into the room from behind the dark curtains. Maddy's body was cramped, still languid from the deep sleep from which she'd awoken. She laid still, her eyes peaking open to discover a new morning. Like sparks, flutters of dust traveled through the intrusive light, flashing suddenly as they came in contact with the light, but disappearing so fast, it was almost as if the light had swallowed them whole.

Her eyes, adjusting from slumber, looked out across the room, panic slowly setting in from the unfamiliarity of the surroundings. Attempting to move, Maddy remembered the evening before ... Aaron coming back covered in blood, being told to go into Aaron's room, the way Aaron had tended to her injuries before forcing drugs down her throat. Finding the ability to turn on her back, she became distinctly aware of someone lying to her left on the bed. Lifting her arms still weighted by the effects of the pills she'd been given, Maddy rubbed at her eyes, brought the room more clearly into focus before turning her head to find Aaron sleeping soundly beside her.

The pure black of his hair was tumbled haphazardly across his face, his lips slightly parted, he appeared childlike, innocent and vulnerable even though Maddy was learning he was anything BUT those things. The skin of his cheeks was rough with the shadow of stubble, his eyes flickering underneath the lids as if he was still dreaming.

Attempting several times without success, Maddy eventually found the strength to push herself into a seated position on the soft mattress of the bed. The comforter, fashioned from silk and the same color black as Aaron's hair, slid to her waist; pooled like liquid as dark as the deepest parts of the sea.

Slowly, she looked around the expanse of the room, seeing for the first time small details previously hidden by the shadow of night. These walls, much like the rest of the house were tinted a deep red, broken by tapestries and paintings held in gilded frames. Small statues and busts of historical figures she did not recognize were placed on bookshelves lining a wall near the door to the adjacent bathroom. Scanning left, Maddy saw a sleek stereo system, silver with multi-colored lights blinking back and forth along the front of the device. Next to the stereo were CD cases stacked in various heights, the top of one laid open, the silvered disc absent from its case.

Curious as to the music preferred by the man lying beside her, Maddy wiggled her toes and bent her legs to force blood back through her appendages before attempting to stand to further explore the room. Traveling slowly across the barely lit space, Maddy kept looking back at the sleeping man, every small sound causing her to jump for fear he'd awakened to find her moving about the room. Creeping past the windows, light flashed across the pale skin of her legs, beams of warmth and illumination brushing against her as she moved.

182

Finally reaching the stereo, Maddy slid her hand against the sleek metallic surface as she passed it to look at the stacks of CDs placed to its side. Her hand shook as she reached out to close the lid of the open case, her breath catching when she realized it was a recording of her music. Tears welling in her eyes, she looked at the picture of the cello that adorned the front, her fingers softly touching the image in disbelief. Her eyes flashed to the stereo, her curiosity heightened as to whether her music would burst forth if she pressed the small play button flashing blue on the front of the machine.

Her finger hovered over the button, her bottom lip pulled tight between her teeth. Nervously, she glanced at Aaron, noticed he hadn't moved from the position he was in when she woke. She knew the sound could wake him, but the desire to hear the deep baritone melody, the harmony of the violin and piano, was too much for her to resist. Quickly she pressed the flashing blue button, and almost dropped to her knees when the sound she missed finally played throughout the room.

Starting slowly, the song wove itself around her senses, emotion evoked through sound, the feeling of the vibration of the string, a phantom memory on the tips of her fingers. A deep melody reverberated through her core, the tempo increasing, drawing her out of darkness but still leaving her enveloped in a feeling of sorrow and loss. The music was beauty that could not be seen, a palpable caress that was not produced by the hand of another person ... and it was lost to her, stripped away and tossed aside so easily when she'd been captured.

Maddy closed her eyes, listened to the sweet sounds as they wrapped themselves around her, seeped into her skin, her bones ... her heart. Her mind drifted back to days spent with her uncle as a child, their laughter as she attempted to handle an instrument that was almost as big as her. It had been just the two of them for so many years; but then, unexpectedly, he'd caught a simple cold that eventually turned to pneumonia, taking his life and leaving her alone. Faithfully, she continued to practice each day as he'd always insisted. Having no one else, those practice sessions turned from two hours to three, and from three to four; on and on until, eventually, Maddy hardly did anything else.

The song ended sweetly as moisture grew cold on her cheeks from where the tears had traveled. Slowly, she peeked open her eyes and found herself staring into green depths so filled with rage she jumped back in alarm. With Aaron so close and towering above her, she could feel the fury rolling off him in waves of heat and negative energy.

"What do you think you are doing, Mouse? Did you have my permission to get out of bed, to touch anything in this room?" His words were spoken in such a controlled manner, the sharp edge to them slicing through her resolve, making her cower down in fear of his rage. He stalked towards her, slowly circling while keeping his eyes trained on the person he could so easily break.

"Answer me, Mouse. I don't have the

patience for your disobedience." The pupils of his eyes swirled with black the color of onyx, the green surrounding it made even brighter in contrast with the red from his anger.

"I ... I was curious." Holding the CD case up so that he could see it, she asked, "Is this why? Is this why I was taken?" She'd barely finished speaking before she was airborne, thrown back toward the bed, landing too close to the headboard, her skull collided with the wood. Pain shot through her head and neck like white-hot lightning, her eyes clenched closed as her mouth released a frightened cry. Reaching back to rub her hand along the sore spot on her head, her wrist was suddenly locked within Aaron's grip, her other wrist caught quickly before both were brought above her head and pinned to the headboard.

"Look at me, slave." The depth to his voice, the ferocity of his tone, it was seduction veined through terror, the continued beauty of the music in the background adding insult to the viciousness of his actions. Her chest heaved as she cried out, his grip on her arms bruising the skin pressed into the delicate bones. Her eyes opened, the tears obscuring the man above her, as if looking at him through water drowning her in misery. Splashing down her cheeks, the tears fell, allowing her to focus on eyes the color of leaves turning up toward the sun, hidden forests touched by bits of light. Her lips parted, forcing the salt of her tears to seep into her mouth, bathe her in the taste of her own her pain, tinged with desire. Staring into the depths of a soul tortured by demons and decay, she gasped when his lips, soft as satin took hers, his tongue

185

invading her mouth, filling her with the flavor of passion and pain, heat and cruelty. But hers was not a body taken easily, the sharp and metallic bite of iron mixed with the salt of her tears when her teeth broke the skin of his tongue, drawing blood.

Aaron pulled back, a wild gleam to his eye. "So you like to bite, do you? That's the second time you've broken my skin." Leaning down, he rested his forehead against hers, his labored breath rolling down her skin. His voice, razors wrapped in fur, "What have I told you about pain?"

Her body shivered at his question, her mind and body warring, the desire for his touch mixed with the absolute terror he was inflicting upon her. The heat and moisture produced between her thighs embarrassed her, sickened her knowing she should fight harder against him instead of enjoying the feeling of his weight pressed down upon her body. Her heart raced in her chest and was suddenly pained when he released her arms to push himself up from the bed. "Stay." A command and warning in one solitary word.

Aaron moved quickly into his closet, emerging with a long strip of chocolate brown cloth, a silk scarf worn by men of esteem, of wealth. His strides were powerful and long as he approached the bed. Maddy huddled into herself, frightened and excited, confused at the conflicting emotions tearing through her body. Crawling back onto the bed, he was a predator stalking his prey, a nightmare overtaking her mind. His movements were hurried as he bound one wrist and then another with the scarf he'd just retrieved. Maddy flinched back, tried to keep him from binding her, but losing quickly as he wrapped the scarf around the posts of the headboard, wrenching it so tight, her arms protested the position they were forced to take. Once she was bound, his hands slid down her body, gripping and pinching in the soft areas they reached. With each flinch of her body, each small cry that escaped her lips still swollen from his kiss, he smiled brighter, looking every bit the savage captor overpowering his conquest. Reaching her ankles, he stripped of her pants. She thought she glimpsed his movements turn more cautious as he used a sheet to wrap the skin of her ankles that had been broken from chains; but it was gone as fast as it'd appeared when her legs were forced apart. Now bound and spread before him, Maddy's chest heaved in and out, her breath, short pants, as she was made helpless to a man who confused and terrified her.

His fingertips dug into her skin as they traveled up her body. She was overcome with shock, yet immersed in seduction. Not knowing what he would do, but recognizing his earlier promise of pain, her eyes widened, a fine sheen of sweat across her skin. His lips, stained red from the blood she'd drawn, were held slightly apart. Every muscle on his chest, shoulders and back tensed and defined, his control slipping from his grip. A beast disturbed, something dark was emerging from Aaron and he had her completely exposed to him, locked down and at his mercy alone. As his face reached hers, he pressed his hips down into the apex of her thighs; only the silk of his pants between them, he let her feel the entire length of him, the hot and hard truth to his masculinity, the reaction her bite had caused.

The warmth of his mouth pressed to her ear, he growled, "I promised you pain for pain, Madeleine, and it only makes my cock harder when you fight back. Keep writhing beneath me, it'll only help me along as I fuck your body and as I fuck your mind." Her shirt lifted at the sides as his hands pushed forcefully up along her torso, his thumbs brushing the peaks of her breasts as he pulled the front of her shirt up over her head, effectively locking her head in a position facing down the length of her body. "Now you'll watch me as I deliver that pain back to its source."

His lips came down on hers, the spice and musk of his scent completely overtaking her as she was frozen in place, pulling against bindings that were tight, yet sinfully soft on her skin. His tongue invaded her mouth, stole her breath from her lungs just before he pulled back suddenly, lightly nipping at her lip while pulling away. Moist heat, and tantalizing suction as his mouth traveled along her throat until finding the peak of her breast and sucking it so far in that the taut skin became nothing but pain and debauched pleasure combined. His tongue skillfully worked at the pebbled nipple, every once in a while breaking so that his teeth could graze and bite the sensitive skin. Electric shocks traveled from her breast, down along some unknown circuit connected directly to her core. Her hips bucked in anticipation while her mind became blank, the panic too much for her to process. When his hand gripped the weight of her other breast a cry escaped her lips from the strength of his grip. She closed her eyes, but opened them again, not able to look away from the wickedly erotic assault on her body.

Stopping suddenly, his eyes briefly met hers before Aaron moved lower on her body. The stubble on his chin scraped against her stomach, until, finally, the burning heat of his mouth covered her core, his tongue snaking out quickly to tease the swollen flesh. She was forced to watch as he kissed her in an area so intimate, her cheeks reddened from embarrassment and shame. Her breasts swelled impossibly full, the feeling so foreign and so satisfying, she felt her body as it reacted to his touch, readied itself for his invasion.

A cord winding it's way up, pulling tight, the feeling reminiscent of a rubber band ready to snap. Just as he drove her to a point where all she could hear was the hum of her blood rushing through her veins, he stopped, turning suddenly and biting down on the soft flesh at the insides of her thigh. A louder cry broke from her mouth, but all she could do was watch with wide eyes, the heavy scent of sex and lust suddenly filling the air from her body's reaction. Not giving her a chance to recover, he took her back into his mouth, swirled the tip of his tongue over her swollen nub, winding her up again and pushing her back dangerously close to the edge. Pleasure so intense, it was painful to endure, he would bring her to an almost release only to drop her back down with small bits of pain that served to excite her body even more; every nerve ending alive, each touch a direct contributor to her frenzied state. Placing his mouth on her one more time, he dipped his tongue between the swollen skin, breaching the entrance to her just slightly, but taking her rapidly back to the peak of an explosion.

189

One more touch, it would have taken one more touch to push her over the edge into ecstasy, but instead, Aaron suddenly pulled away, her juices glistening over his stubbly face.

"I warned you, Mouse." His chest heaved with his own excitement, but there was a chill to his eyes that she'd never before seen. "I'll leave you within the madness that comes before the release, a punishment for your disobedience." He chuckled wickedly. "I'll also leave you bound so that your hand cannot finish what my mouth has started."

Maddy watched as Aaron marched quickly into the adjacent room, leaving her pulled tight both inside and out, her heart breaking for not having been given the release she'd so desperately needed. Split apart, her mind fought against her body, detesting the actions of her captor, yet tormented by the denial of her release. His touch was electrifying and frightening at the same time; his soul, so very dark that the little bit of light she'd thought she'd seen the night before had been all but extinguished. Tears broke free from her eyes as she was left sitting in the evidence of her arousal and left drowning in the misery of a torrent of hormones and anger, pleasure and the torture of the peak he'd left her gripping but never achieving fully.

Aaron's pain was as agonizing as what he'd just inflicted on Maddy. His cock so full and solid that even the brush of his silken pants was too much sensation, the skin too sensitive. He needed relief, something he would not grant her, but something he had to have so he didn't return and finish what he'd started. He'd barely been able to

190

pull himself from the edge of the line that he'd vowed not to cross. Even if she begged he could never take her, not unless it was a choice between that and her life.

Turning on the shower, he set it to pure heat, not bothering to dilute it with cool water. The sunken tiled space quickly filled with steam as he stepped in, allowing the stream of what felt like fire to grate against his skin. His skin instantly turned red upon contact, but it was enough to reduce his length enough that he could grip along its width and milk himself of the deadly desire that the woman had driven into his body. He needed pain, a fight or a good hard fuck, but he would not find those things with the woman tied up in his room. Spending only moments allowing himself relief, he hurriedly turned the water off and stepped out, lazily holding a towel to cover his cock while he stormed back into the bedroom becoming hard immediately when seeing her stretched and spread on the top of his bed. *Fuck!* He cursed under his breath at the sight of her. She was a drug, the soft and supple parts of her body calling to him as he moved through the room. Her eyes widened when he approached, but losing his control again, he turned suddenly to move into his closet and get dressed. He needed to leave this place, and even immediately wouldn't be fast enough.

Quickly pulling on some black slacks, he didn't bother with underwear, knowing he would set out to find one of the immoral women he used frequently when in search of violent relief. Hurriedly he buttoned up a black shirt over his

191

broad chest and started for his bedroom door. It was impossible to not look over at her, to not acknowledge the temptation left sullen and spent on his bed. He stopped, his head dropping to look at the floor, before he changed course, moving over to the bed to tell her why she'd been punished in such a way. He couldn't lose sight that he only had three more days to train her in her role, three more days to keep a tight hold over himself while he broke her down completely.

Her eyes, the color of the sky peaking through the clouds of a storm stared up at him. Her face was streaked red from the tears on her cheeks and her mouth was inflamed and red from his kiss and the way he'd nipped at those deliciously full lips just moments before.

"You are not allowed thought anymore, your choices are mine, your actions are mine, everything you think or do will only be because I have allowed it. You have reached a point of no return, Madeleine, a place in your life where you cannot have the luxury of freedom. Let go of what you were before, what you thought you knew about life. It was all a grand illusion. I'll leave you bound while I go find that which I would not allow you, while I relieve myself on someone who deserves the sting of my bite, the pleasure of my cock as I rid myself of the poison you have left within me. When I return, be ready to listen, to OBEY every command I give." He leaned down, deliberately brushing his lips across her cheek as he moved to her ear. "Your life depends on your submission. Do not fight against me now only to be handed over to men far more cruel than I can ever

192

be."

Turning, he strode out the door and down the long corridor to the living room. Xander stood in the kitchen, the skin under his eyes black and puffy from Aaron's interruption the night before. Aaron simply shot him a look as he reached for the handle of the front doors. Stepping through, his conscience nagged at him, causing him to pause, to consider his mouse. He didn't bother turning back in Xander's direction when he ordered, "In one hour, go in my room and untie her. She'll need to use the restroom and she'll need to be fed. Do not give her clothes. Her training begins when I return."

Chapter Seventeen

Aaron's steps were weighted as he quickly left the building. Reaching his car, he climbed inside, hitting his fists against the steering wheel while throwing his head back against the seat. Forcing Maddy from his mind, he drove off the compound grounds heading out to a woman who'd been available to him over the past several years for a quick fuck. Emily was a socialite and was more attracted to man's wallet than she was his face or personality; but it didn't matter to Aaron. Getting her to spread her legs was as easy as telling her what she wanted to hear. Aaron didn't mind lying to find his release ... the added bonus being that this particular bitch didn't mind his penchant for pleasure spiced with pain.

Pulling up to her sprawling mansion, Aaron parked his car by the front doors. This was going to be a short visit and the ability to leave quickly was a necessity. Emily typically had many visitors throughout the day, but would set some time aside to see to Aaron's needs. It was a beneficial exchange, he got his release and she was left free to continue pilfering off the bank accounts of the other men she'd met by being invited to the more 'formal' events held by The Estate's legitimate business. That's not to say that she wouldn't sink her claws into Aaron if she could, she'd tried on many occasions to sway him into a relationship or marriage. Aaron had declined each and every time. He had no time or desire for a woman in his life, and the last thing he needed was the added

194

weakness of having someone he cared for that could be used to coerce his will when it came to criminal matters.

The door opened as he approached and the doorman immediately alerted Emily to Aaron's presence. In her typical style, she came meandering down the long winding staircase that was to the left of the grand entry room. Aaron watched as she intentionally swayed her hips, pushed out her chest to make her smaller breasts appear larger to his eyes. Her body was covered with nothing more then a blue silk robe, casually left open to reveal the lace-covered slope of her breasts. As usual, her long white-blonde hair was perfectly styled to appear as if she didn't spend hours on her looks.

"Aaaaaaaron ... " Her voice grated against his nerves as she spoke with what he swore was a fake accent, only used by those of affluence and wealth. "It's such a nice surprise to see you. I take it you're here for your usual slap and tickle." Her ruby stained lips curled into a salacious grin revealing perfectly straight, white teeth as she laughed seductively at her own joke.

Steeling himself against the tinkling quality to her voice that she'd no doubt practiced and perfected over the years, Aaron plastered on a fake smile and addressed her, "Emily ... " Reaching out his hand, he assisted her down the last two steps. "This will only be a quick visit as I have business that I must attend to; however, I was driving by and couldn't resist stopping in to say 'hello.'"

She laughed again, the sound irritating and contrived. "I'm so sure that's why you decided to

195

stop in." Looking him up and down, Emily walked toward him, her body held in such a way as to seduce any man in her presence. "Since this is a quick visit, where did you want me? Against a wall? On the couch? Or did you have something a bit more vulgar in mind?" she asked.

Stepping so close to her, he had to look down just to stare into the golden brown of her eyes. "Does it matter where I take you? I thought simply making you scream would suffice," he said.

The corner of her mouth quirked up, her eyes hooded at his sinful implication. "Well, then I have a surprise for you, Mr. Carmichael," she said. "A room I had designed with the *executioner* in mind." Leading him from the foyer, down a hallway to their left, Emily climbed another staircase up two floors. Turning right she pulled a key from the pocket of her robe to unlock the first door they approached. Flashing him a grin over her shoulder, she cooed, "I do hope you like it, I thought long and hard on what would turn you on."

Opening the door, she revealed a room set up for seductive torture; tools and devices tied to the walls that could be used to drive any person who craved the sting of torment to pure, unadulterated ecstasy. Light bounced off the polished steel of the shackles placed randomly around the room; however, that same light was absorbed by the darker colors of the wood and the walls painted a dark, dangerous red and black. Aaron wasn't surprised by the inclusion of whips, canes and floggers, but when his eyes spied the collection of knives laid out on a small table to his right, his brow arched in amusement. Turning to look at Emily as she watched his reaction, he reached out and grabbed the largest knife, unsheathing it and holding it up to inspect the blade. "Do you wish for death, Emily? Or are you truly confident I wouldn't lose control in my *use* of your body?"

The perfection of her face was momentarily marred by her rejected expression, a telling response to his implication that she was nothing more than a tool for his gratification. "I thought the scent of blood might turn you on ... drive you to desire me more than just for play." A scorned pout puckered her face as she slid a single finger along the seam of the zipper of his pants.

Aaron moved into her touch, inviting her to pull him free, to focus on the true purpose of his visit. Running his finger along the edge of the blade, he stated, "Drawing a woman's blood is not something I have much interest in doing ... " His eyes shifted from the blade to hers. " ... to do so would be the sign of an amateur."

Purring, she pulled at his waist and unbuckled his belt, freeing him of his clothing. "Interesting ... except I thought it was the blood, itself, that turned you on. Many men have reported back about the pure ecstasy in the expression of The Estate's assassin when he makes his kill." The warmth of her fingers sent a shiver through his body when she'd finally freed him enough to grip the full width of him. Stroking slowly, her tongue flitted out to run along her lip, her lips becoming full from the heat building in her body.

Aaron didn't respond, didn't feed the

197

perversion of her need to connect the feel of death to that of sex. His head falling back, he allowed her to stroke him, to bring him to a slow fullness that he could use to temporarily drive away the demons created in him by Maddy. As Emily's hand slid forward and back, he imagined it to be the touch of his mouse, her fear finally replaced with a longing only he could fulfill. When his cock had been awakened to the point his skin felt ready to tear, he grabbed Emily's hand, used it to quickly turn her around and bend her over the table behind her.

She gasped at first but her shock was quickly replaced by a chuckle, so wicked, Aaron was instantly sickened with how different this woman was to Maddy. Attempting to shake himself of the thought of his captive, he pulled Emily's arms taught across the table, chaining her and tightening the binds so that she could not move from her bent position.

"Is it torture you seek?" His voice was dangerously low as he snarled into her ear. A smile crept across her face, making her appear thoroughly entranced by his seduction. Pushing back into a standing position he looked down at her body as it trembled ... not fear ... no, this woman anticipated the sting of his touch, wanted to play at the nightmare only truly known by the woman he was attempting to exorcise from his soul. His hand came up to play along the crease of her ass, light pinches as he moved the robe aside revealing the black lace thong running up the center. A pink bow was placed at the top giving the mock appearance of innocence, which was anything but a characteristic of this particular woman. His

198

finger slipped beneath the thin string of cloth that made up her underwear and slid it down so sinfully slow, he could see her body quake with expectation. When he reached down into the soft skin he felt how wet she'd already become, her core greedy for him to fill her, pump her full of his aggression and want.

He continued his caress until he'd found that small bundle of nerves, pressed against it softly, circling around and driving her mad. The musk scent of passion filled the air, her hips undulating against his hand begging for more. Pulling back he lifted the robe more fully up her body revealing an ass that most men would praise, but not one as heart shaped and soft as that of Madeleine's. Disappointment churned through him, his dick becoming soft as he considered what a poor replacement this woman was for the one currently bound to his bed. Where Maddy was soft, this woman was hard, the feminine curves absent in favor of a slender form. Closing his eyes, he attempted to imagine this was his mouse bared to him across the table, that it was her moans and mewls emanating from the head pulled tight to the table. Pulling the sodden string of cloth aside, Aaron inserted a finger into the moist heat of her core, his mouth dropping partially open at the sound of her whimpers.

"Oh, please, Aaron, I need more." Emily begged him to continue, but her voice only served to annoy him. It wasn't the voice of his angel.

"Don't talk or I'll stop and leave you here for your doorman to have his way with you." A threat, yes ... but not exactly the truth. Aaron intended to use her for what she was worth, but if she annoyed him in the process, he would leave her sated and displayed for the help to discover. Aaron pumped his hand into her several times, not impressed by the looseness of her body. He needed something tight in that moment, something more like Maddy. Pulling his finger up, he found the tight pucker of her ass, used the lubrication already dripping from his finger to push in slightly, enjoying the way her body bucked in surprise.

"I believe I'll take you here, where I can feel you along every inch of me." His voice was rough as he spoke of his decision. Pushing farther in, she cried out from the force his finger made through muscles not yet relaxed.

Her voice barely a whisper as she replied, "You'd be my first."

Pulling out, Aaron responded by leaning over her to whisper in her ear. "But not your last, I'm sure."

She giggled in response, her hedonism an amusing thing rather than being shamed by her promiscuous reputation. "We could change that."

A smile creased his lips, the audacity of her to think he'd change was such a comical thought. Dropping his pants down around his ankles, he mocked, "I'd have to want you for more than a few hours to ensure it. Unfortunately, there's no interest in me to have your body much longer than that."

Her jaw dropped just as he quickly pulled

on a condom before lathering his cock in the evidence of her arousal. Pulling up, he pressed against the tight opening of her ass, pushing in slowly to relax the muscular walls. He could see her face furrow from the discomfort he was causing and it made him push against her harder, faster, enjoying the agony inflicted against a women he despised.

"Aaron, you're hurting me." Her voice pled with him to slow down, her ass tightening in response to her panic.

Dipping back for more lubrication, he pulled back up in position at the opening before he growled, "Isn't that what you wanted?" With his last word, he surged forward, burying himself halfway inside her, his girth stretching and pulling at the muscles of her ass. She cried out, but purred as she started to relax. Once stilled, he moved back and forth, enticing her body to allow him entry. His head fell back as he slowly pushed in, his mind not on the promiscuous blonde tied to the table, but rather, on the innocent woman he'd left at his home. While milking his body within the depths of this bitch and after finally burying himself fully inside, he reached around to grab her hips, becoming angry when he felt bone instead of the soft flesh of his slave. He grit his teeth, and gripped her body so hard, he knew he'd leave bruises. No longer holding back, he powered into her, not caring if her cries were from pleasure or pain, only needing a release so strong, it would keep him sated for those moments when Maddy infected his soul.

Releasing her hips, he slapped the smooth

201

contour of her ass, leaving a handprint so red, he wondered if it would welt from the force of the hit. Emily continued to cry out and was barely heard over the sound of her body being hit against the table to which she was bound. He allowed his body to frenzy, didn't dare slow down to think of the needs of the woman whose body he was using. When he found release, he spilled into her heavily, the muscle of his ass clenching from the force of his orgasm, his body quivering as he came down from the high.

He pulled out, grabbed a towel from another table nearby and cleaned himself before tucking himself away back into his pants. When he glanced at Emily, he noticed tears streaking down her satisfied face. Apparently, she'd found her release, although he'd never intended to give her one.

Moving around the table, he pulled the lever that released her chains and quickly moved to remove her from the shackles. Straightening his clothes, he pulled out his wallet to retrieve a dollar bill. He tossed it quickly onto the table before striding across the room to leave. "It's been fun, Emily. We should do this again sometime." His tone was matter of fact, no emotion toward the body he'd just used.

"That's it?!" Her voice shrieked as she pushed herself up before smoothing down her robe. Aaron turned around and immediately noticed how the side of her face was red and creased from the wood grain of the table. "That's all you're giving me?! It's because of that whore, isn't it?!"

The hairs on the back of his neck stood straight as he tightened his spine; every muscle in his body painful and taut from her reference to Madeleine as a common whore. His voice deepened and was dangerously quiet when he asked, "And what do you know of my slave?"

She swept her hand through the air while flippantly brushing off his anger. "Who doesn't know, Aaron? I don't know why you sound so upset about it. So, you've sunk to the level of using the bitches kept at your disposal? So what?" Swaggering in his direction, her hands rubbed along her breasts as she attempted to entice him. "However, I'll be damned to come second to a low class fuck. Bitch has to be pretty loose by now, given how often they are used by the members of The Estate."

She approached him, invading his space and pressing the length of her body to his. Speaking in a tone that should only be used by a child, she begged, "Please, baby, show me what you do to your slave. Teach me what it's like to be your whore."

His hand gripped into her hair, causing tears to burst from her eyes. Backing her against a wall equipped with another set of chains, he turned her around and raised her arms to lock her wrists above her head. Anger rolled off of his body and it took everything in him not to reach for one of the available blades to cut out her apathetic heart. How any woman could make light of the sexual abuse of another was beyond him. However, his reaction was further enraged because it was *his* captive she'd been discussing.

203

"You want to know what it feels like to be a whore?! " Leaning into her, he pressed his hand against the back of her head, shoving her skull up against the unforgiving surface of the wall. Barely understandable, he growled, "Let me fucking show you."

Aaron chose a cane from the wall and did not hesitate to swing it with enough force to leave angry purple bruises across her skin. Over and over, he beat it across her body causing her to howl out in pain before finally breaking into tears and begging him to stop. An audible sigh of relief escaped her mouth when she heard him drop the cane, not realizing he needed an instrument that would draw blood from the skin. Grabbing a smaller whip he slapped it across the backs of her thighs; small crimson streaks appearing before leaking along her legs. Her face was an expression of pure terror as he continued his assault, so thoroughly enraged that he lost himself to the violence. After also dropping the whip, he instinctually grabbed one of the knives and moved to her, holding the dulled blade to her cheek. The edge was not sharp enough for a clean execution, but it was enough to sully the face of the bitch at his mercy.

He held the blade to her skin so that it pressed sharply into her cheek, a line formed where the steel sliced through flesh while he mocked her for her cruelty. "You asked to be treated like a common whore, nothing more than an object to be used and mistreated. I hope you enjoyed it, bitch, because I've made sure you'll never forget what it means to play that role."

She screamed out as he pulled the blade along her cheek, leaving a jagged cut that would scar once it had healed. Emily's beauty was the only thing she cherished and he took it from her without pity; much like The Estate had taken Maddy's freedom from her. Leaving Emily chained, Aaron dropped the knife to the floor alongside the other tools he'd pulled from the wall. Shutting the door behind him, he listened as Emily screamed out, "You fucking bastard! I'll have you killed for this."

A feral smile across his face, he closed the door behind him, not concerned with the threats made by an unfeeling slut. Weaving through the halls and running hurriedly down the stairs, Aaron found his way out of Emily's house and into his car to return home. Laughing as he drove off, he wondered what the doorman would think when he found his lady left bloodied and shackled to a wall.

Chapter Eighteen

Maddy sat at the dining table poking at her food as Xander stood behind her in his usual position at her back. She huddled over the table, shamed by her nudity, but Xander had refused her clothes when he'd freed her, even taking the shirt off her body that Aaron had used to position her head. Her body was covered in the scent of shameful arousal when Xander had entered the room. His eyes, blue as the Caribbean Sea, were filled with a combination of sympathy and anger. He didn't speak as he untied her, or when he led her to the bathroom. The silence remained as he'd led her into the dining room to feed her.

It didn't matter, though. Even had Xander been an excellent conversationalist, Maddy would have been a weak participant. She was angry with Aaron for his behavior that morning, but also angry with herself for having expected anything different. An enigma hidden in a beautiful package, Aaron drew her in when he was considerate and kind; but his ability to lash out in anger, to terrify her with no guilt for his actions, that was the time when Maddy feared she faced the true damaged spirit hidden within him.

Regardless of the torment he'd inflicted on her body that morning, regardless of her shame and her sorrow, the only words she could focus on were his last. She knew he was off loving the body of some other woman. Jealousy creeping along her spine, she stiffened each time the image of Aaron curled together with a woman in the throes of passion haunted her mind. The emotions racing through her were confusing. She wanted to hate him, wanted to vilify him and only remember that he was the reason for her captivity, but yet … there was something about him. Not easily seen, it was when she watched him in those few quiet moments they shared; his caution when treating her wounds, the minute hint of reluctance in his eyes when he was on the brink of rage.

"Are you done eating?"

Maddy jumped when Xander spoke, having become accustomed to his silence over the previous few hours. Dropping her fork on the plate, she pushed it aside, waited for Xander to take it from the table and give her his next command. After Xander had removed the dish and placed it in the sink, he pulled out a chair next to where she sat, surprising her. Sitting down, he rested his elbows against the table and looked at her, a question in his expression.

"Do you mind telling me what happened this morning?" The softness of his voice astounded her. Usually vigilant in his lack of emotion, concerned seeped out in his question, his hard mask removed for the briefest of moments. She sat silently, her head looking down at the fine wood grain of the table. Not knowing if she should reveal the events of the morning, she attempted to avoid Xander's gaze by tracing the veins in the wood.

"Cricket, you need to tell me. Aaron never leaves this place without telling me where he's going. This morning, he didn't look like he was in a

207

good place." His hand reached out to stop hers. "Talk to me, Maddy."

At first shocked by his use of her name, reluctance finally settled like a veil over her heart. Eventually, she spoke up, not knowing how Xander would react. "I woke up before he did. I wanted to let him sleep, but I got curious." She peeked up at him through her lashes to see if she could determine whether he'd already become angry. Finding nothing but a blank expression, she continued. "I looked through his music, found a CD that was mine and I played it." Waiting for an angry reaction, she grew quiet again.

"What did Aaron do when you played the music?" Xander's voice was so foreign, like a counselor speaking to a child, he softly guided her through the details of her confession.

A single tear ran from her eye when she thought of the events that followed. "I became lost in the music ... much like I do when I'm performing." She sighed. "When I opened my eyes, he was standing in front of me ... shaking, he was so mad. He ... he threw me on the bed, tied me up, did things to me ... " The volume of her voice trailed off on those last words, she was not able to admit to what Aaron had done to her body.

Xander nodded his head, but remained quiet for a few minutes as he absorbed what she'd said. Finally reaching some inward conclusion, he asked, "Did he violate you?"

"Does it matter?

208

"It does."

"If you mean, did he have sex with me, no … I wasn't worthy of his … his … of him." She tried to repeat the vulgar words used by Aaron as he left, but her tongue couldn't quite form the sound. "He said he was leaving to go sleep with another woman."

Xander groaned as he ran his hands over his face. He knew exactly which woman Aaron would have gone to see and regretted not having stopped him. Emily was like poison even to the most unscrupulous of men. Standing up, he reached out to take Maddy's hand. "Thank you for being honest with me, Cricket. I'm sure that wasn't an easy story for you to tell."

Maddy took Xander's hand, oddly comforted by his words. She followed behind him as he led her down the corridor to the bathroom he'd taken her to when she'd first arrived. "You need to take a bath. I'm sure Aaron will be on his way back soon enough. The woman I suspect he went to see can only be tolerated for a short period of time."

His words had been meant to lighten her mood, but instead they weighed her down and disturbed her. Before, it had only been a threat, but Xander's words had served to confirm what Aaron had gone to do. Even more disturbing was the fact that she cared.

As Xander drew the bath, Maddy thought she heard the front door open and slam close. Xander must have heard it as well, because he immediately looked up from the water and held up a finger indicating for her to stay put. Having been left alone in the bathroom, Maddy attempted to listen to what the two men were saying, but was only met with the heavy sound of boots walking briskly through the corridor. Xander opened the door and reentered. Turning off the water, he turned to her. "Bath's ready. Be sure to wash up well. I trust that you won't try anything crazy, especially right now. Aaron's not in a good mood."

Maddy nodded and climbed in the warm water, luxuriating in the way it helped soothe her tired body. Once she'd gotten settled, Xander left the room and turned right toward Aaron's bedroom. Knocking on the door, Xander didn't wait for Aaron to answer before entering and finding Aaron sitting on the bed holding the brown scarf he'd used earlier to tie Madeleine to the posts.

"What happened?"

Aaron didn't look up to acknowledge Xander's question. His shoulders weighted, his head roaring with conflicting emotions and thoughts, Aaron just kept staring at the binds he used on Maddy. "We may be hearing from Emily sometime soon, I left her in a … compromising … position." Wrapping the soft material over his hands, Aaron pulled it so tight, the once pink skin turned red, outlined by white. By the time Xander spoke again, Aaron's hand had started to feel like pins and needles from the lack of blood flowing through it.

"I'm not worried about Emily. She's a pretty

face and a fast fuck, she has nothing of value to offer The Estate, and therefore, she has no power. I am, however, worried about you. Your mouse told me what happened this morning. Do you care to discuss it?" Xander's question was not asked easily, there were times when Aaron spoke freely and others where the information was so personal, Aaron became enraged if any person dared to inquire.

As Aaron released the scarf from around his hand, a heavy sigh also escaped his lips. "I treated her like a slave, Xander. There's nothing I can do to avoid it. If she fails when presented, they'll toss her to Emory or Vincent just to spite me. She'll die horribly at the hands of either of those jackals." Pausing for a moment, Aaron gathered his thoughts. "If I have to make her hate me in order to save her, I will, even if it destroys me in the process. I only need to keep her alive until the alliance against my father finally strikes. If we can take the bastard down, I'll set her free."

"It'll come back to you, Aaron. You can't set her free. She'll send the authorities." Xander's concern was apparent in the hurried nature of his words.

Aaron looked up at his lifelong friend. "The authorities are bought and paid for by The Estate. I won't go to jail, Xander. It doesn't matter either way. I'm not sure I'll live for very long after I finally let her go ... "

A weighted silence fell between the two men. With reluctance in his tone, Xander finally responded, "Let's get her trained, Aaron. We're running out of time."

Throwing down the scarf, Aaron watched as it fell, mimicking liquid chocolate spilling down to puddle on the floor. Standing up on tired legs, he walked to his closet to change into a fitted black t-shirt. When he returned to the bedroom, Xander had already left the room. He looked around the room for a moment, in part, stalling the inevitable interaction he was about to have with Maddy, but also in part, attempting to figure out a way to introduce her reward for good behavior. When his eyes caught sight of the CD case laid open on the floor near his stereo, an idea struck him. Quickly moving to the other side of the room, he picked up the case and then reached over to turn on the CD.

Once the melancholy of the music weaved through the air, he strode out into the hall in search of Xander. Finding him in the guest bathroom, Aaron's eyes couldn't help but admire Madeleine while she laid in the bath. His mind instantly traveled back to that morning; the shame that he felt for his actions conflicting badly with the intense heat that grew like an inferno throughout his body while in her presence. When he approached Xander, he leaned over, whispering his question so that Madeleine would not overhear him. "Were you able to retrieve her instrument?"

Xander nodded once in response.

"Please place it in my bedroom, near the stereo. I want Maddy to see it when she enters the room."

Without a word, Xander left the bathroom

to go carry out Aaron's order. The only sound left audible in the room was the light swirl of water as Maddy moved about in the bath. Looking down at the small woman as she bathed, Aaron remained stoic and controlled even though, inside, he was anxious to get Maddy into his room so he could discover if his idea would put even the barest hint of a smile on her face. Neither person spoke as Aaron stood above her, but eventually Maddy lifted her hands from the water and the delightful sound of laughter came from a face that Aaron swore was the most beautiful he'd ever seen. Lifting her palms from the water, she held them up for him to inspect as another soft burst of laughter broke free from her lips.

"I've pruned."

Fighting back the quirk of his mouth, Aaron examined her hands as he witnessed her become amused by such a simple thing. "It appears you have. Perhaps that means you are ready to come out of the bath."

Maddy nodded, a shy smile appearing through the fullness of her mouth. Her voice hesitant as she spoke, Maddy divulged the reason for her amusement. "When I was young, my uncle would always pretend that he was upset when I pruned ... " Another soft chuckle, as the look in her eyes suddenly appeared far away. " ... he teased me by saying that it meant I'd grown old while in the tub, that the water had somehow aged me." Sorrow suddenly broke free on the lines of her face. "I always got so scared that my life had gone by without me having been allowed to live it."

213

A dagger to the heart, her words had penetrated Aaron's resolve, pained him in such a way that he had to actively pull back from taking the small woman in his arms to comfort her. The irony of her words struck him, the foreshadowing of events to come a sad realization revealed to them both at that moment. Stepping away, he used the excuse of needing a towel to separate himself from the woman who was forcing herself into his very soul, adding a small spark of light where only darkness had once existed.

Moving back, Aaron indicated for Maddy to stand just before he wrapped the large white towel around her body. He reached out to take her hand and balance her as her small, delicate foot came over the side to step on the floor. Once she'd been sufficiently dried, Aaron removed the towel and chocked back a growl as his eyes surveyed the warm flush to her skin left over from the heat of the bath. Aaron didn't want to train her, couldn't stand that he had to subject her to more cruelty when all he wanted to do was pleasure her small body, to run his hands and mouth along the pinkish tone to her skin.

"Have you ever kissed a man before, Mouse?" The rough quality to his voice surprised even him. Normally, so very much in control, something about this woman awakened pure lust and need in a way he'd never before known. The blue of her eyes met his, so many shades swirled together to form a tumultuous storm in her eyes.

"No," was Maddy's shy answer, which made the embarrassment over her inexperience apparent in her expression. Looking back up suddenly, she

214

added, "Well, except for when you kissed me."

A quiet laugh followed by a smile Aaron had to quickly hide. "Not in that way." His hands came to her shoulders just as he pushed her gently down toward the floor. "Kneel before me, Madeleine." Her eyes grew impossibly wide as she hesitated at first, but finally relented to going down on her knees before him. When she'd finally taken the proper position in front of him, Aaron slid his hand to grasp his crotch, her eyes following his movement.

"Have you ever kissed a man here?" Hardening under his hold, Aaron tried to think of anything but the warmth and fullness of her lips wrapped around the width of him. He watched as she looked down at the floor before returning her eyes to his crotch and then eventually to his face.

"N …. No. I wouldn't know how … " Her voice became so quiet, it shook as she forced out the words. "I've never even seen a man there before." A confession, one filled with embarrassment and apprehension.

His head falling slightly back, Aaron shook away the overwhelming desire to enlighten her to the male anatomy. Remembering where his dick had been that day, he was able to keep from pulling himself out and teaching her what it meant to kiss a man. There were many ways he would be forced to dishonor the woman kneeled before him, but making her lick away the remnants of a socialite's ass was not one of them.

"Stand, slave. I have something I want to

show you."

Maddy complied instantly, followed behind him as he led her down the corridor toward his room. When wisps of music escaped his door, he sensed Maddy stall at his back. A quick glance over his shoulder and he found that she wavered on her feet, her eyes wide at the recognition of the music. Grasping her hand, he pulled her forward while pushing open the door to enter the room.

He saw the large, black case of the cello positioned exactly where he'd requested. The sudden exhalation of breath behind him told him that Maddy, too, had spotted it. Aaron spun quickly, barely catching Maddy as she fainted.

Carrying her to the bed, he grew concerned at her reaction, lightly tapped her against her cheeks to bring her back to the present. Her eyelids fluttered open like butterflies covering the deep blue of her eyes. "What ... what happened?" Confusion furrowing her brow, she pushed up on her arms, her gaze moving past his shoulder to the instrument.

"You fainted." He laughed quietly. "That was not the reaction, I was expecting." Aaron's voice carried the slight hint of humor as he watched the conflicting emotions play over her face.

216

Chapter Nineteen

Maddy continued staring at the case; her mouth, opening like she wanted to speak, but no sound followed. Aaron moved aside so she could better see the large piece of her life that had been stripped from her when she'd been abducted.

"You may go look at it, Mouse; that is, if you want to." Aaron couldn't help the levity in his tone as he granted her permission to inspect the instrument.

Looking between Aaron's face and the instrument, Maddy finally ... slowly ... crawled off the bed. Her steps appeared hesitant and unsure as she moved closer to the instrument. Aaron watched her like a hawk, every flex of her muscle, every small expression that raced across her face crashing against him as he attempted to hold back his smile.

Reaching the case, Maddy's movements became more hurried as she flicked open the numerous clasps along the side. A slight creak as it opened, and her body trembled when she spotted the cello sitting unharmed inside the case. Her fingers slid delicately along the red colored wood before tracing the outline of the f-hole carved into the body of the instrument. Moving over, she lightly plucked at the strings and frowned upon the discovery that they'd loosened from the heat of where the cello had been stored.

Her body jumped when Aaron suddenly

217

spoke. "Would you like to play for me?"

She was thoughtful for a moment; her silence giving away the trepidation coursing through her veins. Her voice was barely a whisper when she asked, "May I?"

Aaron sighed heavily when Maddy's eyes raced to find his, her question being a great relief when he realized she was learning to look to him for permission. Nodding his assent, she began to remove the instrument from its case before Aaron called out to stop her. "Wait. Put the instrument back in, we'll take it to another room so that you can play."

Begrudgingly, she repacked the cello, quickly snapping closed the enclosures before lifting the case. With Madeleine following behind him, Aaron led her to another door in the corridor. Pulling out a key, he unlocked the door before walking inside in front of her. Before she could enter, he turned to her and said, "Nobody but Xander and I have ever entered this room."

Once Aaron's large body had cleared the doorway, Maddy gasped as her view of the room was expanded. A black grand piano was positioned in the middle of the room; its top left open with music situated above the keyboard, ready to be played. Along one wall was a large black leather couch, but no other furniture took up the space except for a single chair placed next to the piano. Maddy's eyes traveled over the walls as she noticed the padded squares hung over the entire surface, useful in soundproofing and adding to the acoustics of the room. Above her hung a large chandelier.

Much like the one in Aaron's living room, it was a heavy iron circle, dotted with lights fashioned to look like candles. Looking down once again she noticed the beauty of the floors; the wood that was polished to such an extent that Maddy could see her reflection across its surface.

Aaron watched as Maddy perused the room, intently noting her slow understanding that the room had been designed for a musician's use. Placing the large cello case on the floor, she started to move to the piano, but stopped short, turning to look to Aaron for permission before proceeding. A momentary indiscretion, he decided to let it pass, not feeling it worthy of reprimand.

"You may approach it, Madeleine."

A deafening silence fell over the room except for the soft pad of her feet hitting the floor as the sound echoed throughout the room. Aaron held his breath, watching her naked form approach the piano before lightly running her fingers across the keys. Turning to him, she asked, "Do you ... " She gasped, covered her mouth with one hand as her body started to tremble with fright. "I'm sorry. Am I allowed to talk without your permission?"

Interesting ....

Narrowing his eyes, Aaron noticed that after being given the instrument, Maddy's behavior had gone from momentarily brazen to absolute submission. Like a deluge, relief flooded his system. If he could keep her in such a malleable state, they'd both be spared the torment of her punishment and reinstruction.

219

"You may ask to speak if there is something you need to say; but never within the other areas of compound. When we are in my quarters, I'll grant you permission to indicate your desire to speak, but outside of my quarters it is imperative you remain silent. Not doing so could lead to public reprimand, the likes of which you do not want to endure. Additionally, you are to address me as 'Master'; 'yes, master ... no, master .... that is the manner in which you will speak to me." Kindly he spoke the words, although their meaning contained a promise of evil Maddy had never imagined could exist.

Nodding her head in understanding, Maddy appeared to suddenly remember something. "May I speak, Master?"

A short laugh escaped him; amused to see he'd have to be more specific in his instructions. "We're in the middle of a conversation, Mouse, there's no need to keep asking if you may talk. The question is for only when there's been silence between us."

A shy smile, her cheeks reddening from her embarrassment. Aaron groaned when he watched that same blush quickly cover the rest of her alabaster skin.

"Do you play?"

Her words brought his attention from her body to her mouth, his eyes following the perfect lines of her lips. Once again finding the blue of her eyes, he remembered her question. "I do. My mother taught me and Xander both, when we were young." Noting how confusion and disbelief crinkled her brow, Aaron asked, "Is it impossible to believe that a man who's killed also can play a piano?"

"I guess not." Looking down, Maddy avoided the intensity of Aaron's stare as his question reminded her of the true character of the man with whom she was speaking.

"Play for me, slave." While speaking the curt command, Aaron glanced over his shoulder as he moved to take a seat on the couch. Maddy removed the instrument and its bow from its case, walked over to sit in the chair near the piano, and sat down to begin tuning the instrument. Twisting the pegs, Maddy stretched the C and G strings taut and into tune, before moving her hand to the other side to tune the D and A. Almost as soon as the D was tightened into tune, it broke, snapping back to slap a red mark against Maddy's cheek. Aaron was immediately on his feet and moving to her side to inspect the mark left by the broken string. "Are you okay?"

"Yes ... Yes, Master." Her hand went to her face to examine the small welt left by the string. "It's happened before, dangers of being a musician, I guess." She peeked up at him through her lashes. "I have another string in my case, if I may go retrieve it."

After determining that the mark was nothing more than a superficial sting, one that would heal in less than a day, Aaron returned to the couch, waited as Madeleine pulled the broken string from the instrument to replace it with the one she'd fetched from the case. "Mouse, when you are finished, bring me the broken string." A quick facial expression betrayed her confusion, but she complied immediately with his order, not daring to ask why he'd wanted it.

Madeleine crossed the room to hand him the string. Taking it from her hand, Aaron looked up before saying, "Remain standing in front of me." Diverting his attention back to the string, he fashioned a circle out of it by winding it around itself. "Give me your hand." Maddy immediately held out her right hand causing him to chuckle to himself, thinking that if he'd just thought to get the cello on the night she'd arrived, they could have avoided a lot of drama. Slipping the string around her wrist, he tightened it around itself until it fit snuggly against her skin. Looking up, the emerald green of his eyes collided with her perplexed gaze. "Do you know why I'm allowing you to play?"

"No."

He snickered as he arched an eyebrow at her forgetfulness. "No what?"

Another shy smile. "No, Master."

"I let you play because it is a gift for obedience, much like the clothing I've given you in the past. You have done well since I've returned home. If you continue, you'll be allowed one hour a day during which you may play in this room. However, if you falter into disobedience, you'll be punished, and not only by losing your hour for that day, but by other means as well. I can be a kind Master, but I do not condone any rebellion or lack of respect. Do you understand?"

"Yes, Master."

Letting out a held breath, Aaron nodded his head once. "Good. That string will remind you of what you can have. When you misbehave, it will be removed and will be replaced by another type of bind." Maddy didn't respond to his words, just stood looking at him, her eyes welling at the threat of losing something she held so close to her heart.

"Go play."

As she moved back to the chair, Aaron took in the beautiful vision before him as she sat down. Within moments, the room was filled with the baritone sound of her instrument. Sucking in a harsh breath, Aaron had to close his eyes against the beauty of the tone and quality to the music. It was nothing like the CDs, a sound not easily reproduced by even the highest quality stereo systems.

As Aaron sat in awe of the music playing through the room, Maddy's eyes finally released the tears she'd wanted to shed since discovering the instrument in his room. She was spellbound from the feel of the strings sliding along her fingers, the gentle vibration of the wood as she produced sound so exquisite, nothing could compare to its beauty. A single note at first, Maddy added to the deep sound as she played slowly along the strings, building tempo as she also moved along the scale to higher pitched notes. This particular piece had been the one she played on the night she'd been abducted, the music, sensual in its complexity ...

223

hard, yet soft; a driving pulse that was built from moments of anticipation and need. She'd written the piece as an inexperienced woman, never knowing the touch of a man or the desire that could consume her when caressed by the hand of the man sitting in front of her. However, somehow, she'd guessed correctly when composing the piece, had found a way to express the passion that could occur between two lovers in the most intimate of encounters.

Bringing the tempo back to a slower pace, she neared the end of the song while peeking up through her lashes at Aaron. A forbidden forest in the middle of a storm so fierce, the multi-hued greens swirled as his eyes burned into hers, his face overtaken by an expression she'd never before seen. She lost her place in the song almost instantly, mesmerized by the intensity of his stare. Not knowing why, her heart suddenly accelerated and her chest beat against the back of her instrument from her labored and erratic breath. When Aaron suddenly stood and walked to her with a smooth dangerous swagger, the bow slipped from her fingers, clattering against the wooden floor. He stopped just short of where she sat, took the cello from her hands and placed it aside.

Her chest heaved in anticipation, not knowing why he'd looked at her in that way, not knowing if she'd upset him somehow. She kept her eyes trained to the floor, not daring to look up into the eyes of a predator such as him. When he kneeled down, her body trembled at the heat rolling off his skin. He was so close, yet he didn't move, just stared at her, burning trails along her skin as he looked her over. His hands came up to grasp her knees. Parting her legs, he slid his hands along the smooth skin of her thighs, her body quaking even more violently as his thumbs traced along her most intimate parts while moving his hands up further, over her torso, along the edge of her breasts. Moving in between her parted legs, he grasped her head in his hands, held in her in place, while he stared intently into her eyes. "I'm going to kiss you, Mouse, it would be best if you refrain from biting me this time." A flash of a smile before the warmth of his mouth was on her lips. At first tentative and unsure, Maddy allowed him to move over her, have his way with her body. His tongue invaded her mouth suddenly, swirled along hers, soft nips against the edge as he worked her into a frenzy with just his kiss. The silence in the room was staggering as she was engulfed, utterly consumed by the movement of his mouth against hers.

Her heart a fast staccato against the walls of her chest, she gasped into his mouth as his hand moved away from her cheek finding her breast, cupping its weight, his finger and thumb quickly trapping the tight peak between them. His other hand slowly slid away from her face, his mouth still firmly cemented against hers. She felt as his hand slid down the side of her body, brushed along the side of her other breast, it rested at the apex of her thighs. His finger traced along the crease of her sensitized skin, encircling the nub at the top, sending a chill so gloriously violent through her body that she had to pull away from his kiss. Her head fell back as his the wet heat of his mouth traveled along the arch of her neck, eventually

225

settling at the juncture of her shoulder. His tongue teased her as he moved lower, finally finding the pebbled tip of her other breast, taking it between his teeth as he licked over it with the smooth surface of his tongue. His hand continued its torment, one finger continuing the grueling pace over her clit as another finger slid down the slickened flesh until resting just against the opening to her body. She pushed into his touch, desperately wanting him to continue his exploration, to push inside her, introducing to her the sensation of what it felt like to be invaded by a man. But just as she pushed him inside, barely caused him to breach the surface, he'd pull away, only to replace his finger over the surface once more.

"Please, Master, please." Raspy with need, her voice barely broke free of her throat as she begged him to push inside her.

Aaron released her breast only long enough to chuckle wickedly before asking, "So impatient. What do you need from me, Maddy?"

Her cheeks an inflamed pink, she built up the nerve to tell him what she needed. "Please push inside me. I ... I think I need it ... I want to know how it feels."

Fuck! He was a bastard, but Aaron couldn't resist the seductive lilt to her voice, the way her muscles clenched at his fingers, so greedy for his touch. She writhed against him, her hips moving along the chair in erotic rotations that filled his head with images of her moving like that on his lap. Finally losing his ability to resist her, he pushed a finger into the tight heat of her body, the slickened skin undulating against his finger as he pushed up and curled inward to find a spot he was sure would make her scream. If this was the first time any man had been inside her, the first time she would experience what it felt like to be taken by a hand other than her own ... A thought occurred to him at that moment, a wicked joke he wanted to play on the woman approaching ecstasy above him. He stopped suddenly, stopped teasing her breasts with his hand and tongue, pulled out of her to rest the tip of his finger against her opening.

Looking up, he marveled in the lustful expression over her face, her lips, so full, were parted from her panting breath. Her eyes were hooded over and glossy, her cheeks flushed from the way he was making her feel. Clearing his throat, he asked, "Have you ever touched yourself, Maddy ... " Pushing his finger forward, he just barely breached the interior of her core. " ... here?"

The additional blood surging into her cheeks was enough of an answer, but he wanted to make her say it, to speak the words he knew would not easily roll off her tongue. Catching her breath, her breast rubbed against his chin, back and forth as he waited for her to respond. "No ... Master," was her quiet confession letting him know that she was more innocent than he thought.

"Give me your hand. Place the other on my head when I kiss you again. I like to feel the pull of a woman's hand in my hair while I pleasure her." Reaching over to grasp her shaking hand, Aaron growled as he pulled that hand down while the other wrapped itself into the thickness of his hair. Forcing her hand to cup herself, he ran one of his

227

fingers, slickened by her arousal, over hers, pushing her into herself. Pushing inside with her, he kept pressure on her, navigating her to the spot used to tear a woman apart from the inside, out. A teasing rhythm, he moved her to play along that spot, his heart racing as her other hand gripped into his hair, tugged at the skin at the base.

Ecstasy wrapped in sin, Maddy lost herself to the foreign sensation inflicted inside her body; her breathing so erratic she needed to remind herself to pull in a breath. He'd instructed her to touch his hair when he kissed her, but his face did not move from the side of her breast, the warm heat of his skin rolling along her side, his eyes, the color of jade, blazing up to watch her expression as he moved with her, inside her. When his mouth came down over their hands, when his tongue snaked out to circle over the bundle of hypersensitive nerves, she screamed out her release. A volcano erupting within her, Maddy felt like her body convulsed as her orgasm hit her like an avalanche. Her ears rang from the sudden rush of blood through her body, her skin glistening from the fine sheen of sweat produced by the unbelievable heat Aaron was forcing through her. Just as she thought she would tear apart from the intensity of the release, she started to calm, small tremors still traveling along her skin as she came down from a peak so high, she wasn't sure how she'd lived so long without experiencing it.

His mouth continued its suction until the last of her quakes had subsided. When he pulled their hands free, when he sat up and away from her, her body went limp in the chair, her chest

228

heaving ... aching from the tight skin of her swollen breasts.

She looked down at him, her mind nothing but a jumble of mush as he smiled up at her, victory and satisfaction written across his expression. As he stood up, she could see where his pants had become tight against him, it looked painful even from her perspective. He reached down, taking her hand in his and pulling her from the chair. "Let's take a shower, Mouse, we both need to get cleaned up."

He knew he should stop, knew he was skating dangerously close to the edge of that line he dared not cross ... but the temptation was too much. Pulling her behind him down the corridor, they entered his room to the sounds of the CD as it neared its end. Maddy walked dizzily behind him, her occasional missed step endearing to a man not used to the inexperienced woman. Leading her into the adjacent bathroom he struggled to remember that this woman was being trained. Finally corralling his lust, he let go of her hand to further instruct her. "Go kneel by the entrance to the shower. Keep your hands in your lap, your eyes trained to the floor until I instruct differently. Any time that we are in public, that is the position you will take by my side. It doesn't matter whether I'm sitting or standing, when we are not moving, you are to remain on the floor next to my feet."

Maddy complied instantly, slightly relieved to be off her shaky legs, but also uncomfortable with her knees against the hard surface of the stone floor. Despite her discomfort, she held that position as Aaron moved where she could not see

229

him, as she listened to the sound of a zipper being drawn down, to the sound of the material of his pants as they fell to the floor.

Chapter Twenty

Aaron stepped out of his pants and allowed his eyes to trace over the perfect curve to her body as she knelt on the floor by the shower. Her feet tucked underneath her, the full shape of her ass was pure enticement, the fleshy slope of her hip begging for his bite.

With his hand running along the hard width of his cock, he looked her over, imagined himself buried in her depths, introducing her to what it feels like to be taken by a man. Shaking off his thoughts, he stepped back from that dangerous edge, remembering that she was still held captive, still not a true willing participant. But his need got the best of him, propelled him forward into the shower to turn on the water, as she remained kneeling in wait of his next command. Rinsing the last of the socialite off his body, he waited, allowed Maddy to sit in wonder as to what he would do next.

Once the temperature of the water had caused steam to swirl thickly within the sunken space, he called her. He could see as her silhouette moved into a standing position, the supple hourglass curve to her body so lush and exquisitely feminine, his cock swelled even more; anticipation forcing blood south in preparation for his conquest.

When she stepped into the spray of water, the mahogany brown of her hair plastered itself over her skin, the tips of her breasts peeking out from behind its curtain. Aaron's tongue filled his mouth from his desire to pull one of those peaks into his mouth, to leave a telling mark from the suction. Running his hands along the water as it cascaded over her form, he noticed how her eyes looked down, widening to see a naked man for the first time. Aaron laughed to himself, not sure what to do with a woman who'd never even seen a man at his hardest.

"Touch me, slave." His voice was like gravel, rough with need. When her hand shot forward tentatively touching, but then fully grasping his width, he almost released in her hand right then. His head falling back, he ordered, "Stroke back and forth, Mouse; there's no need to be shy." Her hand moved gingerly over his cock, barely a tickle compared to his grip. He reached down to grasp her hand, to force it tighter around his width as he showed her the rhythm he preferred. Her eyes remained trained on their hands, on the intimacy of her touch.

As Maddy was taught how to touch a man, she seemed to marvel at the feel of the silken skin over the engorged muscle and flesh underneath. Finally, pulling her eyes from what they were doing, she looked up into his face, surprise in her eyes to find that he was staring down at her; but when she peaked up, her breath caught, her hand no longer moving on her own accord, but only because he continued to push it along.

"Do you want to know what it means to kiss a man?" This was quickly becoming way more dangerous than Aaron should have allowed, but there was nothing stopping him from his desire to

232

know what it felt like to have those luscious lips wrapped around his width. She blinked in response to his question, small drops of water dripping from her lashes. "Kneel, slave."

Maddy did as instructed, no questions asked, no protest in word or movement. Once she was firmly planted on her knees before him, guilt wound through his veins and into his thoughts. Releasing her hand from his cock, he placed a finger under her chin, pulling her face up to look at him. "Do you want to do this?"

Her eyes searched his, an odd light shining behind them. "I don't know how ... but I can try."

Those words, spoken from lips so pure, they broke straight through Aaron's resolve. "Then kiss me, Madeleine."

Her lips parted as she leaned forward not sure exactly what she was supposed to do. The tip of her tongue flicked out, wetting her lips as she turned her head attempting to find an angle with which to proceed. Having found one, she opened her mouth wider and attempted to take the girth of him into her mouth all at once. As soon as her lips and tongue met the taut skin of his shaft, he bucked, anticipation too heavy a thing for him to remain still as she suckled at the tip. Her teeth grazed his skin from her lack of experience, but he welcomed the sharp sting of pain, had to try harder to keep himself from exploding into her mouth. Hesitantly, she shifted forward, the suction of her mouth, not strong, but enough to work him into a quivering mess.

"Fuck!" His head fell back again, before he immediately brought it forward so he could watch as she worked at his cock. The warm heat of her mouth felt like an inferno on the sensitive skin. He couldn't last must longer, this woman who knew nothing of what she did, but somehow surpassed even the most experienced woman. Was it the best blowjob he'd ever received? Not even close; but it was the woman who delivered it, the woman who had him wrapped so tightly into a ball that his breaking point was as short as it was when he was a post pubescent teen.

"Let go, Mouse, pull off me now."

She moved back just in time for his lust to spill out from the tip of his cock and down the fullness of her breasts. It was almost painful as he watched his seed drip casually off of her tits. She looked shocked for a moment, causing him to smile, once again, at her inexperience. He could have shot off in her mouth, but he didn't want to do something like that until she knew what would occur.

"Clean yourself, Maddy. Wash me off your skin."

Her hands moved over her breasts as she used the gathered water to wash him off her body. It was an innocent enough activity, but to him, it was the most sensual thing he'd ever seen. "Stand." Maddy stood up, her eyes seeking his as if searching for some sign of approval. "You're a good girl, Madeleine. There is no need for you to question what you've just done for me." Not wanting this to go any further, Aaron kissed her softly on her

234

swollen mouth before reaching around her to turn off the water.

Aaron led his slave up the steps of the shower, leaving her at the entrance as he traversed the room to retrieve a towel. His breath caught in his lungs when he turned back to find Maddy knelt down in the position he'd instructed her to take before. When he approached her, he bent down to wrap the towel around her, gripping along the side of her body to pull her up to her feet. She looked up at him with something *different* in her eyes, the blue so serene it mimicked a long forgotten mountain lake ... a crisp blue, reflective like a mirror.

Once dried, Aaron walked into his bedroom, Madeleine following closely behind. "Go kneel by the bed, Mouse." As Maddy complied without hesitation, Aaron moved into his closet to get dressed. Pulling on a pair of slate grey dress slacks, a plain leather belt and a black fitted t-shirt, he finished dressing quickly and stepped out to discover Xander standing in his doorway. Dread instantly crawled up Aaron's spine when he noticed the look on Xander's face.

"I have news, Aaron. You're not going to like it." Xander's voice held an edge to it that told Aaron his reaction was going to be much darker than simply not liking what he had to hear. When Aaron didn't respond, Xander quickly took it as a hint to continue. "Your slave is to be presented to The Estate within the hour. Your father has reneged on the week of training he'd granted you."

Silence, a razor sharp blade slicing through

235

the nerves of every person who stood in Aaron's bedroom. Xander understood that when Aaron was silent, he was lethal; but Maddy couldn't understand why she was suddenly terrified, she just instinctively knew that the darkness within Aaron had surfaced; that the *assassin* had taken over.

Without speaking, Aaron moved to his bureau to pull out his guns and to select five blades. He would be fully armed walking into that ballroom tonight; the fact that his father had broken their agreement, a clear indication that games were to be played. While arming himself, Aaron observed Maddy in the large mirror. Secretively, she lifted her head at times, attempting to glance in his direction. Fearing she would fail during her presentation with behavior such as that, there was no room for mercy in his reaction to her noncompliance. Quickly spinning in her direction, he grabbed her by her wet hair and pushed her face to the floor, her lip busting open from the impact with the ground. His voice was overbearing and cruel as he growled, "You are to remain looking at the floor, DO NOT steal glances in any other direction when you are out there." The sound of her loud cry shot through him like ice. Her voice, smothered in fear and the shocking pain of his grip was tearing him apart, but there was no room for error; it was either train her or watch her die. "Stop crying, or so help me, I will ensure the pain becomes much worse!"

Steeling herself to the immediate shift in Aaron's behavior, Maddy bit her tongue, attempting to hold back the sobs that shook her to her core. Calming her breath, she quieted, waited out the agony of what Aaron was doing to her. She was released only when Aaron was satisfied with her compliance. Even when he let go of her hair, she did not dare sit up, having quickly learned the truth to his words from that morning; every action she took, every thought in her mind could only happen if he had allowed it.

"Good, Mouse; very smart. You may sit up now." Aaron's chest still heaved from his spurt of rage, and when he looked from Maddy to Xander, he was met with a concerned stare. Like the sea churning in a violent storm, the blue of Xander's eyes had darkened to a dangerous black; bits of light bouncing through like waves. Brushing off the obvious concern of his guard, Aaron ordered, "Follow me, slave."

When they reached the living room, Aaron ordered that Madeleine kneel next to the couch while he continued his path to his office. Xander following closely behind, Aaron waited for him to fully enter the room before shutting the doors. "Why is she being demanded now? What happened to the agreed five days?"

Xander turned toward Aaron, took a position with his feet spaced slightly apart, his hands folded together behind his back. "There was no explanation given by Vincent when he delivered the directive; only that she was to be presented within the hour rather than at the end of the week."

Aaron ran his hand through his still damp hair. "When did he arrive? How long has it been since you spoke with him?"

"We have twenty minutes from now to present her in the ballroom, if that answers your question. He arrived while the two of you were in the music room. By the time I stepped back into the apartment from the hall where we spoke, you'd already moved along to the shower. I couldn't be sure, but I believed it would be unwise to interrupt." The implication in his tone was loud and clear; Xander was concerned about how far Aaron had taken his desire for Maddy.

"What happened between Madeleine and I is nothing when compared to what will be done to her if she fails in her presentation. Your concern is ill placed at the moment."

Xander nodded, understanding that this particular conversation would have to wait until after the presentation. "Is there anything we can do within the few minutes we have left?"

"No." Walking back toward the door, his hand gripped the handle as he turned back to order, "Go retrieve the blindfold I keep in my room. It's in the third drawer of the bureau on the left." Exiting the room, Aaron found Madeleine kneeling by the couch, her hands folded together in her lap and her head pointed down toward the floor. Her hair had dried some, but still appeared bunched and matted from the moisture of the water. "Madeleine, come with me. We need to prepare you."

Obediently following behind him, Maddy's body shook as he led her toward the bathroom in the corridor. When they entered the room, Aaron immediately pulled a brush and a hairdryer from

238

the cabinets below the sink. Placing them on the counter, he plugged the hairdryer into an outlet before turning to her. Her breath caught when she noticed it was panic etched across his face and not rage.

"Dry your hair and comb it. Your toothbrush is in the drawer."

"May I speak, Master?" She didn't know why the scent of fear rolled off Aaron and intermixed with his cold anger, but she did not want to falter and find out first hand.

Dark green, muddied eyes looked back at her, a lethal red edge surrounded the rims of the color. Pain flickered across his expression as he swiftly approached her and reached up to run his thumb across her bottom lip. Maddy saw the pink stain on his thumb from the blood he'd wiped away. Just as swift, his concern was gone, replaced with a blank mask much like the one he wore the night he'd unwrapped her. Not looking at her but at his thumb, he answered, "You may."

"Does it matter if I'm beautiful? I am nothing more than a slave."

The slice of steel through his heart, a quick death had it been made by a blade rather than by her words. This woman, one who was far better than any person within The Estate, was so much *more* than she could ever know; this woman was reducing herself to garbage, to an object not worthy of care or concern; and he was forced to allow it. His voice was controlled and so dangerously low as he responded, "Any person

239

within The Estate would know that if I were to fuck a woman ... a slave, she would be kept in pristine condition to ensure that the sight of her would serve to make me hard. That is your purpose, Madeleine. Now do as I ordered and fulfill your role."

Aaron took a sentinel position at the other end of the room as Maddy dried and combed out her hair. When she'd finished with her hair, she retrieved the toothbrush as commanded, just as Xander entered the room to pass something to Aaron. Once her teeth were clean, she watched in the mirror as Aaron approached her.

"Tell me why you love music, Madeleine; how it affects you." Aaron already knew the answer to this question, had discovered it when he'd seen her on stage, and again when she played in his music room.

"I can hide within it, surrounded in beauty, rather than a witness to the cruelty of the world." A quick response, one that took no thought before being said.

Unrolling the blindfold, he watched as the lights in the room bounced off the small metal beads that were pulled over leather cording to make up the front. Those same cords were tied at the sides to secure the beads and were left long enough to be used to tie the mask to the face. "I'm going to blindfold you, Mouse, allow you your hiding place. It won't be the same as the music, you'll still be able to hear the nightmare that goes on around you, but you can at least pretend that you're shielded and outside of view."

Aaron walked up behind her, reached over her head to pull the mask across her face, securing the cords in a knot at the back of her head. Through the mirror, he looked at the vision of her body, her silken hair as it cascaded in waves down the front, only partially obscuring the swell of her breasts. He hated to admit it, but the addition of the mask made her even more appealing, a mystery veiled in leather and metal.

Finishing up his inspection, he straightened his spine, pulled his shoulders back and placed a mask of indifference over his face. There was nothing else that could be done; no additional time with which to prepare her. "Xander will lead you behind me, slave. When I'm at rest he will place you where you need to kneel. People may approach you, may touch you and I will allow it. If I hand you off to another person, you are to go with whomever I say. Do not hesitate for a moment in your obedience, Madeleine. If you do, there's a good chance you will not be returning to my quarters."

Chapter Twenty-One

The weighted sounds of their boots echoed through the halls of the building as Aaron and Xander led Maddy to her presentation. Maddy couldn't see anything. Although shielded by the mask Aaron had given her, she could still feel the energy as it rolled off of the men, her other senses awakened in response to her lack of sight. Their pace was hurried yet steady, her legs faltering every so often from her fear. Not knowing what to expect had her terrified, her insides knotted in dread. She was thankful she'd not eaten much that morning, afraid that her nerves would cause her to get sick, to fail in her presentation.

When their steps slowed, Maddy heard a loud click and the distinct creak of doors being opened. Stopping suddenly, the sounds of laughter rolled out from in front of where they stood; unruly male voices, excited and loud. Maddy wasn't sure whether she should kneel because they'd stopped moving. Just as she started to bend down, they moved again, stepping forward into what she believed was the ballroom where she'd been gifted to Aaron. The rowdy behavior of the men calmed almost instantly when they entered the room. A few more steps forward, and she felt how Xander pushed against her, indicating to her where she should kneel down. Doing so, her skin was struck by the chill of the stone floor, her knees feeling bruised from the amount of time she'd spent on them that day. Her body trembled and shook, her mind racing with images of what the men looked like around her. Terror overtook her when she finally heard the voice of the man who'd abducted her.

"So good to see you, Aaron. I'm sure you have questions as to why I ordered the presentation of your slave so soon." His accent was familiar, an air of entitlement and refined taste dripping from each syllable that he spoke.

Aaron bathed himself in apathy and boredom, effectively containing the boiling rage within his mind and body. With his body held straight and strong, his green eyes met the steel grey of his father's, the corruption a wild thing running rampant in the stare of the man who'd raised him. "It is of no concern, father. If you wish to admire my slave sooner rather than later, I bear no ill feelings toward your request."

A dark chuckle, evil pouring out of each sound that was produced. "I'm so sure, Aaron. I'll enlighten you then. There have been some strange rumors running rampant through The Estate. Men have whispered that you allow your slave to be clothed, that you treat her as more than an object for your use." Standing up from the large, throne-like chair placed in the front of the room, his father moved about with a feline swagger, a strut that had been practiced and cultivated over his many years. "I sent my men to you, Aaron, in an attempt to squelch the ridiculousness of those rumors." Stopping suddenly as he stood by Emory and Vincent, he smiled. "They reported to me that you gave your slave pleasure instead of taking your own." A weighty silence. "It concerned me, to say the least."

243

"Do you question my methods?" Aaron asked.

A throat clearing, a hushed murmur amongst the men that sat within the room; his father looked between Emory and Vincent before returning his attention to Aaron. "I do. Explain why these reports are circulating; reveal to me the method to your madness."

"The whispers of clothing are a fabricated rumor. Your men can attest that when they arrived at my quarters, the whore was not only naked, but also bound in shackles to the bed, her body soaked from the ways I had used her. When I *forced* pleasure from her body, it was in the presence of three other men, it was a means to embarrass her, to shame her, to make her get off on the torment of her Master." Aaron paused, his mind reeling at having to speak about Maddy in such a way, his rage a blazing inferno that she'd been present to hear those words. "While I appreciated Emory's excitement to see my ass and cock, I do not fuck in public, that is my choice and my right in the position I hold within The Estate."

His father's shoulders shook with silent laughter, having been amused by Aaron's insinuation regarding Emory. Behind him, Emory's face took on a vengeful scowl, the scar along his cheek reddening from his anger. "Very well, Aaron; put in those terms I can understand why you demonstrated her to my men in such a manner. However, I would like to inspect the whore myself, see how well you've trained your slave."

His steps echoed through the hushed

silence of the room, the click against the wooden floor as it approached a jarring sound to Madeleine's ears. She remained motionless, her head facing down, her hands wanting to wring over themselves as she forced them to remain still. The fast beat of her heart conflicted with the slow beat of the father's steps; the sound of blood rushing through her head, the only thing muting the terrifying sound of his approach. When she felt Aaron move aside, panic coursed through her veins, her skin cooling from the sheen of her perspiration, while the intense heat of fear threatened to burn her to ash inside.

"Remove the blindfold."

Hands quickly moved to her head, loosening the strings knotted at the back immediately upon the father's command. When she felt the cool metal pulled from her face, she didn't want to open her eyes, didn't want to witness the monster who stood before her. Forcing them open, she kept her eyes trained to the floor, the order not having been given that she look up into the face of depravity and contempt.

A hand reached below her, a finger pulling her face up to so that she could look into the cold grey eyes of a man far older than she. The angle in which he held her face caused pain in her neck and spine, and her hair to cascade down her back until it reached the upper swell of her behind. A sardonic grin, the corners of his mouth turning up until the lewd expression of his face made her want to retch from her disgust. Turning her face back and forth to examine her features, his smile grew brighter when he saw the red mark across her

245

cheek and the swollen and broken skin of her lip.

"So, you've been a violent Master to your slave. She's marked all over her pretty face." A deep chuckle saturated in the filth of his amusement. "Why am I not surprised the executioner favors drawing blood when spilling his seed?" The father's hands moved down her body, causing her skin to crawl from his touch. Cupping her breast he pinched the nipple so hard, she had to bite her tongue to keep from crying out in pain. He grinned again when he saw the bite mark left by Aaron the previous day.

"What full breasts this one has. Not used and spent like the other whores of the house." His hand released her breast, crept slowly south along her torso stopping as his fingers explored the flesh between her thighs. Bile rose into Maddy's throat from his touch, the effect not near the same as when it had been Aaron's hand caressing her skin. Every muscle in her tensed when he slipped a finger inside her, circled it around to test the strength of the muscles of her core. Forced to keep her eyes trained downward, she watched as that disgusting finger pushed farther inside, the delicate flesh burning from her lack of arousal.

"My, my, Aaron, I do believe I outdid myself on my gift to you." He pulled his hand away before using his other hand to pull her face back to his, to make her watch as he licked her clean of his fingers. "I do believe I want to ride her myself. Unlike you, I have no qualms about fucking in public."

Maddy's body clenched, her gaze returning

246

to the floor once the father had released her. Tears threatened her eyes, but she wouldn't let them fall, wouldn't disappoint Aaron. She wondered if he would allow this to happen, then realized it was a certainty based on what he'd said to her before they left his quarters.

"String her up, I want her shackled to the table, her ass bared to me to take what I want." Several sets of hands grabbed around her arms as she was pulled up into a standing position; her knees almost giving out from the weight of her fright. Led to a wooden table, Maddy was pushed forward into a kneeling position atop the rough surface of the wood. Splinters dug into her skin as she was forced down onto her elbows, her hands shackled in metal rings set into the table. The intimate parts to her body were completely exposed to the view of the room as she felt the sting of steel wrapped and then locked around her ankles. The position was painful, her muscles not used to holding her up in such a manner. Shame enveloped her as the men behind her hooted and hollered at the sight of her. The rhythmic click of the father's shoes approached her from behind, her body flinching when she felt his finger run down the crease of her flesh, stopping just against the entry to her ass. "Maybe I'll take you here, it would be a sweeter sting to the skin of my cock."

The distinct sound of a belt being unbuckled and loosened followed by that of a zipper being unzipped. Violent trimmers tore through her system and she couldn't stop the tears that escaped her eyes, her agony a suffocating blanket that covered her.

247

"Have your fill, father. It is of no consequence to me. Just know that if you shove your filth inside her, I won't touch her again. You might as well throw her to your dogs so they can lick off the taste of your dick." Aaron's voice boomed throughout the room, the tone emotionless and without concern.

Hushed silence followed Aaron's words, each man's breath held to see what would happen in this exchange between father and son. Within seconds, she heard the deep laugh as it rumbled out of the chest of the man positioned behind her. His laughter growing in volume and intensity until finally joined by the laughter of the group. Once the merriment had calmed, she heard him zip up his pants and rebuckle his belt, before the sounds of his feet could be heard walking away.

"Now, we can't have that. I so enjoy the fact that you appreciated my gift. I'm in a bit of a bind, however. I would love to hear the sounds of lust roared from your slave's mouth, her screams as someone takes her to the peak of her orgasm. Emory and Vincent reported to me that it was like music to their ears. However, since you will not fuck in front of an audience, and if I may not touch her without your resultant rejection, whatever shall I do to finally have the demonstration that I seek?"

Quiet. Deadly silence a heavy weight throughout the room. Aaron's voice, so dreadfully calm, Maddy's skin prickled from its implied violence. "I see no solution to your conundrum. I will not touch her here, you do not want me to cast her aside, and no person within The Estate is

248

allowed to touch her per the directive you gave on the night she was gifted."

A dark laugh, delight in the game between father and son. "But that's where you are wrong, Aaron. I never stated that no *person* would be allowed to touch her, I merely ordered that no *man* within The Estate would be allowed that privilege." A pregnant pause as Maddy was unable to look up to see the expressions of the men bartering regarding the form of cruelty that would be used. "Bring me a slave."

Murmurs erupted again amongst the members of The Estate.

Aaron's shoulders rolled back as he tried to ease the tension from his spine. His skin inflamed by the fury that filled him, he remained outwardly calm and detached as the large doors opened for Vincent to go retrieve a slave as instructed. Ever loyal, Aaron knew Xander stood just behind him, ready to fight every man in this room if it was what Aaron determined should be done. A high pitched shriek sounded as Vincent dragged in a blonde slave, her body covered in welts and bruises, her skin hanging from her bones from lack of nutrition and care. Until Maddy, the slaves who'd been taken by The Estate had known the risk. Accepting drugs without the ability to pay, getting involved in other criminal acts with members of the units, but failing in their tasks. They'd been warned, had seen the other slaves kept chained throughout the large building, but had taken the risk regardless, so sure that they would not end up like the other spent hags that littered the interior of the building. Most were kept drugged to keep them quiet, the volume

249

of their screams was a nuisance to the men who weren't using them at that time. Aaron had little compassion for their plight, knew that it was by their own actions, they'd ended up the lowest members within the compound.

As Vincent dragged the slave to stand before the crowd, Aaron kept his eyes trained on his father. The game had been played well, a small slip of semantics and Aaron had been bested by a man who delighted in tempting men into evil, who excelled at leading people to their own self-destruction. The face of a debonair man of privilege, the mannerisms of someone who'd led a life of luxury and wealth, his father was the ultimate deceiver, a poison so potent, that even the most intelligent of men succumbed and were eventually destroyed by his father's games.

The evil in the steel grey eyes that stared back at him twinkled within the insanity of his gaze. His lips curling at the ends before he ordered, "Have the blonde work over Aaron's slave, not stopping until her face and hands are drenched in the evidence of the other whore's orgasm."

A tremor ran through Aaron's body, pure anger igniting within him by the fact that Madeleine would be touched in such a manner by someone other than him. He'd risked pretending his father's threat of rape didn't affect him. He'd been able to save Maddy from the shame that'd almost been inflicted, but there was nothing he could say to stop this assault. His father's order fell within the established rules for Aaron's slave, did not breach the decree that had been given the other night.

250

Vincent let go of the blonde woman's hair, pushed her in the direction of Maddy as she remained bound to the table. Aaron's eyes followed as she approached the table, wished he could look into Maddy's eyes to let her know he was tormented alongside her.

When the blonde reached Maddy, a filthy snicker sounded from her body, almost as if the thought of tormenting another made her feel more powerful than the used up whore that she was. Her yellow stained fingers brushed up to Maddy's head, pulled through the silken mahogany waves of her hair. The blonde leaned in as if to whisper, but spoke loud enough so the people in the room would be able to hear. "Don't shake, beautiful girl, I'll make sure you like it." Reaching around she slapped her hand against Maddy's ass so hard that just the sound of the slap made Aaron's teeth clench. Forcing himself to remain still, Aaron watched as the blonde continued to torment Madeleine, images flooding his head of stepping forward and breaking the bitch's neck for every action she committed against his slave.

The blonde smiled wickedly, enjoying the torment she enacted against Maddy. "Come on, baby girl, you need to get wet for Momma, I'm going to show you that taking a woman for a lover is so much better than a man." Her fingers slicked down between Maddy's thighs pressed in and out as she attempted to elicit arousal. Her other hand found Madeleine's breast, her fingers teasing the nipple into a tight point before again caressing the weight of her breast. "This isn't doing it for you, baby? Let Momma take care of that for you."

251

When the blonde moved behind Maddy, she instantly moved her face closer to lick at the sensitive nub, her hands continuing to work over Maddy's body. Aaron watched as a flush of color broke out along Maddy's skin, he knew full well that an orgasm was building in her despite her disgust and shame. He watched as her jaw loosened, her hips beginning to writhe under the flick of the blonde woman's tongue. Each man in the room moaned at the sight of the two women, some pulled themselves loose to jerk off as they watched the display. Aaron made sure to note which men took the most pleasure in the scene played out before them, promised himself that the dicks they stroked would be removed from their bodies when he killed them. The room only held a few of the men that were part of Aaron's alliance and he noticed how they would turn their heads, ashamed to be witness to the rape of a young, innocent woman.

Soft moans began to sound from the table, the blonde successful in her mission to force pleasure through Maddy. When wound to the peak, when pushed to the point of eventual release, the blonde took her thumb and pressed it into Maddy's ass just as she screamed out in the fits of her orgasm, her body quaking from tremors as hormones surged through her veins. Winding her down, the blonde finally pulled away, cackling at her achievement. She stood up, turned so that the audience could see the evidence of Maddy's orgasm as it dripped down her face.

Walking back over the Vincent, the blonde leaned in for a kiss, her pride allowing her to

252

believe that she was anything more than a tool. Vincent grabbed her by the hair again, pulled a rag from his pocket to wipe her face clean before dragging her back out the doors to lock her back in whatever hole she'd crawled out from.

Looking unimpressed, Aaron turned to his father, saw a glimmer in the eye of the man who just ordered Maddy's rape. "Are we done here?"

His father's keen eyes searched Aaron's face for any hint of emotion. Not finding the reaction he wanted, he snapped his fingers, ordering that Maddy be released. "We're done for now Aaron, take your whore and return her to your quarters. I will call again soon if I have need for another demonstration."

Chapter Twenty-Two

When Aaron, Maddy and Xander returned to their quarters, Aaron ordered Maddy to sit on the couch while he indicated for Xander to join him in his office. Maddy sat down as instructed, not able to hold back her tears from the events of the presentation. Aaron did his best to ignore her sobs, slamming the door out of anger, but not closing it entirely. Moving to his desk, he sat down in the large leather chair as Xander took a seat on the opposite side.

"I have to release her, Xander, she can't be forced to endure another presentation. He will only get worse, will come up with new ways to torment me by abusing her body." Aaron's voice was distant, controlled so that he didn't go back to that ballroom to kill every man who occupied the room.

"You can't let her go, Aaron." A truth spoken softly, but the heavy weight of those words hung amid the momentary silence between the two men. "If she escapes, it will be your life. The alliance is not yet strong enough to overpower those who still hold allegiance to your father. A few more months and we'll be ready to strike. We have to hold out until then."

Pounding his fist against the wood of the desk, Aaron sat up in his chair, anger seething within his veins. "She will not live through another few months. At some point he will push my patience too far, will overstep bounds that will cause me to lose control. I'll die either way. If I free her, at least she stands a chance. She'll be able to get to someone who can help her, she'll be able to escape the disease that The Estate has become."

"And she'll have to live in hiding for the rest of her life, a prisoner to The Estate even then. If you release her, he will not stop until he's found her. Whether you are alive or dead, he will torture her just to spite you once she was found. There is no place on the face of this Earth that isn't infected by his influence."

Silence again, a blanket of hopelessness and futility settling over the two men as they argued over the fate of the young woman currently crying in the room on the other side of the office walls. Aaron finally spoke again, his voice rough and cracked through by the despondency he felt. "If I was to be her only abuser, if it was me she would learn to hate while I fought to keep her alive, it would be different. I could protect her from the worst; ensure that she remained whole. But that is not the option I've been given, at least not now that he has found ways around the agreement we'd entered. He'll rape her at some point, Xander, he'll pass her around to the slime that serves him before ending her life as he has every other woman he's wanted to use."

"We'll find a way around it. We'll ... "

"THERE IS NO WAY, XANDER!" Aaron stood up from his desk, knocking aside whatever objects cluttered the expanse of the wood. Walking away he punched the wall, knocking a

255

large hole in the plaster before moving to the window to look outside. Thoughtful for a few moments, Xander didn't dare disturb the beast that was slowly wrapping it's claws around Aaron's soul, didn't dare disturb a man who could kill within seconds.

Finally breaching the silence, Aaron spoke again, "Retrieve what clothes she has left, I'll walk her to the perimeter of the property, take the paths through the woods away from the cameras. I will not let Madeleine's life slip away in order to save mine. She is light while I am darkness, she is raw beauty and so blessedly pure while I am nothing more than a poison to humanity. She deserves her life far more than I deserve mine."

Maddy calmed herself while sitting on the couch as Xander and Aaron spoke. As she stopped the flow of tears from her eyes, tried to still her trembling body, she could hear the conversation between the two men, her skin prickling at the realization that Aaron would set her free. Enveloped in shame and disgrace, her mind flitted back to the events of the presentation; the inspection by Aaron's father, the feel of the other slave's hands and mouth on her body. But it was Aaron's voice and words that had disturbed her the most. The lack of emotion and the reference to her as nothing more than garbage, she would have rather died than endured the mockery from the men in the room. As they'd walked back through the halls toward Aaron's quarters, she felt more anger at herself for having believed he cared anything about her, she cursed him silently as she watched him through her tears as he walked in

256

front of her and Xander.

His words just spoken to Xander were in stark contrast to the man he'd been at the presentation; her confusion now a deep and dark chasm tearing through her mind. During the presentation, she'd been so sure that he cared nothing for her that he'd fooled her into believing that even a spark of humanity could exist within him. After he'd stepped aside, allowed her to be chained to a table, gave permission to his father to use her as he saw fit, Maddy believed that she'd been deceived, that he'd used kindness to train her, that his kindness meant nothing more than ensuring she was ready for the presentation.

She listened intently as Xander argued against Aaron's decision, heard Aaron when he described her as a thing of beauty, a light in comparison to the darkness of his soul. Her eyes widened at the realization that he'd never wanted to train her, that he'd rather lay down his life than witness her endure further abuse, that he would lay down his life to set her free. Tears again, but this time not from the pain and torment of abuse, but from the realization that she hadn't been deceived, that the tiny spark of light she saw within him hadn't been extinguished, it had just been disguised.

Aaron came storming through the office doors, the dark green of his eyes swirling with rage and despair, the droop to his shoulders revealing that, at this moment, the decision he made was his acceptance of defeat. Xander walked behind him, but rather than stopping in the living room as Aaron had, Xander continued on until he

257

disappeared down into the shadows of the long corridor.

While waiting for Xander to return, Aaron stared at Madeleine, his eyes taking in the vision of her in an effort to commit the image of the only good thing he'd known in his life to memory. The image wouldn't need to last long; as soon as it was discovered that she'd been released, his father would order his death. Although Aaron was a skilled assassin, the *executioner*, as he was dubbed within The Estate, he could only survive for so long when fighting the army of men his father would undoubtedly send to ensure his death.

"We're going to take a walk, Madeleine. I will have to get dressed for the cold weather, unfortunately I will not be able to provide you clothes to protect you. I want you to stay here while I change, don't move from your seat until I return." He didn't wait for her response, knew that she'd been broken enough that he wouldn't have to worry about her attempt at disobedience, hoped that when he set her free, she'd find her way back to the innocence The Estate had taken from her. Moving quickly to his bedroom, Aaron put on a large coat, took Maddy's clothes from Xander, shoving them in his coat to hide them until he could get her to the perimeter of the property. Xander's eyes were bleak and he remained quiet while Aaron armed himself with more blades and walked out toward Maddy so that he could set her free.

Approaching the front doors, Aaron turned to Maddy. "Stand slave and follow behind me. At no time should you walk beside me as if you were my equal. Until we get to our destination, all eyes will be on us as we pass. Be sure to stick to your role."

Maddy nodded her understanding and took her place behind him. Letting out a heavy sigh, Aaron pulled open the large front door, stepped out into the halls and shut the door behind him once Maddy had followed him out of his quarters. They walked in silence through the halls, the men they passed wearing expressions of shock to see Aaron and his slave out in public so quickly after the events of the presentation. He hated parading her around in her undressed state, but he had no choice. Exiting the building, the bite of cold air stung his cheeks. Early evening had begun to settle over the land and a thick mist hung in the air obscuring the distant tree line. Although relieved to know that once they entered the woods they would be hidden from sight, he couldn't imagine the discomfort Maddy would feel from the cold air hitting her skin. The only solace he could find was that soon she would be free to return to her life. Once they passed the exterior walls of the building, Aaron led Maddy into the woods, cringed every time a branch broke under his foot when he realized what the ground, littered with twigs and rocks, must be doing to Maddy's bare feet. He wanted to slow down, to pick her up and carry her as far as he could, but he had to keep the appearance that she was only a slave, nothing worthy of his care.

Once veiled deep within the thickness of the mist and fog, Aaron stopped. Turning to Maddy, he pulled the clothes from inside his jacket.

259

Her skin had taken on a blue tint from the cold air against her body, her lips and cheeks already chapped from the wind. Holding the clothes out to her he said, "Put these clothes on, you'll freeze to death without them. They're not much to protect against the cold, but they're better than nothing. He attempted to hand her the clothes, but Maddy just kept her arms wrapped around her body, refused to reach out to accept them.

Aaron tempered back his annoyance with her disobedience, remembered that she was not the slave she represented. "Please, Maddy. Take the clothes."

"May I speak, Master?" Her voice was shy as she trained her eyes to the ground.

Letting out a sigh, Aaron watched as the warmth of his breath steamed out before him. "I'm not your Master, Madeleine. You are not a slave, you are nothing as low as I've made you believe."

"Will you die?" Her head shot up, her eyes the color of a summer sky burning into his as she shocked him silent with her question.

"Maddy ... "

"No!" Her voice firm, she stepped out of character to find out the truth to Aaron's plan. "Tell me now. If I leave here, will you die?" Her voice shook as she found a hidden strength within her that she'd never known existed.

"How did you know, Maddy?" The soft tone to his voice was confession enough, his continued refusal to answer the question she asked. "How did

260

you know I intend to set you free."

"I overheard your conversation with Xander. You didn't close the door all the way; I heard everything. Xander said it would cost you your life if I were released ... you agreed. I can't let that happen, Aaron, not after ... not after everything you've tried to do for me." Tears streaked down her face, their warmth quickly diminished by the cold wind, they felt like ice by the time they dripped from her cheeks.

Aaron stood dumbfounded, not knowing what to say to the woman who appeared to be crying for him when he'd done nothing but torture her. His voice was softened by disbelief when he said, "I've tormented you, Maddy, and I've treated you like nothing more than an object, allowed others to treat you that way."

Holding her chin up, she continued to lock her eyes with his, not shying away from the dark soul of the man who stood in her presence. "Have you enjoyed it, the torment you've inflicted on me?"

Her question struck him. Now was the time for Aaron to answer her truthfully, but he didn't know what it was. Had he enjoyed it? Yes; when her body was writhing beneath him, when she'd bitten him and fought against him; when she was kneeling before him making him feel things that no woman ever had. "Yes."

Her body tightened at his answer, the realization of his honest character apparent in the way she held herself. "I'm not a good man, Maddy.

261

I'll never be a person worthy of you, of the beauty and light you provide to this world. I kill, I steal, I lie and I cheat. I take pleasure when I bathe in the blood of another man's demise, when I watch the life drain from their eyes as they die. I enjoyed you as well, Maddy, not when I had to hurt you, but when I took things from your body that weren't mine to take. I've done nothing for you, Mouse, nothing but what I wanted to do."

She thought about those encounters, at first disgusted with the feel of his hands on her body, that disgust had been reduced to ash by the way he made her body feel. Not the first time, not when she hadn't yet been exposed to his gentle side; but after that, yes, she'd wanted the fire he ignited within her, wanted the feel of his skin, his mouth, his tongue on her skin. Her heart had been lost to him during those quiet moments between them, when he tended to her wounds, when he watched her play in the music room. He had given her something; he'd attempted to give her the only modesty that he could. More importantly, he'd given her back her music, showed that he knew, on some level, how important it was to her. Pulling her hands in front of her, one hand moved to spin the circle of the string around her wrist. Staring down on the silver cord, she shook her head, refusing to believe there wasn't a small glimmer of goodness within him. "Did you enjoy it when you allowed other people to touch me, to rape me while strapped to a table, to display me to a group of horrendous men who were turned on by my pain?"

"No." A simple answer, one so true to its

262

core, it struck Aaron to realize that he'd become possessive of this woman, couldn't stand the thought of any man or woman laying another hand on her.

Nodding her head, Maddy knew he wasn't as indecent as he believed himself to be. "If I stay, if I endure the acts of The Estate, continue to be your slave, will the alliance that Xander spoke of be able to destroy your father? To destroy those vile men who watched as I was raped by another woman?" She didn't look up from the cord around her wrist, too afraid to see the green of Aaron's eyes.

Reaching out to touch her, Aaron pulled back when he remember she wasn't his. "It's not for you to be concerned, Maddy. Once you leave here, you never have to worry about this place again, you can live your life as you should, play your instrument, get married and make babies if that's what you want. The affairs of The Estate are beneath you, you are so much more than any member of this godforsaken hell hole."

"But I want him dead." She finally looked up, saw the shock in his eyes at the vengeance in her tone. "Don't I have a choice? Or are you as entitled as your father, feeling like you have the right to make decisions for me, the right to tell me what will happen to my life."

Aaron shook his head, not comprehending what she was attempting to say. "I have taken no choice from you. I'm trying to let you live your life as you see fit, not under the command of men so corrupt they blanket the world in violence and death."

"Then I choose to stay, to remain as your slave, to allow you the time that you need to ensure that your bastard father dies. If you are giving me back my choice, then I choose to stay."

Shaking his head in refusal of what she was asking, he watched as Maddy fell to her knees on the ground. Her head held in her hands, she sobbed so violently, that her small body shook with the force of her sorrow. Aaron dropped to his knees beside her and took her small body into his arms. Her skin felt like ice from the frigid temperature outside, the small bits of light reflecting beautifully off her alabaster skin. He allowed her to cry, completely overtaken by the woman who dared care about him when he'd been her nightmare. Something flickered within him, a light breaking through the black recesses of his soul, a small glint of hope where before, there'd been none.

"They'll torture you. If I let you stay, they'll get to you eventually, Maddy. I can't protect you when we're in the ballroom, it will only be so much time before they push me too far ... "

"So then, why let me go?" Her tear streaked face turned up to his, the blue of her eyes glistening with her tears yet unshed. "If you release me, I have no where to run. I heard Xander when he said that your father's reach was all over the world. You'd die and he'd come after me just to enslave me again. I'd be right back in the same position as I am now, except I wouldn't have you to help me through it. I'd belong to one of those

264

monsters ..."

"I AM one of those monsters!"

Pushing up on her knees, she brushed her lips softly against his, the difference in their body temperatures a startling feeling. "You may be one of those monsters, but there's something else inside you, a kindness that you didn't have to show me. I don't believe you are exactly the same as those men."

Aaron stared down in wonderment of the woman in his arms. Amazed that she would choose to endure torture, the possibility of rape, and that she would walk naked through a building full of ruthless thieves and murderers, just to see justice done to the man who'd abducted her. Such strength for such a small woman, such courage for a woman who once preferred to hide. "Maddy ... "

"Please, Master." Her beautiful blues sparkled as she looked up into his. "Let me help you bring down the man who torments us both." Not waiting for a reply she rose again, taking his mouth with hers. Her tongue invaded his mouth, shyly teasing the edges of his tongue, until he lost himself to her kiss. Deepening the kiss, Aaron pulled her up into his lap until she straddled his legs with hers. Heat blooming within him, he allowed himself to become absorbed in the moment, not caring if it was wrong to allow her to stay, not caring whether he could endure watching her undergo torment at the hands of The Estate. Not only would she risk herself to exact vengeance for what his father had done to her, but in revenge of what his father had done to him. Her need for

265

vengeance was something he could understand. Begrudgingly he pulled away from her kiss, his hand traveling down the cold skin of her back.

"Yes, Mouse. Yes, you can stay."

Chapter Twenty-Three

Two weeks had passed since that night in the woods, two weeks where Aaron and Xander worked fervently to build up the alliance against Aaron's father; two weeks since Aaron had allowed himself to touch his captive. Maddy remained the diligent slave to her Master when they'd traveled the halls, but she was allowed more freedom when safely hidden away by the walls of Aaron's quarters. Not quite treated as an equal, she was allowed to roam the apartment, was given clothes to wear when she was outside of the public eye. Aaron asked that she sleep in the spare bedroom where she'd spent her first night here, her heart breaking at his rejection of her in his bed. Keeping busy with work, Aaron avoided Maddy as much as possible, while Xander kept her company most days and nights. Xander had been surprised when Maddy had returned with Aaron that night, couldn't believe that she was willing to exist within a nightmare in order to ensure the death of the man who dragged her into it. Her presence was welcomed by Aaron's best friend; but was also a burden because Xander had to stay with her and couldn't escort Aaron to the meetings between the alliance members, or to the executions on behalf of The Estate. Often Aaron would return home, his shirt stained with blood, the darkness in him still attempting to keep tight control of his mind.

On one such day, Maddy sat with Xander at the table. Discussing nothing of importance, they laughed easily with each other, Xander still prone

267

to calling her 'Cricket' rather than using her real name. While Xander made jokes regarding the size of the cello in comparison to Maddy, the front door creaked open as Aaron snuck inside. As usual, he silently looked her over, as if ensuring she was well, before walking away without a word, disappearing into the corridor that led to his room. Her heart fell when he avoided her, her eyes tracking his path before returning to the startling blue of Xander's eyes.

"He hates me." The hurt of rejection stained her words, easily discernible to the man sitting across from her at the table. "He's barely spoken to me since I chose to stay. I feel like he doesn't want me here."

Xander sighed heavily, slid his hands across the wood of the table to touch hers. "He doesn't want you here ... but not for the reasons you think. He's worried about you, Cricket, he doesn't know what his father will plan next." Pausing momentarily, concerned etched its way across Xander's expression. "You are his weakness and I don't think he knows how to deal with that fact."

Pulling her hands free from Xander's, Maddy leaned back in her chair, looked down to spin the cello string she still had wrapped around her wrist. Silence loomed over them as they sat for a while longer.

Standing up, Xander looked down at her and winked while tucking his chair back under the table. "I'm going to talk with him. He had a meeting today with some of the members of the alliance; I need to know if there are any tasks I should complete as a result."

Nodding her understanding, Maddy stood as well, and walked alongside Xander as they approached the corridor. "I think I'll go into the music room for a while, see if I can ease the pain in my heart by playing." When they reached the room, Maddy turned to enter, closing the door behind her as Xander continued down the hall.

Picking up her bow, she spent a few minutes applying a healthy sheen of rosin to the hair before picking up the cello and making sure it was in tune. Sliding her fingers along the strings, she allowed the harmonics to take her back in time, when life had been about nothing more than music, when the world was only a scary place that existed on the outside of the small house she called her home. Wondering what happened to that home, she started playing a song that her uncle had taught her when she was a child, a soulful lullaby from some other country for which she couldn't remember the name.

Pulling her bow across the largest string, the deep bass of the notes vibrated throughout the room. Sorrow spilled from the sounds of those notes, her emotions transformed into sound so beautiful, and she couldn't keep from shedding a tear as she played. A string of higher pitched notes slowly leading down to one low, soulful tone, the vibrato tightening her out-of-practice wrist. Slow and steady the notes changed, a touch of sunlight covered in the black clouds of a building storm. She knew happier songs, small tunes that would make most people smile in delight, but those were not the songs she chose this day, her heart needing an

269

audible expression of her melancholy, a release from the built up tension in her muscles, bones and spirit. After going through three or four songs, her shoulders dropped with sadness, her head not finding the usual escape provided within her music. Placing the cello down on its side, Maddy sat quietly for a moment, stared at the couch where Aaron had sat just a few weeks before, remembered watching his seductive stride to her from across the room, the way his body and mouth felt when touching her skin.

Finally standing up from her chair, she moved to sit on the piano bench to look over the music, surprise alighting her face when she saw that it was by a composer she didn't recognize. Reading over the music she discovered that it would be a sad piece, but powerful in its intensity; fitting for the environment in which Aaron had been raised. She reached up to the music, ran her hand along the notes of the bass clef in the piece, imagined the song if played by piano and cello together. Looking back down to the keys she ran her fingers over the surface a few times, finally daring to press down on a key. The tone of the piano was exquisite, the acoustics in the room helping it echo throughout the space. She played another key and then another, before running her fingers along them, not unlike a child who didn't know how to play.

"Isn't that the wrong instrument, Madeleine?"

Spinning so quickly, she nearly fell off the bench, Maddy's eyes met the emerald green of Aaron's. A light in his eyes glimmered, the corners of his mouth twitching as he attempted to hold

270

back a smile. Maddy looked at him, struck dumb by his beauty, the air about him speaking of danger and passion all at the same time. He was entrancing; an enigma of sorts, but one where the mystery within him revealed itself when you were least expecting it, when you swore that only darkness truly resided in the body of the man who enjoyed killing. Aaron laughed quietly, his shoulders shaking slightly with the sound. Maddy just kept staring, not understanding how he could go from being barely able to look at her to a man able to laugh at the effect he had on her.

"Are you going to answer me?" His head angled to the side, he continued to make light of her shock in that moment.

Finally finding herself, Maddy shook her head before saying, "I'm sorry, Master, I ... I thought it would be okay if I ... I shouldn't have touched it." Why she reverted back to her behavior as his slave, she wasn't sure. It made it easier for her to communicate with him, sheltered her from having to make decisions that went against her shy nature.

Shock at her response flickered across his face quickly before being replaced by the expression of a man who wanted nothing more than to dominate. His voice lowered sinfully deep, the light that once glimmered in his eye turning into the beginning of a slow heat. "You know what this means, don't you slave?"

Her body shuddered at that word, moisture building between her thighs, she couldn't believe how easily she responded to him, how much she wanted him. "No."

"No, what?"

"No, Master." The corner of her lip peeked up, this exchange placing her back in familiar territory, a place where she knew how to associate with him, how to communicate with him. Although she wasn't sure why, but by acting as his property, by surrendering herself fully to him, it made her feel safe, the weight of the world lifted off her shoulders, allowed him to make the decisions she was too afraid to make.

"You've touched something of mine ... so, now, I get to touch something of yours." Moving from the doorway so that he could close the door and ensure their privacy, he slowly stalked her. Keeping his eyes trained on hers, he let the pressure build between them so that he could watch her body tremble as he approached. Even while she was clothed, he could imagine the curves of her body, her supple and weighted breasts, the way her mahogany hair contrasted sharply against the pure white of her skin.

Just as he approached her, his hands tightened into fists as he held himself back from touching her right then and there. Standing over her so that she had to crane her neck to look up at him, he smiled, enjoyed the way her lips were slightly parted from anticipation, the way her skin flushed from his scrutiny of her face and body. Stepping quickly aside, he surprised her as he moved to sit in her chair.

"Come here, slave. Stand in front of me."

272

Maddy pushed herself up on shaking legs, used her hand to grip the side of the piano so that she could steady herself. Her heart raced making her lightheaded, her chest heaving as the rate of her breathing increased. Hesitantly, she stepped toward him, moving so slowly, until stopping a short distance from where he sat. Her eyes searched his, her body awakening, nerves coming alive with trepidation and want.

Aaron's eyes slowly looked over her body. She pulled her bottom lip between her teeth, forced herself to remain still for his perusal. She'd enjoyed this feeling, knowing that she was his to play with, knowing that while he took his fill of her body, he gave her such extremely rewarding pleasure in return.

"I want you on your knees." Broken up with hoarseness caused by his need, his voice rubbed itself along her senses, made her quiver in anticipation of his touch.

Maddy immediately lowered herself to the floor, the sting of the hard surface against her knees a sweet feeling when mixed with the eagerness for what was to come. Aaron reached down to gather the bottom hem of her shirt in his hands; a slight grin on his face as he pulled it up to remove it from her body. Maddy obediently lifted her arms, would allow him any liberties with her body that he wanted to take. She was so new to this, so completely out of her league that she preferred submission, luxuriated in the trust she granted him by allowing him to own her completely.

273

Once he pulled the material from her body, he placed it on the floor beside them. His lips parted slightly as his eyes devoured her breasts. Reaching out slowly, he took the weight of them into his hands, pinched the tips between his fingers enticing them into tight buds. Maddy's head rolled back with the feeling, her body readying itself for whatever it was he wanted to do.

Releasing her, Aaron pulled his hands back to his sides, continued to admire the stunning woman who, at this moment, was *choosing* to give herself to him. A strange difference, her choice to give herself to him rather than taking what he wanted; it was enough to floor him as it stoked the flames of the inferno even higher than they'd ever been.

"Unbuckle my pants, Mouse, stroke me with your hand."

Maddy hesitantly reached for the buckle of his belt, the warmth of him against her hands a heady sensation. Loosening the leather from it's metal clasp, she brought her hands closer to his body, could feel the tightening in his pants from his excitement. Satisfaction blooming within her at the realization that she affected him just as he affected her, a smile threatened her lips as she quickly unbuttoned his pants. Pulling down the zipper, she found that he wore nothing underneath, her ability to pull him free made easy and quick. Gripping her hand around the width of him, she stroked along the satin feel of his skin, the muscle underneath engorged to such fullness, it felt so unforgivingly solid within her hand. Her breaths now coming in short pants, she jumped suddenly when his finger

274

came under her chin to pull her gaze to his. He grinned seductively, the chiseled quality to his face softened by the expression; however, his eyes gave away the lust that burned within him.

"Kiss me, Madeleine." Barely a whisper, his command pleased her, let her know that this exchange was going to end in exquisite passion.

Aaron had intended for Maddy to push up, to bring the fullness and warmth of her lips to his, but when she wrapped those lips around the head of his cock, started suckling the tip allowing her tongue to dart out to stroke along the shaft, he melted into his seat. The realization that she needed more specific instruction at times, that she was so new to this that she wouldn't always understand what he'd intended, didn't escape him; but he was so undone, so completely overpowered by the feel of her mouth wrapped around him that he let the misunderstanding go, favoring the moist heat of her mouth where she'd placed it. He groaned, leaning back in the chair, he allowed her to explore him with her tongue, to please him in such a selfless way that it was endearing. She didn't have her head in his lap in an effort to get something from him, she did it out of the pure desire to please him. So different from all the other women he'd been with; his angel, a woman who had unknowingly taken him captive in return.

Wanting to extend this encounter, Aaron reached out to stroke his hand down the soft silk of her hair as he ordered, "Stop, Madeleine. Lean forward, press your breasts into my lap, hold the sides of the chair with your hands and use your arms to press your breasts tightly together."

275

Confusion flashed across her face, but she obeyed Aaron's command, not questioning what he intended to do to her. When he moved her up so that he could insert himself between her breasts, Maddy looked up at him, a shy expression crossing her face as she waited for him to instruct her what to do.

"Push yourself up and down, slave; please your Master." Fur across her skin, the deep baritone to his voice seeping into her pores heating her blood to a point of boiling heat.

Maddy did as he said, was shocked by how the feel of his hard length, slickened with the moisture of her mouth, made her feel, turned her on to such a painful point of need, she had to fight from reaching down to touch herself to find relief. She bounced on her knees in front of him, purred at the satisfied moans that escaped his throat. She watched his lips part, fought back the desire to climb up and take that mouth with hers. Not having to fight long, Aaron suddenly looked into her eyes, locking her in a stare so hot, her skin flushed as a fine sheen of sweat broke out along her skin.

"Stop ... pull off my pants and then climb up and straddle my lap, Madeleine."

She did as instructed, pulled the pants free of his legs, left them lying on the floor as she climbed up before straddling his legs with hers. His hands gripped the flesh of her hips as he pulled her forward, pressing himself against her sensitized flesh, against that point that he'd found would make her writhe and moan. When she was in place, he released her hips to slowly run his hands up the

276

sides of her body, teasing her breasts as he passed them, finally gripping his fingers into the thickness of her hair. He pulled her head forward, forcing her body even more tightly against his cock so that small bursts of electricity shot through her nerves from the pressure against her. His mouth moved over hers slowly, his tongue darting out to lick along her bottom lip seeking entry. When she opened her mouth, his tongue invaded hers as a growl resonated from his chest. Pulling away suddenly, he pressed his mouth to her ear as he whispered, "I can taste myself on you."

Her body trembled as his hand slid out from her hair to reach around behind her, finding the point of entry to her body. While her sensitized nub was pressed firmly against him, he ran his fingers along the crease of her slickened skin, propelled her body to rub along the length of him as he teased the opening to her core. "I want to bury myself inside you, Madeleine ... I want to finally make you mine."

Another violent quake as she listened to words that made her heart sing while he pushed her toward a release she'd craved for the two weeks he'd refused to touch her. He wanted her, wanted to own her, to never let her go. "Then take me." She would give herself to him, needed to give him whatever he wanted, trusted that, in this moment, he would take care of her, would slowly ease her out of her inexperience. Even more she wanted him, could feel her muscles grip along his finger, wanting ... needing more than his hand could give.

Resting his head against hers, Aaron fought

277

against lifting her body so that he could spear himself into her. His conscience warred with his desires, the reason he'd avoided her since they'd returned from the woods that night. She was not his to take, a captive. To take her would be to cross that line he'd firmly set when she'd first arrived.

"No, beautiful. It's not mine to take. That is a piece of yourself that should be yours to give freely, not to be taken by a man such as me." The rasp to his voice broke apart his words, betrayed the fire burning inside him as he fought for control.

Maddy struggled to think as he continued to work her up and down along the length of him, his fingers, moving in circles around the muscles of the opening to her body, tremors ran through her as she fought to respond.

"I want to give myself to you, Master; I *have* given myself to you." Peaking through her lashes, she found his eyes; saw the conflicting emotions swirling within the depths of the green. "Will you accept what I give you?"

"You are captive ... "

"Not anymore. I chose to stay, I'm here of my own free will."

He let out a heavy breath, his body shaking under her hands, his strong arms lifting her, still rubbing her against him. "You stayed for vengeance."

Maddy pushed back against his hands, stopped the motion of their bodies and reached up to cup his cheeks and lock her eyes with his. "I stayed for vengeance, yes; but I also stayed for you."

His breath catching, Aaron's resolve shattered at the sound of those words. Fighting the urge to spear her right then and there, he picked her up instead, standing while guiding her legs to wrap around him. He marveled at how light her body was as he quickly carried her out of the music room to take her to his bed. His mouth barely left hers as they moved between the rooms.

Laying her down on the bed, Aaron explored her body with his mouth and hands, teased her skin with soft pinches and nips as he worked her into such a frenzy she dripped in anticipation. Spreading her legs before him, he looked into her eyes, stared in awe at the woman who'd been so shy but somehow had become braver than him. Reaching over to the side table, he opened a drawer, removed a condom and pulled it on. Looking back down into her eyes, he said, "This may hurt, Maddy, tell me if it's too much, I want you screaming my name from your enjoyment and not from your pain."

Maddy nodded her head, nervous of how the width of him would fill her, but she trusted him, knew that he would go as slow as she needed in order to please her. He positioned himself at the surface of her, pushed slightly in, but waited as her body adjusted to his girth. The sting was divine, a spice added to the sweetness of their passion. Grabbing his hips, she pulled him toward her, forced him farther inside. Her body burned where the muscles were forced apart, but she still wanted

279

more, wanted him as deep as he could go. He braced himself motionless above her, looking over her body, watching every hint given by the expressions that flitted across her face. Leaning down, he leisurely laved at the peak of her breast, pulling it into his mouth to suckle the tip. Slowly, he moved back and forth within her, working the muscles loose enough to avoid hurting her when he buried himself to the hilt. Losing his control, he leaned down, nipped at her earlobe before whispering, "Are you ready?"

Nodding her head, yes, Maddy was struck silent by his movement within her body. A final push forward and Aaron was fully inside her. Pausing again, he waited for her muscles to relax, to adjust to the width of him, but then he began to move, and a heat like she'd never experienced bloomed within her. Losing herself to the intensity of the moment, Maddy's heart beat out a staccato rhythm, her breath held as she was driven to an edge so sharp, she feared it would slice her in two. Almost too much, the sensation gripped her body, her muscles tense as every nerve ending came alive and sparked along her skin.

The feel of air against her heated skin was almost too much as Aaron worked her body, drove her to a point of complete abandon, loved her like no other person had before. Moans escaped her lips, sounds of pure passion erupted as the inferno he built inside her took over. Pushed higher and higher, she was barely able to think, fought to keep her eyes open so she could watch the flex of his glistening muscles as he moved above her. When Aaron grabbed the backs of her thighs to push her bent legs up higher, he moved impossibly deeper within her. Her hands gripped the sheets as she was forced to a peak that seemed so high it would be painful to finally reach. When his mouth took hers, when his teeth nipped at her bottom lip, she came undone. A fevered storm roaring across her body, the intensity of her release caused her to scream out his name. Her muscles quivered around him, gripped along the fullness and width of him as he continued to pump into her. Her body quaked uncontrollably as it felt like she was being ripped apart from the inside out. When he finally let go, when he finally shot himself inside her, when his mouth pressed hungrily against hers as he joined her in exquisite release, Maddy melted beneath him; her body occasionally trembling with the aftershocks of her orgasm.

Aaron stilled above her, his eyes searching hers for any sign that she was in pain. She smiled up at him, her expression so sated and satisfied her beautiful blues were barely visible under the droop of her eyelids. Pulling himself out of her, he removed his weight from her body, but pulled her into his arms and against his chest.

Maddy found sleep while enveloped within his heat, found peace while safely tucked against his body.

Chapter Twenty-Four

Only having slept for a few hours, Maddy woke up to find Aaron passed out beside her. She moved to look at him better and noticed soreness in her body she'd never experienced before. After turning over, she gingerly reached up to brush the errant strands of silky, black hair away from his face before running her hand down along the stubbly skin of his jaw. He looked so peaceful, so reposed as he slept. His perfect lips were held slightly apart and Maddy resisted the urge to lean up to run her tongue along the crease. Even in his sleep, there was a unique quality to him, a majestic air that frightened her and tempted her at the same time. While most men feared the man that lay beside her, she couldn't help but feel comforted by his presence, a feeling of safety that she'd never had. Even before her abduction, when she was hidden away in her house or within the studio walls, she still felt lost, so terribly alone in the world. But now ... now, while in the middle of a nightmare, she found solace in a damaged soul, one who'd showed her a part of him that no other person had ever seen. There was light in him, one so bright it could illuminate the entire night sky if only it wasn't covered over by the shadow of his darkness.

Maddy was startled when Aaron's eyes peaked open, when his arms suddenly pulled her tighter against him, when one corner of his mouth curled up in amusement at her shock. His mouth changed into a wicked grin as he said, "Hello,

Mouse." His voice, still rough from sleep, rumbled from his chest, her body vibrating from being pressed up against him. Before she could respond, he rolled her over so that he was on top of her and brought his mouth to hers. Heat bloomed in her chest, her heart dancing against her ribs. They lay there leisurely as they kissed, no need between them to rush the moment, simply happy to be in each other's arms. Eventually, Aaron pulled away, rolled them both to their sides so they were facing each other.

"I'd like to take you somewhere; wine you … dine you … show you the world, but given the present circumstances, I'll have to settle for having Xander fetch us something to eat and bringing it back here." His hand came up to brush against the smooth silk of her hair. "It's so frustrating, not being able to treat you as you deserve." Aaron whispered his confession to her as the sun set beyond the thick curtains of the room. The eerie glow of the red light created a safe hideaway for two lovers, a respite from the terrifying environment within The Estate. Never completely at ease, Aaron looked over the features of the woman in his arms, found that it was the light that shone in her eyes when she was near him that turned him on most of all. Most women had always wanted for him for his looks, his status, his money and his reputation … but not Maddy, never Maddy. She saw something in him that made him feel like, maybe, there was something that existed in him that was more valuable than all those other qualities combined. She made him feel like he was loved, something he'd not known since his mother disappeared when he was a child.

283

The perfect pout of her mouth moved seductively as she answered, "I have no idea why you're frustrated, you've taken me to the place where I most want to be; you've taken me into your arms."

A hit to the chest, Aaron's wind was knocked from him briefly, her words ... poetry like none he'd ever heard; this woman who was burying herself within his soul, her purity enough to chase away his demons. He smiled, took her lips with his once more. Pulling back, he chuckled. "Maybe there is something I can give to you, something that will show you what you mean to me."

Thoughtful, Maddy took her bottom lip between her teeth and thought of what she would want. Her eyes widening, she realized exactly what Aaron could give her. "Play for me."

His body tensed, his brow furrowing in confusion before realization shown in his eyes. "You want me to play the piano for you? I ... you don't want that, I've never played for anyone before. I'll butcher the music just from having an audience."

Her smile grew so large, her cheeks hurt. "You? Afraid of an audience? I find that hard to believe." Her whispered voice had a teasing quality to it, a softness meant only for the man beside her. "I was able to go on stage in front of hundreds of people and play. There's no way that you could be scared of just one."

Quiet laughter erupted between them, magic found in a peaceful moment they had all to themselves. Maddy continued to goad him into playing, but they were interrupted by a knock at the door.

Pushing up on one arm, Aaron grabbed a blanket to pull over their naked bodies. "Come in." The softness to his voice long gone, once again replaced with his usual business-like tone. Xander pushed open the door, paused for a brief second at the sight of them curled together in bed before delivering his news.

"Emory just stopped by. You've been ordered to present Maddy in the ballroom within the next half hour." He paused, his expression darkening from his thoughts. "He had a smile on his face, Aaron. I have a feeling something very bad is happening."

Every muscle in Aaron's body tensed as suspicion and fear ran along his spine. He looked down into the wide-eyed expression of his mouse, could see the terror as it flooded her eyes. Having no other choice, Aaron steeled himself for what was to come. "Leave us, Xander. We'll be in the living room momentarily."

Once Xander had closed the door, Aaron immediately ran his hand along Madeleine's cheek, his eyes, the color of light streaked forests, were alive with his panic. "I don't think I can do this ... " He shook his head when Maddy went to interrupt. "No, Madeleine, I'll kill any man that touches you …."

She placed a finger against his mouth, forced a small smile on her face despite her overwhelming

285

fear. "I know what we're walking into, but you have to stay strong ... for me. Regardless, of what they do to me, you are to stand there, to pretend like you don't care, because in the end, we'll have vengeance against the man that's brought such great sorrow into both of our lives. You can't react, you have to be strong so that I can remain strong through you."

"What if they want you dead?" He didn't want to spend what could be their last moments talking about the horror that awaited them, but he needed her to know, he needed to know that she understood what could come.

A single tear ran from her eye as she looked up into the face of such a dangerous man. "Then you offer to do it; just kiss me as I pass so that I can give you my last breath. We'll become one and when you succeed in destroying them, I'll be part of you when you do."

Wiping away her tears, Aaron's heart melted at her words. Such bravery for a woman who faced the unknown; it amazed him to see that her heart had changed from that of a mouse into that of a lion in a matter of weeks, that her strength was enough to heal them both. One more kiss ... he placed one more kiss on her beautiful mouth before pushing up of the bed and getting dressed.

After meeting Xander in the living room of his quarters, the three left together, traveled solemnly down the winding corridors in route to the ballroom. Striding elegantly through the halls, Aaron took the lead while Xander led Maddy

286

behind him. No longer needing the blindfold, Maddy's eyes followed the lines of the stone floor as they moved, once again donning the mask of Aaron's slave. The sound of doors opening, the loud and unruly behavior of the men on the other side quieted, a hush falling over the room as Aaron stopped and Maddy down knelt by his side.

Aaron looked up at his father as he sat on his throne. A smug look over his face, his eyes appeared hazy as if recently drugged. Even still, the slate grey of those eyes mimicked the polished steel of Aaron's blade, were still shrewd in their scrutiny of the troublesome son. There was no sound, the tense silence in the room rubbing against Aaron's nerves as he waited to hear what his father planned to do next.

"You look good, Aaron; as does your slave." An accent of affluence and wealth, a deep voice that commanded the room. "Something quite unsettling has been brought to my attention. It appears my *executioner* has been having some fun outside of business."

His spine like an iron rod, the muscles in Aaron's back protested his stance. He tucked his arms behind his back, folded his hands one over the other to relieve the tense muscles. "Enough with the riddles, just tell me why I'm here."

"Very well … " A sardonic grin, broke over his father's face as he looked to Emory and signaled. "Emory, please bring in our witness."

Aaron cast a flippant look toward the door as Emory moved to open it. Once the large

287

wooden surface was pulled free, Aaron's eyes landed on the blonde hair and stick-thin body of Emily. Holding her hand out to Emory, he bent down to kiss it before leading her into the room. Emily looked over at Aaron, a sickening grin across her face as she was led to stand next to his father. Aaron sneered at the ugly jagged scar that ran down her face, stitches still in place from where the blade had cut the deepest.

"You remember Emily Hart, don't you? I believe it will be hard to forget a face like this." A mocking tone, his father obviously had something purely evil in mind. "You see, the problem is that Ms. Hart didn't look like this before having relations with you several weeks back." Standing up, his father held out his hand so that Emily could take it before leading her down the stairs to stand in front of Aaron and Maddy. Not faltering in her obedience, Maddy kept her eyes trained to the floor even when the tips of expensive high heels, revealing perfectly manicured, pink polished toes, came into her line of sight.

Not receiving a response from Aaron, his father continued. "Ms. Hart tells me that you had come to her house for a visit, that the two of you had sex. Apparently, this is what you did to her when you took her, and I was wondering … if you are capable of this type of brutality against a fine woman such as Ms. Hart, whatever are you capable of doing to a lowly slave?"

When Emily began to sob, Aaron's lip curled into a taunting grin. Her eyes trained on him, he mouthed the word "whore" before returning his bored gaze to his father. He was able

288

to return an indifferent mask on his face, while inside he was fighting back the raging desire to pull a blade and finish the bitch off. "My slave has no such marks. I haven't needed to punish her as brutally as I did Ms. Hart. It's not my fault that one bitch knows to keep her mouth shut while the other doesn't know when to shut the fuck up."

The amused shake of his father's shoulders indicated to Aaron that he cared nothing of the woman to his side, this was just another opportunity for him to play his hand in the game. "Unfortunately, Aaron, your punishment was inflicted against a *lady* of The Estate and I cannot condone your use of such brutal force against an acquaintance of the network. It sets a bad example. If I let this pass without retribution, soon everybody will be at each other's throats. We are a collective, Aaron, we don't fight amongst ourselves."

Fisting at his father's words, Aaron had to force his hands open in an effort to give no outward sign of his rage. His father was a master of reading a man's mind by carefully watching facial expressions and other small gestures that could betray a man's innermost thoughts. "She is not part of the network, she is merely a piece of ass that is available to the community. She is of no benefit, therefore she has no right to seek retribution."

Laughter, cruel and mocking, erupted from his father as he moved to grip Madeleine's face. Aaron flinched just slightly, forcing himself from breaking the old man's neck right then. Pulling her head up, his father forced Maddy eyes to look at Emily's face.

289

"Do you see what your Master has done to this woman? He's been a very bad boy, and I'm afraid you will have to suffer as a result. She tells me that Aaron did that to her because she called you trash." His father released Maddy, just as Emily reached down to grab Maddy's face again, pulling it up so that she could spit at her. Releasing her before wiping her hand clean on her skirt, Emily looked down at Maddy as if she was nothing more than diseased filth at her feet. Aaron's eyes narrowed, his jaw slightly ticking from the force of his clenched teeth, he took a deep breath, replacing the mask of indifference on his face. Promising himself that he'd make sure that Emily didn't live beyond the night, he was able to calm himself back to a point of appearing bored.

"What is the retribution?"

"One mark on your slave for every one on Ms. Hart's body. I've examined her scars. It appears a whip was used to create those lines across her skin. The same will be used for your slave."

Maddy's heart beat so fast, she was worried the rush of blood would knock her unconscious. Her knees shook as she was pulled up on her feet, the father's guards stepping forward to take her from Aaron's side. She wanted to look at him as she passed, wanted to see the emerald green in his eyes, to know that he was standing beside her, but she didn't dare glance over, didn't dare appear disobedient in front of the crowded room.

Murmurs erupted throughout the space as she was led to the side of the room and placed facing a wall between two wooden posts. Shackles were placed around each wrist, the chains pulled tight so that her hands were stretched out above her. When she was secured in place, she heard the two men walk away, leaving her alone between the two posts.

"At her request, Ms. Hart will deliver the lashes." Spoken without emotion, his father's voice filled the room.

The rhythmic click of heels as Emily approached Maddy, Aaron's eyes followed her every move, made note of every flex of her fingers around the whip, and every flutter of her hair as it was blown back by her movement. He would kill that woman the next chance he had. He would make it slow and superbly excruciating, tearing her apart piece by piece, limb by limb before finally ending her pathetic life.

Emily approached Maddy and allowed the length of the whip to unravel from her hand and drag along the floor. Finding her position, she pulled back her arm, used her wrist to flick the length of the cord behind her as she prepared for the strike. Just as her arm flexed with her intent to bring the whip forward, Aaron's father called out. "Stop!"

Emily faltered on her heel at his sudden command. Pulling herself back into balance, she turned to him, her face overtaken by a loathsome scowl.

Locking eyes with Aaron, his father smiled, the purist form of malevolence dripping from his next words. "I've changed my mind, and I take back my agreement with Ms. Hart's request. I believe it would be more fitting if you wielded the whip. After all, it was your hand that caused those marks across Ms. Hart's back." Ever the devil who could lead a man to his own destruction, his father assigned him with the cruelest torment off all ... forcing him to torture the woman who'd buried herself within his very soul.

Aaron's eyes dropped to the floor, a momentary lapse of strength as his father delivered the ultimate insult. Not only would Maddy have to endure the slicing pain of a whip, she'd have to do so at Aaron's hands. Looking back into his father's eyes, he smiled, imagined how the old man's face would look when his neck was torn open by his blade. He refused to back down, to reveal even the smallest weakness. The woman tied to the wooden posts had the inner strength of an army; he'd be damned if he let her down. "Fine."

Moving toward the posts, Emily's face twisted into open hatred. Reaching her, he gave her no chance to hand the whip over, but took it from her still clenched hand causing her to lose her balance and fall. The room erupted in laughter as she looked up at him with red flames in her cheeks. Pushing herself back up, she brushed down her skirt and stood back from him. "Enjoy whipping your fucking whore." Spitting in his face, she quickly walked back to the edge of the audience; her spite, an inferno behind the browns of her eyes.

He wanted to go to Maddy, to explain that he'd rather die than raise his hand to swing the whip; but to do so would be to fail her, to be weaker than a woman much smaller than him.

292

Pulling his arm back, he swung out, dying inside when he heard the slap against her skin followed closely by her bloodcurdling scream. Her body trembled, her knees giving out instantly, he almost stopped when he saw her body buckle from the agony of the blow. Blood dripping in trails down her back, Aaron fought the urge to reach out to her. Raising his arm, steeling himself against the torment he shared with Maddy, he pulled the whip back again, bringing it forward for the strike; dying inside each time the leather hit her skin and she screamed.

When he reached a total of ten lashings, his body trembled with hers, his arm protesting the continued movement. He was fighting with all he had not to break down, his emotions too much against the fake mask that he wore. Reaching back for an eleventh strike, he was stopped by his father's booming command.

"Enough!"

The mixture of relief and guilt a heavy weight on his shoulders; he dropped the bloodied whip to the floor, straightening his spine before turning to face his father.

A malicious grin, the father knowing what he'd just done to the son. Satisfaction in his voice, he commanded, "Retribution has been paid, now you may take your slave back to your quarters."

The sound of Emily's shrill scream grated against Aaron's nerves. Spinning so that he could look in her direction, he watched as she pulled a blade from another man's belt before running toward Maddy. Stepping in her way, he pulled his gun from his side, his sight directed between her eyes. "I wouldn't take another step if I were you."

She stopped, staggered back in her step, before turning to his father, a plea in her eyes. "She does not have the mark on her face, that is the worst scar of all!"

Amusement again in the shaking of his shoulders, his father faced Aaron when he asked, "What is it, exactly, that Ms. Hart said to you before you attacked?"

Aaron grinned, understanding creeping along his mind as he discovered the true depth to his father's game. "She said she wanted to be treated like a slave; that she wanted to know how it felt to be a whore." Keeping his voice steady, Aaron glanced at the confusion on Emily's face as he repeated her words.

"And did you feel slighted by her words."

"I did."

Snapping his fingers, his father indicated for Emory and Vincent to take hold of Emily while he finished what he had to say. "It seems there is some additional retribution owed to my son for dishonoring his property. Given the words you used that upset him, I see nothing more fitting than to grant the request that you made."

Only when Emily was firmly in the grasp of his father's guards, did Aaron lower his gun. Emily's face contorted in terror, her body falling from the weight of his father's words. "No! Please, you can't

294

do this to me, I'm more than a common whore."

Laughter erupted throughout the room, his father waited for the sudden noise to hush before continuing. "You forget Ms. Hart, The Estate does not benefit those that do not benefit The Estate. You've been living off the hard work of my members for years, spreading your legs for any man who was willing to open his wallet. However, my men have moved on from what you can offer, have found other *ladies* who would love to take your place."

"No," The one word barely understandable outside the force of her sobs. Aaron looked across the room and indicated for Xander to help him release Maddy as Emily was dragged and strapped to the wooden table in the front of the room. Once released, Xander gingerly took Maddy into his arms, trying not to touch the wounds on her back. Her light body sagged against him, her feet dragging across the stone as they removed her from the room. Once in the corridor, Aaron paused a moment to listen to Emily's screams as she was made into the whore she'd asked to become. He walked away laughing, knowing full well that those screams would continue until every man in that room had been allowed his fill.

Chapter Twenty-Five

"Set her down face first on my bed, be careful not to brush anything across her wounds." Aaron allowed Xander to carry Madeleine to the bed. Watching as Xander carefully laid down her unconscious body, he turned and hurried into the bathroom to get out his box of medical supplies. Hurrying back beside her, he flinched when he saw the jagged cuts that tore across her back, blood red rivers polluting the dove white perfection of her skin.

Kneeling down on the floor, he dared not sit on the mattress for fear of jostling her body. Even though she wouldn't feel it while passed out cold, he still cared too much to risk causing her any more pain. Pulling the antibiotic cream from the box, he set up the jar near her on the bed, unrolled several strips of gauze and moved back to the bathroom to retrieve a damp cloth. When he returned to her, he noticed how her head turned slightly, her eyes squeezed tight as she started to gain consciousness. Kneeling by her side, he brushed his hand against her cheek, shushing her moans, praying she would fall back into the arms of slumber instead of awakening into pure agony. She settled as he whispered to her, appearing to find a place in her dreams, stilling enough so that he could tend to her wounds.

Slowly, he used the damp cloth to remove the blood from her skin, flinching each time he noticed her brow furrow. After applying the

296

ointment, he bandaged her back with butterfly bandages and gauze as best as he could, giving the ointment time to work its way into the cuts. He knew the wounds would need air, but at the moment he was more concerned with stopping the bleeding while protecting her against infection. After repacking his medical kit, he sat on the floor, his back and head leaned on the bed where her legs hung down; he waited for his angel to awaken.

Hours must have passed, the night sky an unforgiving black against the windows of the room, Maddy woke up in excruciating pain. As she tried to move, her leg kicked out landing against something solid, just before a hand reached up to keep her still. She jumped at the touch, not understanding whose hand had grabbed her. Aaron pushed up from the floor, wiped his hand across his face to chase away his exhaustion. Standing beside her, he placed his hands on her back, steadied her while whispering, "Don't move, Maddy, you need to stay as still as possible, at least for tonight. The wounds are too fresh for you to be moving around. I've closed up the cuts as best I can, If you remain still, there's a chance the scars won't be too deep."

"Aaron, oh God, Aaron, it burns so bad!" Tears ran from her eyes as she spoke. "What happened after we left? All I remember is that horrible woman screaming, but I remember nothing that happened after that." Her pain was apparent in the tone of her voice, the tears flowing freely from her eyes. Aaron soothed his hand down her hair while she adjusted to what must have felt like fire across the skin of her back.

"You passed out as we carried you back. I

didn't wake you, preferring that you sleep through the time it took me to tend to your wounds." His voice shook with emotion, his concern for her becoming his greatest weakness. "Are you hungry or thirsty ... why don't I get you some water? Maybe you could take something to help you keep sleeping."

Nodding her head, Maddy would accept anything he offered if it would deliver her back to delirium and away from the pain overtaking her body. Aaron traveled quickly across the room, going through both his closet and the bathroom, he returned to her with a pill in one hand and a glass of water in the other. Maddy moved as much as she could to take the glass from his hands. Aaron held her down, bringing the edge to her lips so she could drink. Returning the glass to the bathroom, Aaron turned on the stereo system as he passed; let the haunting sounds of Maddy's songs fill the room as she fell to sleep. He sat down on the floor beside her, stroked his hand down the back of her leg attempting to sooth her back into sleep. Within minutes he heard her deep, even breathing and relaxed against the side of the bed. Closing his eyes, he kept a sentinel position at her side, a snake coiled to strike out at any person who tried to disturb her.

~ ~ ~

Morning light, the reds and pinks flitting past the edges of the curtains, Maddy's eyes peaked open as she watched the dust swirl with the beams of light. She attempted to move, but was struck so

298

suddenly with pain, she instantly remembered the events of the previous day. Instantly aware of her movement, Aaron opened his eyes as well, placed his hand on her leg to let her know that he was there beside her. Pushing up on his cramped legs, his muscles protested the movement. "Maddy, are you okay?"

Wiggling around on the bed, she let out a small cry as she tried to push herself over from her stomach. "No ... I need to ... "

"What, what do you need? I'll get it for you so you can stay still."

A deep breath escaped her, her hair blowing out from the exhaled air. "I need to pee."

Aaron didn't mean to, but he chuckled at her statement. Her cheeks had become pink with her embarrassment of the request. Leaning down to her, he whispered, "Stay here, I'll get a cup and hold it between your legs."

"No!"

He chuckled again. "Fine. Let me help you up, try to keep your back as straight as possible." Lifting her from the bed he watch her wince with the movement of her body. When he had her standing, he put his hands under her arms to steady her, keeping her upright with each step she took. Lowering her down onto the toilet, he stood above her, waiting for her to finish.

"I'm going to have to wipe you, Maddy. I don't want you moving if you don't have to." He smiled when he saw the dejected look on her face about what he'd said, but instantly felt guilty for finding any sort of humor in the situation. When he was done cleaning her, he flushed the toilet and placed his arms under her to pick her up. Shaking her head, she tried to push him away.

"Just let me sit for a moment, please, just let the pain go down some before I have to move and make it worse. I don't think I can handle anymore right now." She sounded breathless, her heart beating erratically at the intensity of her pain.

Nodding in understanding, Aaron knelt down on the floor in front of her, his eyes holding hers as he gave her the time she needed. Sitting quietly, he watched her face, searching her eyes each time they opened briefly, grabbing her hand to comfort her when she flinched from the pain. Examining her wrist, he saw where the string wrapped around one had cut into her wrist from the shackles she'd worn the night before. Aaron instantly attempted to unwrap the string, but Maddy pulled her hand away, covering the string with her other hand. "What are you doing?"

"The string, it's cut into your skin, I have to remove it."

Shaking her head in refusal, Maddy pulled her arm to her body, cradling the injured wrist. "I don't care if it cuts my hand off completely, I never want it removed." Pausing she appeared as if she thought of a far away place. "I always found freedom within music, Aaron, and then to be taken captive ... to have it stripped from me ... " Looking deep into his eyes, she continued, "You gave that back to me when you gave me my instrument; somehow you knew. Do not take the freedom away, no matter how it injures me." Her expression, a plea as she begged to keep something as simple as a bracelet fashioned from a broken cello string.

Seeing that she was becoming upset, that panic was settling into the lines of her face and the muscles of her body, Aaron backed off, nodded in understanding of her request. "Okay, I'll treat and dress the wound under it, I'll leave it, if that's what you want."

Finally, calming, Maddy was able to keep her eyes open longer, the deep-sea blue meeting his as she asked, "Did it work? Were they fooled?"

"Yes. Yes, my brave girl, they were. Emily ended up the ultimate victim in his game. My father was never concerned about what I did to her, he was just using her to get to you." A dark part of him started to sneak out in those words, his anger resurfacing at the thought of what his father had done.

"Don't let your anger control you now, Aaron. I can hear it in your voice. Hold onto it until a time where you can use it to finally end his life." Still strong. Even with her back ripped apart and her nerves screaming out in agony, Maddy still remained strong.

Silence fell between them, Aaron's voice only a soft whisper as he finally dared to breach it. "I'm sorry, Maddy. I'm sorry that I had to use that whip on you. If I could have traded places with you, I would have. I would have laid down my life not to

301

have to do what I did." Pain flickered across his face as he remembered what he'd been made to do, a pain so deep it only added to the darkness within him. For years, his father had been cruel, unjust, and had fashioned Aaron into the assassin for The Estate, had stripped from him the ability to love or to be loved.

Reaching down to cup his cheek in her hand, Maddy pulled his eyes to hers, let the serene blue wash over him, giving him back some parts of himself that his father had stripped away. "You did what I asked you to do. You remained true to what we hope to accomplish. No matter what happens, if I live or if I die, you can only help me find justice by eradicating the man who took me from my life."

Aaron pushed up so that he and Maddy were face to face. "Let me help you back to bed. You can't stay here forever, you need to lie down and rest."

A shy smile, the expression on her face one that reminded him of the woman who'd first been gifted to him, the one who'd dared to reveal herself during the quiet moments between them. "I don't want to spend anymore time on that bed ... " Her cheeks heated from some inward thought. " ... Not in this condition, anyway."

Her words reminded him of the events before the presentation, the words she'd said to him in the music room, the moment she'd given herself to him on the bed and the whispered conversation that occurred when they woke up. Sex had been a first for Maddy, a part of herself she'd given to him .... but his words ... those had

302

been a first for him, a part of himself he hadn't even known existed. The memory of those moments brought back a request Maddy had made; one he'd denied her then, but one he wouldn't refuse now.

"Let me take you to the bed so that I can redress your wounds; after that, I'll take you somewhere else."

Nodding her assent, Maddy tried to cover up her pain as he helped lift her into a standing position, but Aaron knew. Every flinch of her body, every wince that furrowed the perfection of her face; he knew she wanted to cry out, couldn't understand why she wasn't screaming, a warrior wrapped within the beautiful shell of a musician, a strength in her that no one could have suspected.

After laying her down on the bed, Aaron retrieved the supplies. Pulling the gauze from her back, he died a little more inside each time he revealed one of the deep cuts made by the whip, cursed himself for having been the one to inflict them. Her hands gripped the blankets by her head, her muscles clinching with each strip of gauze he removed.

When he finishing cleaning and redressing the wounds, he helped her into a standing position again, caught her as her knees weakened below her due to the pain. Tears streamed down her face and Aaron swore vengeance for each tear that escaped her eyes; pain for pain, that was a promise Aaron made to himself, to his father.

Leading Maddy down the corridor, he

eventually took her into the music room and laid her down on the large leather couch. Quickly retrieving pillows from another room, he brought them to her, placing them around her so that the position she was forced to lay in was as comfortable as it could be. Brushing his hand along her cheek, he wiped away tears still flowing freely from her eyes. When she'd finally calmed, her eyelids drooped as if trying to stay awake. Eventually closing, Aaron looked over her face as she gave into the exhaustion from her agony, pleased that her body knew when to block her mind from a pain so excruciating, no person should ever have to experience it.

Only when her breath deepened and evened out did he leave her side. Slowly he moved over to the piano, looked over the music opened above the keyboard. His mother had written this piece for him when he was born, had been so proud of her accomplishment that she'd had it sent away to be transcribed and printed under a fake name. Before she disappeared, she'd made sure to teach him this song, to ensure that even if they were parted, Aaron would have a piece of her she'd saved for him alone.

Running his fingers lightly across the keys, he thought of how long it had been since he played. Over the years, he'd slipped so far into the shady dealings of The Estate, into his position as the executioner, that he recognized his father had been able to corrupt him, had been able to turn a spirit that at one time had been pure, to one that was infected with the poison of death and decay. He'd begun killing at the age of fourteen. Barely a man, he'd been taught the basic use of a gun, of a blade, but it had been the poison that'd grown within him, the one that eventually would fill him during each waking moment, that had driven him to prefer the use of the blade to a gun, to enjoy the bloodbath and carnage of the kill.

Pressing lightly down on one key, the sound reverberated throughout the room. With his right hand, he slowly played the notes as he remembered them, softly at first, the song that reminded him of another pure soul in his life. Recognition took over his instincts; his fingers placed themselves, notes played out of habit and memory, rather than from reading the music in front of him. Finally bringing his left hand to the keys, he added bass to the treble, harmony to the melody, until he was playing a song so beautiful; it mimicked the song of angels. He became lost in the sound as it consumed him, his hands moving along the keys as if of their own will. Within the song, he heard the voice of his mother, the laughter when she'd taught him and Xander both to play an instrument she'd mastered as well as Maddy had mastered hers. Birthed by a woman who was beauty, purity and light, he wasn't lost to the irony that if there had been a kindred soul born into the world, the woman sleeping near him had been that spirit.

When the song ended, when he played the final notes, he sat quietly, reflecting on the loss he'd suffered through his life, the darkness that had smothered the light of his youth, had all but extinguished the spark of life within him.

"That was beautiful."

305

Aaron spun around on the bench to lock eyes with the deep recesses of a mystical blue sea. Maddy's eyes sparkled with tears, her expression one of wonderment and awe. "Who is the composer? I didn't recognize the name when I read over the music yesterday."

Crossing the room to kneel by her side, he took her hands into his. "My mother wrote it, had it transcribed under a false name so that my father wouldn't discover that she'd continued in her love of music when he had started to slip further into corruption. He'd loved her, loved her gift of music when they'd met, but like everything else, he attempted to destroy it, attempted to take a thing of beauty and turn it into a nightmare."

Maddy noticed the pain and loss etched across Aaron's expression, reached out to smooth the lines of his face. "What happened to your mother?"

"She disappeared one day. She'd been teaching Xander and I to play a new song when my father came home unexpectedly and ordered that she follow him from our quarters. I never saw her again." The shadow of a child's agony flitted across his face before the darkness could once again take over.

"And Xander, is he your brother? How is it he's been part of this place for so long?" Maddy tried to distract him, to bring him away from the memory of the loss of his mother.

"No. His father was a member of The Estate. He had attempted to steal from the business, to make himself a rich man. When he was caught, he and his family were dragged in as punishment. Xander watched as his father and baby sister were executed ... as several men raped his mother before she too was executed. Before they died they were told that Xander would be kept and made a member of The Estate. They died knowing their son would be trapped in this place. Even in death, they were not granted rest."

More tears shed by the angel in front of him, Maddy wept for Aaron, his mother, Xander and his family. Aaron tried to wipe them away, but they fell so fast, so furiously he couldn't catch them all. Her face looked so sorrowful, so utterly lost as she absorbed the details of his life, of the place that she'd been dragged to, of the nightmare that he'd lived that had become hers as well.

"You never did answer me that morning in your room," she said through a quiet whisper; the hesitancy in her statement made obvious by the tone of her words.

"Answer what?" Aaron thought back; at first not knowing what she was referring to, but understanding soon seeped into his thoughts. "About why you were taken?"

She nodded, the tears still flowing so freely that he wondered if her sobs were choking back her ability to speak.

A sigh of resignation floated across his lips, his forehead dropping to hers as he closed his eyes. His voice was also a whisper as he confessed to her, to himself, the reason for her captivity. "Yes.

Your music is the reason you are here, the reason you were taken." He paused, not wanting to admit the correlation between her music and her abduction; not wanting to admit the *connection* he felt to her before she'd even known he existed. "My mother, her music was always so ... so sad. I understood the music, I somehow knew that it was her way of lamenting what my father had become, what he was still becoming. He was a different man when she met him and married him; a businessman at that time. His slip into madness was subtle, barely noticeable until it was too late. She hid behind her music much like you do, used it to block out the ugliness of the nightmare that was manifesting itself around her. When I heard yours for the first time, I *connected* to it, I understood it; I understood you." His eyes opened as he looked deep into hers. "I'm sure my father had me followed, probably had his men grab you after seeing that I'd gone backstage to speak to you. You see, he would have known that you meant something to me, that your music meant something to me. He hated the connection between my mother and I when it came to music, he did what he could to destroy it, to make me dark like him. I never intended for this to happen, Madeleine. But you were a bit of light in my life that my father couldn't allow to exist."

Finally, a sharp glimmer of anger filled her eyes, a streak of silver through the blue. "Your father must die, Aaron. No matter what happens from here on out, keep that goal in mind. Know that you will succeed in ridding this world of the corruption of his evil." She grabbed his hand. "Together we will destroy him. If I have to endure

308

decades of pain, of torture, I will. I'll give you the strength you need while you will give me mine."

Nodding, Aaron smiled, amazed yet again at a woman who possessed such a beautiful soul, she could cry for murderers and thieves, but one who could also fight in her own way against the devil himself. "Yes, Madeleine, he will pay for what he's done, and we'll bring that justice to the world ... together."

Chapter Twenty-Six

Four months passed, uneventful for the most part, Aaron and Maddy kept to their routine, he as the executioner and she as his strength. Xander, ever the loyal friend to Aaron, protected her in Aaron's absence, becoming her friend, her confidant in those moments when she grew concerned that the darkness in Aaron was winning, was taking over the man she'd grown to love. Xander swore she had no need to worry, that Aaron had been an assassin since he was young, had bathed in the blood of other men for longer than she could imagine. In that time, he'd not been overtaken by corruption, hadn't become the monster his father had wanted him to be. Each day, each night, that Aaron returned home, Maddy followed him into the shower, helped wash away the blood from his body, brought him back into the light. They'd become dependent on each other, he as her Master and she as his slave, except, in their case, Maddy freely gave to Aaron what the other women in The Estate had not been given the choice to give. Maddy trusted Aaron, enjoyed her submission to him, and knew that he'd always ensure she felt worshipped.

The alliance continued to grow over the passing months, each unit within the network of The Estate aligning themselves with Aaron, vowing to stand behind him when the day came to bring down the monster that his father had become. By the time Winter had loosened its grip on the Earth, they were in a position to strike, to take down an evil so deeply entwined in The Estate, he'd become drunk with his power, had made decisions and acted in ways that'd turned some of his own men against him. He still possessed a large number of men loyal to him, the most despicable of whom were entranced by his insanity, gluttons to the malevolence he spread throughout the network.

"Are you ever going to tell me why you call me Cricket?" Maddy frowned as she sat at the table eating dinner with Xander and Aaron.

Xander sat back, a silly grin across his face. "Nope. I thoroughly enjoy annoying you by not telling you. Why would I willingly give up something that brings me so much joy?" Smiling brightly at the woman who had become like a sister to him, Xander pushed his plate away, patting his stomach to indicate he'd eaten too much.

Aaron laughed, appreciating the back and forth between Maddy and Xander. He could step in, could whisper to her in the dark of night the truth behind Xander's name for her, but he too enjoyed the sullen look she gave whenever Xander refused to give her the reason behind it.

The three enjoyed their time together, laughed and spoke of times past and times to come when they were interrupted by the pounding of someone's fist against the front door. Aaron's entire body tensed, knowing that no man would pound against his door in such a manner, except for one. Allowing Maddy the time to strip off her clothes and take a kneeling position at the foot of his chair to ensure that whoever saw her would believe she was the same slave in Aaron's quarters as she was when present with him in the halls of the mansion, he paused before he walked briskly to the door. Pulling it open, he found Emory and Vincent both standing on the other side. Instantly, his rage bloomed within him, knew that if these two men were at his door, that a nightmare would soon follow.

"Aaron, so good to see you."

The slime of Emory's tone rubbed against Aaron's nerves as his hand moved toward one of the many blades he had hidden about his body. Stopping himself, he stepped back to allow the men entrance.

Cutting to the chase, Emory eyed Aaron when he delivered his message. "The executioner has been ordered to the ballroom within the next ten minutes."

Relief lessening the weight from his shoulders, Aaron remained impassive, absolute in his refusal to allow any emotion to be seen underneath the mask of indifference that he wore. He could handle anything his father ordered him to do, as long as it didn't involve Maddy, there was nothing that could break him down, nothing that could bring him to his knees. "I will be there." Moving to the door, he opened it to allow the men to leave. Walking through the doors, Emory sneered at Aaron, turned before fully leaving the doorway.

"Also, the executioner's slave has been ordered to appear as well." A filthy laugh. "Sorry, I almost forgot to mention that part." They

312

continued their path, disappearing down the hallway as Aaron closed the door.

Xander stood up, immediately moving to Aaron's side. "Why would they request Maddy if you are being called in as the executioner? You don't think ... "

Holding up a hand to stop Xander in his thought, Aaron crossed the room, pulled Maddy up from the floor and into his lap as he sat down in his chair. Burying his head into her hair, he allowed her to soothe him as she brushed her hands through his hair and down the side of his face.

Seeing that the two lovers needed a moment alone, Xander moved toward the corridor. "I'll give you two a moment. When it's time to leave, call for me. Remember, Aaron, we have ten minutes only."

Nodding, Aaron pulled Maddy closer to him, his silence effectively dismissing Xander. Once alone, Maddy leaned up to brush her lips softly across Aaron's, an attempt at comfort that neither of them would truly find. "Could this be it? Will he order you to take my life?" Maddy whispered the words, too frightened by their meaning to give them any strength.

"I don't know." A confession. Aaron could imagine his father ordering the death of his slave, wouldn't be surprised if his boredom had supplied him with the need for such entertainment.

"Remember to be strong, Aaron. If that is what you must do, than I'll never hold you accountable. You are so close, so very near the day when you can finally erase your father's evil from your life and this world. If my death must occur for that to happen, I ask that you allow it. Take your vengeance knowing that I watch as a phantom, my spirit standing beside you always." Placing another kiss on his lips, Maddy shed a single tear as Aaron deepened the kiss, held her to him like they were the same person, as if their entwined bodies could somehow become one.

Having run out of time, Aaron pushed up from his chair, called for Xander and opened the door to exit the apartment when Maddy had taken her place beside his friend. They marched through the corridor, Aaron allowing the infinite black to consume him. No emotion could be present in his mind as he led the woman who was the light within him to the possibility of slaughter. If he was ordered to kill Madeleine, he would; he wouldn't fail her by giving up on the possibility of destroying his father. However, it couldn't be done without the black mask he wore, if he were to feel her death as he was bathed in the warmth of her blood, he would go insane, would die attempting to kill each and every man in that room. They approached the large wooden doors of the ballroom and, as usual, two men were stationed to open them, giving him easy entry into the heart of meeting room for The Estate.

There was an odd hush over the room, the usual chaos not present amongst his father's men. As they entered, Aaron saw makeshift gallows that had been built, six ropes hanging down from a wooden beam that lined the top. Taking his position in the center of the room, he faced his father as Maddy took her position kneeling at his feet. The silence of the room was ominous, Aaron's skin crawling from the odd ambiance of the ballroom.

His father sat in his usual throne, his eyes burning into Aaron's. His voice betraying nothing of his insanity, the refined tone of a businessman, a façade used to mask the demon that resided within him. "I have requested the executioner tonight for a very specific purpose. My men and I have grown bored with the slaves kept on the property, have become sickened by the skin that hangs off their bones, by the way they've loosened from overuse. As such, each slave will be executed tonight, and you will be the blade that ends their life."

"Will my slave be executed as well? She still remains in my service, and I have not had the opportunity to grow tired of her ... she's not been stretched out from overuse as your slaves have." No emotion, not a miniscule sign of the terror swelling in his heart at the thought that Madeleine could be executed along with the other women.

"No," Mr. Carmichael replied, "I assume that you'll eventually kill her yourself, your tastes being as violent as they are. She will not die tonight because I have another need for your slave. Well, because of that and the fact that I'm still allowed to taste her when I see fit." He laughed briefly, before adding, "Having no others at my service, I may have needs one night that only she will be able to fill."

A growl started to erupt from Aaron's chest, but he was able to swallow it back down

315

before it could escape. "Of course, father. What is your purpose for my slave at this time, if not to be executed with the rest."

"I realized that once you are done performing your task, we'll have no slaves left, so who would clean up the mess you leave behind?" Mocking laughter bellowed from his father's chest, his depravity an amusement to him alone.

Relaxing only a small amount, Aaron looked down at Maddy's back as she knelt by his feet. He noticed the way her skin prickled, the slight tremble of her body. She would be made to wipe clean the blood of his kill once again. Looking back up to his father, Aaron said, "Fine, let's get this over with. There's no need to delay my task."

"Ever the professional, Aaron; I'd expect nothing less of my son." Reaching his hand up, he snapped for Emory to bring in the slaves. The door opened and Aaron watched as each woman was led to the gallows. Blindfolds covered their eyes; their hands bound behind their backs. He particularly noticed when Emily was led out because her body bore the marks of several men; teeth marks and lashes littered her flesh, bruises and cuts scored skin that had lost the kiss of the sun while locked up as a slave.

One by one, the women were led up the wooden steps, placed underneath a rope, and each one's arms bound by the rope above their head before they were lifted into the air so that their feet were barely above the floor. When each had been placed and secured in position, Emory and Vincent traveled back across the room to take their places by Aaron's father. Pulling his blade from the sheath secured to his back, Aaron started across the room to deliver a quick end to the women who had outgrown their usefulness.

Climbing up the steps, Aaron moved toward the first slave. His hand moved quickly as he sliced his steel across her throat, waited for her blood to spray out onto his clothing and skin, and then waited for it to pool down below the slave's feet hanging inches above the stage. The executioner wiped his face clean with the sleeve of his shirt, and took a step toward the next slave, but was stopped by the booming voice of his father.

"Halt!" Walking slowly from the stage, Aaron's father traversed the space until he stood next to Maddy. Aaron's shoulders rolled back, his spine becoming a steel rod with his fury. Every muscle in his body tensed up with anticipation of what his father had planned next.

"Now what kind of entertainment is that?" His father reached down and took Maddy's hair into his hands, pulled her up into a position where she could see the carnage of the executioner. "You are too quick to kill, my son. Moving at that pace, all of our preparation for today's events would have been for nothing more than a show that lasted only a few seconds." Looking down at Maddy, he smiled with a lascivious grin. Pulling against her hair with more force, his smile brightened when a cry escaped her lips. "Don't you want to see what the man you call your Master is capable of doing? How very cruel he can be when taking someone's life? You are to watch him, whore. Do not look away because if I see you so

317

much as blink while he executes the slaves, I'll request that you be strung up when he's finished."

Maddy looked into the steel grey eyes of the man she detested most in this world. Her heart was already breaking for the women whose lives were being ended for entertainment, who'd been enslaved the same she had. If not for the knowledge that the man holding her head would soon die, she would have fought against him, welcoming the death sentence he threatened. Turning her eyes to the stage, she locked them with Aaron's, providing him strength with nothing more than her presence.

"I want them disemboweled, Aaron." His father released Maddy's hair to turn in the direction of the gallows while giving his instructions. "Let their entrails fall to your feet while the light dies in their eyes."

Maddy shuddered, trying hard not to imagine the agony that would accompany such a death. That she was made to watch as Aaron was delivered into the darkness, forced into an act so cruel, that no man could be expected to come back from it — this was the final insult to the injuries inflicted upon her. She would watch, however, and remain steadfast in her role as Aaron's slave.

Aaron turned his back to her and moved along to the next woman strung up on the gallows. She could only see that his arm moved, but the woman whom he slaughtered screamed out in terror and suffering. Maddy could only watch as the blood red organs from the woman's body splashed across Aaron's feet. Maddy had to hold back her

318

tears as she was forced to watch Aaron move from one slave to the next. In his position as The Estate's executioner, Aaron was required to commit these vile, horrible acts. She knew the darkness surrounded him — penetrated him — and pulled at his soul while he carried out his father's orders. Maddy wondered if Aaron enjoyed these kills now like he had before she'd been abducted. She knew what he was, she knew the things he'd done — the things he continued to do — and she knew that those acts would one day destroy even the small spark of hope she'd seen come alive inside him during the time they'd spent together.

As Aaron moved from one woman to the next, he leaned into them pretending that a closer angle was necessary in order for him to carry out their execution; in reality, he was whispering an apology to them as they died. The stage was slick with their blood, their entrails kicked about as he moved across the wooden floor. Finally reaching Emily, he pulled the mask from her face before reaching up to turn her head so that she could see what had become of the other women. Her eyes widened with fear and her mouth suddenly sprang open as she vomited on his shoes. Aaron smiled, leaned into her as he did the others, but this time, it was not an apology that he gave.

"How does it feel to be a whore, Emily? I do hope you discovered that answer and I hope you enjoyed it." His knife pierced her abdomen just below her ribs, he pulled down slowly, tearing at her flesh with the blade; he did not grant her the swiftness he'd given the other women. Once her

319

belly was open, he pulled the organs loose, wiggling them free from the abdominal cavity in her body until they splashed down at his feet. He kept his eyes trained on hers as she screamed, locking his gaze with her eyes so he could watch the life leave her body.

Once the task had been completed, he turned to the audience. His shirt, once white, was now stained crimson from the blood of the slaves; his boots covered completely by bits of the organs he'd removed from their bodies. When his eyes found Madeleine, he saw the horror written across her features at having bore witness to how truly dark he could be. Had that been his father's plan? Had this entire show been a ruse to make Madeleine fear him by showing her what he really was inside?

"Very good, Aaron. I'm pleased to see that you haven't become so accustomed to death that you lack style in your method." Settling himself back into his throne his father motioned for Aaron to return to his position in the center of the room. His steps across the room left dark crimson puddles, a trail of carnage from the stage to his place next to Maddy. She'd remained in the position his father had placed her, her eyes glued on the scene of the empty shells that had been made of the slaves hanging from the gallows. She appeared frozen in her horror, a place where the waking nightmare had taken her ability to move, to scream ... to escape.

"Face to the floor, slave." Aaron's voice was terse as he ordered her to look away. Allowing the audience to believe that he cared nothing for the woman at his feet, he immediately granted Madeleine the ability to look down, to huddle over herself, to come to terms with the bloodbath she'd just witnessed. Returning his eyes to his father, he waited for the next command.

His father's eyes were glued to Aaron's as he spoke. "Xander, take Madeleine to the gallows please. She is to remove the entrails and place them aside to be fed to the dogs. Once that is done, I want the blood wiped clean from this room."

Xander picked Maddy up, provided her with as much balance as he could while he led her to the gallows. Aaron didn't allow his eyes to follow their path, instead he kept his gaze glued to the epitome of evil that sat in its throne.

When Xander and Maddy had gotten close enough to the gallows that she could see the remains of the women strewn about the floor up close, she got sick. Her body violently expelled the dinner she'd eaten earlier that night, the audible heaves of her contorting body filled the quiet room.

With a disgusted and bored tone, Aaron's father ordered, "And make sure all that *vomit* is cleaned up as well. If she gets sick again, I will order her execution so that I do not have to hear it."

Aaron waited for Maddy and Xander to reach the gallows before speaking again. "Is that all you require from the executioner?"

His father didn't answer immediately, his

eyes staring at Madeleine as she cleaned up the stage. As he took in the sight of Aaron's slave, something within his eyes shifted before a smile creased his face. Turning back to Aaron, the smile was lost as he responded, "No ... actually, I have a job you must do tonight as well. Emory will supply you with the information regarding your target and his location this evening when it is time for you to go."

A warning rolled along Aaron's spine as he nodded his assent, but he brushed it off as he turned to walk to the gallows. Taking a place by Xander's side, he looked on as Maddy struggled to clean up what was left of the women. Her body retched with the vomit she couldn't spill. Diligently she moved from one to the next, wiping up the blood and picking up the organs until at last the stage was clean. After finishing the floors of the ballroom they were excused to leave so that they could return to Aaron's quarters.

As soon as they were inside the apartment, Aaron picked up Maddy and ran to the bathroom carrying her in his arms. Placing her in the tub, he pulled the nozzle out from the setting and washed the blood that covered her body. Violently, her body continued to retch as he cleaned her. Once the crimson stain had been erased from her skin, he filled up the tub with warm water, hoping the heat would help soothe Maddy's tired and weak body. Pulling his own clothes from his body, he washed the stains off himself in the other shower before returning to pull her from the tub.

Walking into his room, he laid Maddy down on the mattress of his bed, before climbing in

322

beside her and pulling her tight against his chest. They lay in reticence for over an hour, the shock of what they'd just seen and done had frightened them enough that their words had been silenced. Every so often, Maddy would be reduced to tears, the violent sobs took control of her body. The cries that escaped her throat worked like a knife that twisted itself into the heart of the man that held her.

When she'd quieted, finally succumbed to the exhaustion left behind by witnessing such horror, Aaron finally spoke. "I will kill him, Madeleine, I swear to you, he will die."

Maddy didn't respond except to close her eyes and lose herself to sleep wrapped in the arms of a man who could commit the atrocious acts of an executioner.

~ ~ ~

A faint knock on the door woke Aaron. Opening his eyes, he watched as Xander entered the room, a piece of paper held in his hand. "Emory dropped off the information for your job this evening. It's about an hour away from here. I'll stay with Madeleine while your gone."

Begrudgingly, Aaron removed his arms from around Maddy, slowly crept off the bed and covered her with a blanket once he was standing. Once Xander left the room, Aaron moved into the closet to quickly dress in black pants, a black shirt, and his black leather coat. Arming himself, he continued to look over to Maddy as she slept on

323

the bed. Like an angel at rest, her dove white skin shimmered in the low light of the room. Her features were not quite at ease, but not locked into the look of horror she'd had since the ballroom. Aaron approached the side of the bed, leaned down to place a kiss on her cheek, before turning to exit the room.

Finding Xander in the living room, Aaron barked out his order. "While I am gone, I want you to contact the leader of each group in the alliance. The time to strike is now. My father has gone too far. The only hand he has left in this game is to take Maddy from me and I'll die before I allow that to happen. I want him dead tonight, Xander."

"I'll start making the calls," Xander replied.

Reaching for the door, Aaron turned back to his guard. "If anything happens, you are to contact me immediately." With that Aaron swept out into the halls of the corridor on his way to take another human life.

After Aaron had left, Xander spent more than an hour coordinating the strike, each unit given a time and place to meet. Xander paced the living room floor waiting for Aaron's return, his nerves on fire from the anticipation of the evening's battle. When he heard boots outside the door he moved to open it expecting that Aaron would be on the other side. Once he had moved aside the large door, however, his eyes locked with those of Joseph Carmichael.

Mr. Carmichael didn't bother with a greeting as he stepped into the apartment, followed

324

closely by Emory and Vincent. He rotated slowly as he looked over the room, his eyes pausing every so often on a statue or other similar decoration. When he'd finally turned back to Xander, a grin stretched over his face. "Where's the slave?"

Instantly tensing, Xander stood motionless as he tried to think of anyway he could refuse to answer. Finding none, he responded, "She's sleeps."

"Well, then, wake her and bring her to me. I have use for her tonight." Mr. Carmichael's words were slightly slurred, but still dripped with the malicious intent toward Maddy.

Xander paused. Wanting nothing more than to kill all three men where they stood, he realized his efforts would be wasted, he be killed before he could take them all. Recognizing that Aaron was the only man who could save her, Xander begrudgingly walked to the corridor, but stopped suddenly when Mr. Carmichael said, "Better yet, Emory and Vincent, why don't you two escort him? I don't have time for dillydallying tonight. I want my needs met sooner rather than later."

Except for the sound of their steps, the corridor was quiet. Reaching Aaron's bedroom, Xander let out a deep sigh and pushed the door open. Emory and Vincent came from behind him to wrench Maddy from her sleep. Xander stepped aside as they passed back out into the corridor, Maddy's feet dragging behind her as she awoke and discovered that she was being removed from Aaron's quarters. Mr. Carmichael and his guards left without another word and as soon as the doors closed, Xander was on the phone letting

Aaron know that Maddy had been taken.

"Aaron .... your father ... he just took Maddy." Xander's voice shook with the rage that was teeming inside him.

Almost wrecking his car when he heard Xander's words, Aaron's foot slammed into the gas pedal. His mind went blank with rage as he drove — except for one solitary thought: tonight, his father would die.

Chapter Twenty-Seven

Madeleine regained full consciousness as she was being dragged down the halls toward the ballroom. The grips of the men who held her were so firm, she knew bruises would form easily beneath her pale skin. Joseph Carmichael walked quickly in front of them, ordered the doors to the ballroom be opened, but traveled through the large room to another set of doors on the other side. As she was dragged through the second set of doors, Maddy's eyes took in her surroundings. She'd never been on this side of the house, had never seen the different corridors that led to the rooms where those loyal to Joseph stayed. The walls of the corridors were the same burgundy red as on the other side, but chains were attached at evenly spaced intervals. The walls beneath those chains were stained a darker red, almost black; handprints smeared along the paint, footprints smeared along the floors. Ominous and terrifying, it was apparent that an untold number of evil and bloody things had occurred in these halls.

Realization dawned on Maddy that she was being led to her rape and probable death. Aaron's father had played his last hand, choosing to take the slave, not caring that Aaron would cast her aside as a result. There was no longer the need to maintain the façade she'd kept over the last few months, and she allowed herself to shed the tears that swelled in her eyes. Weakly she pulled against the men that held her, but she was too small to fight physically. The skin on her toes burned from

327

being dragged against the stone floor, her stomach still had spasms from being sick earlier that day. When they reached a room at the end of the hall, Mr. Carmichael produced a key from his pocket, quickly unlocking and opening the door so that Emory and Vincent could drag her into the room. The loud click of the lock sliding into place made her jump, made her realize that her fate had been sealed.

Mr. Carmichael's space was even larger and, at one time in the past, would have been more luxurious than Aaron's. Littered among the books, fine statues, and other decorations that spoke of classical times and educated taste, however, his quarters housed tools used for torture, glasses still half full of liquor, and drug paraphernalia on every counter and table. Her eyes widening, Maddy glimpsed the lifestyle that led a powerful man into fits of insanity. His home displayed his fall into the abyss of the depraved. Blood pooled in different areas of the room, in others it was dry and like dust; it looked like the place hadn't been cleaned in days or weeks. The three men who'd taken her didn't seem to mind the filthy conditions of the home, they didn't seem to notice that their environment had taken on the appearance of Hell itself. Almost every sin possible for a man to commit, every temptation that can lead a man to evil, was given its own space.

Terror flooded her system as she was dragged through a set of doors and down a long corridor that led to the back bedrooms. Glancing in each room as they passed, Maddy's heartbeat sped up faster and faster, her breathing became more erratic when she saw the bodies — rotting and long dead — laid out across beds, on floors, and even chained to walls. Blood lay in dried pools, the putrid smell of decaying flesh assaulting her nose, causing bile to rise into her throat, the cramping in her stomach become unbearable as she attempted to hold back her need to retch. Even more horrifying was the way these men didn't seem to notice the squalor and repugnance of the apartment: they walked passed the rooms without even a glance toward the outward manifestation of a man gone mad.

The door creaked loudly as they entered the room at the end of the long hall; a room illuminated by dozens of blood red candles set in sconces on the walls. Every wall bore shackled chains. Crimson-stained whips and canes, ropes, and phallic-shaped objects littered the tables and floors. Mixed among them needles and mirrors, pills and white powders that reflected the scant traces of light in the room.

The large bed in the center of the room was raised up on a platform so high, steps were required to climb in. The posts at the four corners of the bed bore the scars of fingernails scratched down their lengths, ligature marks across their breadth; ugly white scars of exposed wood, evidence of the agony women had been put through at the hands of the man who now intended to take her. Chips of a pink fingernail polish were buried within those scars, the same color as the toes of a woman she'd seen in the ballroom many months before.

Climbing the steps of the platform, Mr.

329

Carmichael sat on the edge of the mattress near a small round side table that held a large pile of white powder and the paraphernalia to match. Emory and Vincent dragged Madeleine up the stairs, their fingers digging into her skin and the muscle underneath from the strength of their grip. Pain shot through the fine bones of her feet as they hit against the sharp edges of the stairs. Reaching the top, she was thrown down on the mattress, Emory and Vincent took seated positions on either side of her. Their rough hands taking liberties with her body, vice grips on her breasts, fingers invading the flesh between her thighs, barely, but not fully forcing themselves inside. Vincent, becoming too caught up in his excitement, leaned down to bite the tip of her breast. Maddy cried out in pain, drawing the attention of the man for whom she was being restrained.

Mr. Carmichael's hand reached out suddenly, the back of his hand slapped against Vincent's face, knocking his guard back on the bed. "Not yet, Vincent! You and Emory will have your turns when I've had my fill of the bitch; and it is my preference to fuck her WITHOUT your spittle across her body!" Turning his attention back to the objects littering the side table, Mr. Carmichael measured out some of the powder, scooping it into a spoon, the bottom of which he held over the flame of a candle to heat.

Even though they'd been warned, the temptation of Maddy's body was too much for the two men holding her down. Emory licked his lips as his eyes traveled the length of her body, his hand reaching down to fondle her between her thighs,

330

his fingers pushing even deeper into her and she saw him visibly harden underneath his pants. Each man grabbed one of her legs, spreading them apart so that they could gain access to her more easily.

"I cannot wait until I get you back to my playroom, whore. My dick has never been so hard as it is at this moment." Vincent's finger breached the opening of her ass, the lack of lubrication causing the skin to burn from the intrusion. "Oh, I think I'll be taking you there, it is so fucking tight."

Pulling the liquefied powder into a syringe, Mr. Carmichael stood up. Speaking through laughter, he said, "It won't be when I'm done with it, I plan on ripping this bitch apart. Such a sweet piece of ass, it'll be like Heaven itself in comparison to the whores I've used up over the years." He placed the syringe aside, stood up with the spoon in his hand; the spoon's bowl was still red from the heat. He stood in front of her as she was held to the bed, her legs pulled apart so that she was completely bared to him, not a single bit of her wasn't exposed. His eyes roamed over her skin, his gaze fixated on the flesh at the apex of her thighs. "Oh yes, I'm going to thoroughly enjoy this."

He leaned down over her, supporting himself on one arm, while the one that held the spoon remained behind his back. Pressing his mouth to her ear, he whispered, "I want to hear you scream for me." With his last word, he pressed the back of the spoon into her inner thigh. Maddy released a bloodcurdling scream, she could smell her flesh as it burned underneath the spoon, her legs shook violently from the agony tearing across her skin, through her nerves, sinking itself deeply within her bones. Mr. Carmichael hissed while standing up; his eyes closed as if listening to the sound of something so sweet it placed him in a state of ecstasy. His eyes opened once she stopped screaming from the pain, the unforgiving steel-colored eyes filled with malice as he looked down into her eyes. "Like music to my ears," he scoffed. Another chuckle as he moved back to the table to put down the cooled spoon, before retaking his position in front of her.

His hands moved to his crotch and he squeezed himself. Looking over her body, he shook his head, "Tsk, tsk. It appears my son didn't know how to properly use a whore. There isn't a single mark on your body. He is such a failure — such a disappointment — preferring to indulge in his desire to kill rather than the splendor of a whore splayed out before him."

Leaning down, he took her breast into his mouth, swirled his tongue over the tip, and sunk his teeth into the tender skin surrounding it. Maddy's throat felt torn from the volume of her scream, tears saturating her skin as they ran in rivulets down her face. Mr. Carmichael sucked on her breast, drawing blood from where he'd broken the skin. A loud popping sound resonated when he let go and stood back up. "So fucking sweet."

His hand reached down as he forced his fingers over her clit and within the crease of her soft skin folds. Pushing his fingers inside her, he pulled them apart, spinning them along the muscles of her opening. "Remember when I did this to you in the ballroom? I've wanted to fuck you ever since I had the pleasure of tasting you that day. You should have never been given to Aaron. When I'm done with you, I'll abduct another woman and be sure not to make the same mistake." Bringing his fingers to his mouth, he licked her off each one, slowly and suggestively as a chuckle rumbled from his chest.

~ ~ ~

Arriving at the compound twenty minutes later, Aaron immediately went to his quarters, Xander following closely behind as Aaron entered and moved down the corridor to his room. Grabbing and arming himself with as many knives and guns that he could carry, Aaron barked out orders as Xander stood diligently nearby.

After retrieving a pair of longer knives from the closet that could be used as short swords in a fight, Aaron emerged and asked, "Are the men on their way?"

Xander nodded indicating that they were. "They will be here within the hour. Once they have formed their group we can move to strike."

"I will not wait for them, Xander. I'm going after Madeleine now! She may not have an hour. If that bastard kills her, I swear to you, neither he nor I will remain alive for much longer." Rage burned behind the green of Aaron's eyes, fury so intense his muscles shook with the force of it rushing through his veins. The darkness that Maddy had tempered over the last few months returned with such a fantastic vengeance that Aaron felt like, if he did die, he'd detonate and take hundreds of men with him.

"Then I'm going with you. I've told you before: 'If you die, I die.' And I'm not letting you go against a hundred men on your own." Xander's tone was firm, the sound of a man who would not be swayed to change his decision.

Green met blue as the two men stared at each other; both knowing it was futile to argue against one another. Aaron turned and grabbed another long blade for Xander to use. Tossing it to his friend, he said, "Then let's be quiet as we go in. If we can keep the element of surprise, we might stand a chance. Use your gun only when it's absolutely necessary."

Once they'd entered the halls, the only sound between them was the pounding of their boots against the stone floor; the rhythmic beats sounded strong and assured as the men moved toward the wing of the house that was occupied by Mr. Carmichael's men. Approaching the doors to the ballroom, the two guards who usually would pull them open so that Aaron and Xander could pass now blocked the doors instead. Aaron went against the man on the right while Xander swung out toward the man on the left. Their blades quickly decapitating the guards, Aaron watched as their heads fell from their bodies and rolled along the ground. Grabbing the handles to the door, Aaron pulled it open. He was not surprised to find twenty men waiting on the other side. Just as their boots moved into the ballroom, the sound of twenty guns being cocked reverberated throughout the large space.

Aaron looked to Xander then back at the men in front of him. "I guess we won't be remaining quiet for much longer." Both men ducked to the sides, seeking shelter behind furniture as twenty guns were fired in their direction. Aaron and Xander both pulled their guns in return, more capable of finding their targets among the chaos than the ones they were fighting. One by one, they took down the men, but were met with a wave of reinforcements that came pouring through the doors on the other side of the ballroom. Between the two of them, they'd killed more than forty men. Running out of ammunition, Aaron took advantage of the chaos in the room and ran into the crowd slicing away at arms, legs, and heads as he passed through. Blood ran like rivers through the ballroom. The fetid stench of expelled excrement, which spilled from the bowels of the dying men, became a suffocating stink that permeated Aaron's skin as he continued to fight.

Xander stood guard by the doors, firing at any man who approached Aaron's back. At least fifty men had been killed before another wave of men came running through those doors. Aaron looked up from the carnage littered across the floor of the ballroom and he feared he'd be overtaken. Using the bodies of the dead to shield himself from the spray of bullets, he continued hacking into each man that he approached. Some died immediately upon contact with his sword, others lay in pools of the own blood, the sounds of their death rattles mixed with the shouting throughout the room.

Another wave of men arrived, but this time,

it was the alliance members flooding through the doors where Aaron and Xander had entered. More guns were fired, more bullets flew through the air as Aaron moved quickly, executing each man who dared cross his path. His body was covered in the crimson shade of death, trails of sweat running through it, turning the red into a muddled perversion of pink. His shoulders burned as he swung the long knives in front him, his teeth gritted as he tore into the flesh of bodies that stood before him. He was a monster in that moment, the darkness finally being allowed to take over so that he could reach his target. No emotion in him for the souls being delivered to the gates of Hell, no concern for his own life except that he be given the opportunity to kill the man who'd played him his entire life.

With the help of the alliance members, Aaron was able to reach the doors of his father's wing of the building. Waiting for Xander to reach him, he held the handles, but pushed forward into the tight corridors that made it more difficult to fight. The men he encountered screamed out when they were met with his blade. Some were not sure they wanted to approach, but knew they would face death eventually if it was found that they acted as cowards.

Powering forward, Aaron had to spit the blood from his mouth as it seeped in from the crimson streams running down his face. With Xander by his side, they slaughtered every living thing that crossed their path. If those men were still breathing by the time Aaron and Xander passed by, the men of the alliance that were

336

bringing up the rear would certainly strike them down. The screams were deafening as they charged through the halls, their vision obscured by the gunfire smoke. Like a runaway train, there was nothing that could stop them in their search for Madeleine, and Aaron knew *exactly* the room where she'd been taken.

One single objective, one thought in his mind; he would find Madeleine, and he would kill any man who got between them.

Chapter Twenty-Eight

After taunting Maddy with the truth of her helplessness, Mr. Carmichael crossed back to the table and picked up the syringe. Holding it up so that he could see its contents by the illumination of candlelight, he flicked it a few times. Testing the syringe with his fingers and finding it cool to the touch, he picked up a rubber strap and wrapped it tightly around his arm. "I can't wait to have you, slave, but first, let me get myself to a place that will make the sex so much better for me. There's nothing like the feel of a whore's nails across your back under the influence of such a wonderful drug." He tapped his vein before inserting the needle and shooting the drug into his bloodstream. Pulling the tourniquet from his arm, his head fell back and his body visibly trembled from the rush of the substance through his body. A heavy sigh left his mouth, his tongue flicking out to lick along his bottom lip.

While Mr. Carmichael was busy adjusting to the drug in his system, Emory and Vincent took the opportunity to continue molesting Maddy's body, leaving bruises and scratches all over her skin as they manhandled her. Maddy bit her tongue, trying not to cry out and feed the sexual frenzy of the two men.

Mr. Carmichael, finally coming back from the initial rush of the drug, moved back between her legs, let her watch as he slowly undid his belt, pulled the button loose from his pants, and slid his

338

zipper down. "It's time, my dear, for you to learn what it means to be a whore." Reaching his hand into his pants he appeared to be fondling himself while his expression grew into one of frustration. Although terrified, her body shaking violently as she awaited her fate, confusion bloomed in Maddy's thoughts ... he was not pulling himself out of his pants.

A sound like that of firecrackers could faintly be heard from the direction of the corridors to the apartment. Mr. Carmichael's head turned suddenly as Vincent and Emory immediately released their grips from her legs and sat up straight to listen intently to the noise. Emory spoke first. "It sounds like gunfire."

A wicked grin lazily spread itself over Mr. Carmichael's face; his eyes were glazed over from the drug, yet still alight with understanding; his shoulders shook from his low, malevolent laugh. "It appears Aaron has returned home." His words were slurred, the effects of the drug snaking its way through his system.

Maddy's heart blossomed with hope, but was overshadowed with dread. While anxious for Aaron to reach her, she still feared for his safety, feared that he'd not waited for assistance, feared that his darkness propelled him into battle against an army that he couldn't hope to win on his own.

Sounding distant and wishful, Mr. Carmichael, commented, "What I wouldn't give to see the carnage that the executioner must be creating outside my door." Turning his attention back to Emory and Vincent, he added, "It's a shame

339

he'll never make it, go finish him off and make it quick. I'm sure there is going to be a large amount of bodies to burn if he's made it through the ballroom, let's not give him time to add to the pile."

The two guards obediently rose from the bed, but looked back at Madeleine not sure if she would attempt to run now that she'd been released. Mr. Carmichael's expression became annoyed with their hesitation. "Don't worry about her boys, I'm perfectly capable of handling a woman, especially one her size." The two guards left the room, leaving Madeleine alone with a man who was anxious to perform unspeakably atrocious acts against her, to use her and toss her aside like she held no value to the world whatsoever.

~　~　~

When Aaron and Xander finally cut through the majority of his father's men, the door to which Aaron was charging came into view. It opened as they approached. Two men, Emory and Vincent, stepped through; savage smiles smeared across their faces as they lifted their guns and opened fire.

Pain erupted on Aaron's arm — the feeling of flesh splitting — from a hot lead bullet. Ducking down a hallway on their right, Aaron and Xander got out of the path of the bullets from Emory and Vincent's guns, allowed the men of the alliance who still had ammunition to charge ahead. They watched as men fell into piles at the juncture to the hall, not able to match the marksmanship of his father's top guards. Waiting out the two guards,

340

they listened as bullets flew past, the high-pitched whistle as the air itself was torn open by the lead. His back against the wall, Aaron got Jason's attention as his men charged through the corridor, he waved his hand to ask that Jason and his men fall back. The alliance started to back up, still having to fire their guns to keep up with the weapons used by Emory and Vincent; weapons which had undoubtedly been altered to hold as many rounds as possible.

When Jason's men had retreated as far back as they could, Aaron glanced around the corner, noting that Emory and Vincent's attention was diverted by the few men who still fired every so often from around the wall of an adjacent hallway. Grabbing a small blade that was strapped to his ankle, Aaron aimed his weapon, throwing it expertly toward Vincent's face, the blade embedding into his left eye. Vincent howled from the pain of the injury, went down to his knees, and eventually lost consciousness from the blood loss and probable injury to his brain. An expression of confusion mixed with contempt shadowed Emory's face as he looked around for Aaron. No one else could have been more accurate with a blade and there was no doubt Emory knew Aaron's hand was behind that throw. Slowly, he stepped forward, his boots kicking against the dead that lay in his path.

"Aaron? I know you have to be around here somewhere; only the *executioner* could've pulled off a throw like that. Why don't you come out and fight like a man rather than hide like a scared woman?"

341

The hall became so quiet during the standoff between the two men, a high-pitched scream could be heard emanating from Mr. Carmichael's room. Rage, a red film over his mind, covered the darkness already consuming Aaron when he recognized that cry as Maddy's.

A sickening chuckle sounded before Emory said, "You hear that, Aaron? Your father ruts himself on top of your whore as we speak. By the sounds of those cries, I do believe she likes it." The sneer to his lip curled even more as he attempted to goad Aaron into walking in plain sight. "I'll have to hurry this up so that I can get back and have my own fun before he fucks her to death."

Aaron remained with his back against the wall, shoulder to shoulder with Xander. Just barely, Aaron could see Jason barricaded behind the wall of another hallway. When Jason looked his way, he used his hands to silently indicate where Jason should fire his weapon. As soon as the shot was fired, Emory focused his attention toward the distant hallway, giving Aaron a chance to come around the corner without being noticed. Creeping forward, he kept his long blade at his side, which allowed Xander to create another distraction that kept Emory occupied. Just as Emory looked down, the scar running along his face throbbed red with anger, Aaron swung out with his blade while still crouched, striking Emory across the knees.

Blood poured out of the guard's legs as he fell hard to the ground. Ever the warrior, he bit back the pain and lifted his weapon to fire, but Aaron was faster. Pushing himself up into a standing position, Aaron drove the blade downwards, forcing it through the top of Emory's skull. Burying the steel deep into Emory's brain, Aaron had to twist the hilt to get his blade back; he pulled upwards with such force that it dropped Emory to the floor once it broke free.

Aaron's chest heaved out in front of him from the physical exertion he'd just been through, but there was no time to catch his breath, not when his father still had Maddy. Spinning on his heel, he moved toward the door. Xander came up beside him just as he broke the handle off the locked door and opened it to go find his slave.

~ ~ ~

Mr. Carmichael appeared sinister in the dancing candlelight's shadows — sinister and cruel. His refined looks suddenly became those of a demon. His cheekbones ran like sharp blades across his cheek, the cut of his nose and lips made even more pronounced by the faint illumination. Maddy's vision began to tunnel from the rush of adrenaline and fear rushing through her battered body. She had to fight not to faint, not to pass out and leave herself completely at the mercy of a sadistic hedonist.

Expecting Mr. Carmichael to immediately attack, Maddy watched as he seemed to sway on his feet, his body slowly moving back and forth before he shook his head. His eyes appeared confused, hazing over as his breaths became more erratic, his lips parting to take in more air. Slowly closing her legs, Maddy crept back on the mattress, her eyes glued to the man standing in front of her.

343

When it appeared that he'd finally shaken himself from his haze, his eyes narrowed as he noticed she'd moved from her wide-open position on the bed.

"And just where the fuck do you think you're going?"

Lunging toward her, he caught her ankles in his hands and pulled her down while spreading her legs out towards his sides. She screamed and she wouldn't stop screaming as she desperately gripped and scratched at the blankets and sheets, but she didn't have the strength to keep from being pulled into the position that he wanted. Wrestling her back into a position where she was bared to him, he again reached into his pants, this time allowing the crisp material to fall to his ankles, his boxers still covering his hand and his cock. Eyes narrowing, he appeared frustrated again as he worked himself beneath the material. The slight sway returned to his body, his eyes hazing over as he grew even more impatient.

"Fuck this." Pulling his hands free, he leaned over on the bed. The sudden movement must have caused his blood to surge from his veins because Maddy watched as his eyes slowly rolled back in his head, his eyelids fluttered open and closed and his full weight fell still over her body. Pushing at his heavy weight, Maddy struggled for a few seconds to roll him off of her and onto the floor. Her heart pounding against the walls of her chest, she crept off the bed, not sure what she should do. Checking his pulse, she found that he was still alive. Considering her options, she feared that if she ran — if Aaron had been defeated — she'd be dragged

344

right back into this room so that Joseph could finish what he started. There was no other choice but the one so obviously laid out before her. She had to kill him.

Looking around the room, Maddy spotted a heavy bronze rod lying on a distant table. Hurriedly, she retrieved it, swinging up with both arms, she brought the weight of it down onto his head. Blood broke free of the skin; flesh broke free of the skull, but she wasn't strong enough to cause much damage to his skull. The bone was too thick for Maddy to pierce or shatter. As she threw the weapon aside in search for another, light from a candle flickered along her wrist, catching her attention. Her eyes widened when she realized the cello string, the makeshift bracelet that she'd refused to allow Aaron to remove, was still on her wrist. Quickly she unwound the string, feeding it below Mr. Carmichael's neck before pulling the end up from the other side. Lodging her knee into his back for leverage, she pulled at the ends of the string in an attempt to choke him, but even with the extra leverage she couldn't get enough weight into the pull to have much affect. Growing frustrated, Maddy reached over to retrieve the rod she'd cast aside and tied the ends of the string on either side of the rod. Turning the rod in circles, Maddy watched as the string wound itself around into a single spiral line that appeared to slowly travel toward the back of his neck. When the weaving wire reached his skin, she continued to turn the rod, round and round, until finally she could see it cutting into his skin. Finally, she could hear his choked struggle for air, his body convulsed with violent spasms from the loss of oxygen. Just as

345

his hands flinched and moved toward his throat, his body gave out. Maddy continued to hold the rod and her knee in place, refusing to allow the tension to dissipate in case he was still alive. She didn't know how long it took for a person to die, she just held on wanting to ensure that his type of filth was erased from the Earth and quickly sent to the pits of Hell.

As she held the tension, as her arms started to quiver from the exertion of holding the rod tight against his neck, she heard a loud bang against the doors in the front portion of the apartment. Recognizing the sound of wood splintering, and finally the sound of the door's weight being thrown against the wall, she knew someone was coming for her. Perspiration broke out all over her skin, but she held tight to that rod — her knuckles turned white from her adrenaline-fueled grip — and continued to drill her knee into his back. She refused to look toward the door as the sound of boots approached her, she was too afraid to look up and see that Aaron had been defeated, that the other men had come in to take her captive once again.

The boots stopped suddenly when they reached the doorway, an audible gasp from the mouths of the men that stood witnessing Maddy as she held tightly to the weapon she'd fashioned from a bronze rod and the string of her instrument.

"Maddy ... " Fear and shock were inlaid in the tone of a voice that Maddy would recognize for the rest of her life.

346

Dropping the weapon, she turned, instantly pushed up to her feet, and ran into the arms of Aaron. He held her for a few moments, his chest heaving against her cheek. She didn't care that he was covered in blood, didn't care that she could feel the heat of anger and rage still rolling off his body. She buried herself within those arms, delighted in the sound of his heart as it raced in his chest.

His voice awash with concern, Aaron asked, "Are you okay?"

Maddy nodded 'yes' into his chest as she pulled him closer to her body. "I am now. I think I killed him. I think that vile bastard is finally dead."

Xander squeezed around Aaron and Maddy as they embraced in the doorway and immediately moved over to inspect the body of Aaron's father. Unwrapping the string from his neck, Xander felt for a pulse. Finding none, he rolled the body over to discover that his eyes had bugged out from his desperate struggle to breathe. Whistling low, he shook his head in amazement. "My, my, Cricket, whatever have you done?"

Aaron opened his eyes and peered over Maddy's head while still keeping her cradled to his body. He caught his breath before it gasped at the sight of his father: eyes wide and dull from death, mouth agape in search of air. Xander picked up the weapon, a smile appearing across his face as he pulled the string from the rod, held it up so Aaron could see it. "Remind me not to piss off your mouse, Aaron."

347

His eyes widening, Aaron pulled away from Maddy and grabbed her arm to inspect her wrist. "Was that ... ?"

Nodding, Maddy looked over her shoulder at Xander as he held the string up. She shrugged her shoulder, looked back over toward the man she loved. "Not only did you give me freedom with that string, you gave me a weapon to use against him, Aaron, you gave me justice."

Looking down at his gentle musician turned assassin, Aaron picked up her small body, winced from the pain from where the bullet had torn his skin, but still cradled her against his chest when he turned to leave his father's apartment. As they spun around, Maddy caught a brief glimpse of Xander kicking the body on the floor before laughing and following along behind them.

As they traveled through the corridors leading back out to the ballroom, Maddy closed her eyes to avoid seeing the carnage that littered their path. She knew there had been a bloodbath, knew that Aaron had killed countless men as he battled through the halls to get to her, but she didn't want to see the evidence of his brutality, the victims of his darkness cut into pieces along the floor. Reaching the ballroom, Xander stepped around them, opening the door so that Aaron would not have to put Maddy down.

When the doors opened, and Aaron walked through into the expanse of the large room, the deafening boom of cheers rolled throughout the room. Maddy's head shot up to see several groups of men — some injured, others covered in the

348

blood of their victims — with their arms raised in the air, their war cry now a shout of victory for their new leader.

One man stepped forward from the crowd, his hair was pale white and his eyes an eerie silver. Reaching out, he shook hands with Xander, his other hand coming up to clap Xander's shoulder. "Is it done? Has the old man finally met his maker? Please tell me the last thing he felt was Aaron's blade as it pierced his rotten heart."

Xander shook his head and pulled his hand free to motion his thumb toward Maddy and Aaron. "Sorry, Jason, but Aaron never had the chance. His slave took care of it before we could even get in the room."

A hush fell over the celebrants like a wave, each man turning to look at the small woman cradled in Aaron's arms. Aaron stepped forward, took a position in the center of the room, before speaking out to the crowd.

"Joseph Carmichael is dead, the leadership of The Estate is now in my hands. Tomorrow we will meet to discuss changes that will need to be made to the network, but tonight, I want you men to rest and to celebrate while I take my slave back for my own bit of merriment. Know this: The corruption has been extinguished, a new leader is among you."

With their fists pumping in the air, the men cheered for Aaron as he moved toward the exit. Nothing could be heard except his name being chanted even as they walked down the halls toward his quarters. Maddy reached up, wrapped her arms around Aaron's neck as she whispered in his ear, "Together, Aaron. We defeated him together. We are free and tomorrow we will finally wake from our nightmare and we can open our eyes to a new day."

Epilogue

"May I speak, Master?"

"Yes."

Pulling her legs apart, spreading herself open before a man so lethal, she should be terrified of him rather than turned on. Maddy smiled seductively at Aaron as he crawled his way up the bed. Her skin blushed from the intensity of his stare as he took in her body, the growl that emanated from his chest as she opened herself before him.

"Have I been a good enough girl to deserve your kiss?" Her voice cooed as she teased him, enticed him into doing things to her body that left her drunk on the waves of ecstasy only he could create within her. She couldn't help but smile as she watched the side of his mouth quirk up while he attempted to narrow his eyes and appear stern. His hands grabbed her ankles and pulled her down to a point where her bottom brushed against his bent knees. Reaching up, he took hold of the brown scarf ends that were tied to the posts of his bed. Wrapping her wrists within the scarf, he locked her in place, preventing her escape. Holding his upper body over her, he brought his forehead down to hers, his eyes, the color of forbidden forests, glistening with mirth.

"I don't know, Mouse, have you been a good girl? Tell me how you've pleased your Master." His voice held humor in its tone, Maddy's heart delighting in the way they played when they had moments alone.

Opening her mouth to speak, Aaron quickly leaned down, taking her lips with his. His tongue licked across her lips seeking entry, and when she opened them for him, another growl vibrated across his chest. Aaron deepened the kiss before his mouth moved along her neck, down across her breast and abdomen, and finally kissing her in the most intimate of ways as his hands kept her legs fully spread apart.

Her head fell back from the sensation. The heat of his mouth, the movement of his tongue against her, causing her body to tremble and quake. Heat bloomed within her, electricity that shot along her skin and through her core. He'd been correct that day when he'd first forced pleasure in her body; his kiss was something she craved so intently, she'd be willing to crawl to his feet if that was what she had to do so she could feel it. This man, her warrior ... a dark knight, if anything, but not really a knight at all. He wasn't a good man, he'd committed countless acts of violence in his life, and he was still considered the most lethal man of The Estate. When it came to Maddy, however, he was another man entirely, a man that would kill to set her free, who would lay down his life if it would save her.

It has been six months since Aaron took control of The Estate. Throughout that time, Maddy still appeared publicly as his slave, still knelt at his feet as he addressed the murderers and thieves that he ruled over. On the night that his father had been killed, they'd gone back to Aaron's

352

apartment, helped wash the blood away from each other's bodies, and had entangled themselves on the bed as they whispered their innermost thoughts and feelings to each other. The following morning, Aaron, Maddy, and Xander met before the assembly was to take place in the ballroom. Reaching the decision that Aaron couldn't show weakness — couldn't have something that was so meaningful to him that it could be used as a weapon against him — they decided that Maddy would continue to play the role as his slave before the other members of The Estate. It was their hope that if another man had the idea to challenge Aaron's rule, their first target would not be Maddy, as they would not believe her to be of much value to Aaron.

So far it has worked, however, Aaron didn't like her naked body displayed to the men who served him. Covering her in expensive materials and jewels, he had clothes made that would entice, but would also allow her modesty while in public. Under his rule, many of the activities in the house were changed. The wing where his father had resided was stripped of all chains, stripped of all tools intended for cruelty, stripped of all evidence and corruption Joseph Carmichael had spread among the men who'd been loyal to him. The bodies of the dead men, the dead slaves, and finally the dead Mr. Carmichael and his two guards were burned in a giant bonfire the night after the slaughter. The smell of burnt flesh filled the air while the carnal screams of The Estate members rallied around Aaron.

The units were also instructed of new rules

regarding the severity of their crimes. Aaron couldn't stop the men from continuing in their practices, but he gave a stern warning regarding the method in which they were performed. There would be no more abductions of innocent women, no more slaves that were tortured and mistreated from any of the units within the network. The unit that dealt in prostitutes and the sex trade was eradicated, the members of that unit dispersed out to serve in other areas controlled by The Estate.

Bringing the network to a quick end was impossible. These men were not the type to quietly walk away when told. If Aaron had attempted to immediately dismantle The Estate, he would have been ambushed, killed, and replaced with another leader.

Aaron led the men during the day and had hushed discussions with Maddy at night. Although he was technically the leader, she was the voice that whispered in his ear, the conscience that influenced his decisions and directives, the angel on his shoulder that grounded him to their task.

Her story didn't end with her escape; she didn't go back to the life she'd known before. Even knowing that it was possible the world still searched for her, perhaps still grieved for the loss of her, she'd chosen to stay. She needed to support the man that was bringing down the network slowly, whittling away at the most corrupt areas first before moving on to the other units. She'd chosen to seek her vengeance, to deliver justice, by tearing the network down from the inside out; and for all intents and purposes, Aaron ruled The Estate. He was the esteemed leader whose decisions were followed without question, the executioner of those who failed to act in accordance with his rules; but it was Maddy who sat quietly in the background, who whispered suggested directives, and who was able to help guide Aaron as he slowly demolished the house and organization built by the devil himself. In a sense, it was Maddy who had taken command of the organization that had abducted her, and she did so by taking possession of the heart of the man who was the most brutal of them all. She stayed not only for her vengeance, but also to ground Aaron, to ensure he remained free of the corruption and madness that had slowly destroyed his father.

It could take years, maybe decades to finally bring it all to its end, but Maddy understood the need for Aaron's caution, knew that there was never true loyalty between murderers and thieves. Eventually they would succeed, eventually they would make sure that there was nothing left but the legitimate business they used to launder money through.

Ever loyal, Xander followed Aaron's orders, knew full well that Aaron intended to bring a little piece down day by day until, finally there was nothing left. Maddy had been worried that Xander would oppose such an objective, but when he'd finally been told, when Aaron had sat him down and explained what they'd planned to do, he smiled. The destruction of The Estate was his justice as well ... for what had been done to him and for what had been done to his family. Tirelessly, they worked together. Xander, once again Aaron's spy, was impressive in his tasks now that he was no longer bound to the apartment to protect Maddy.

Regardless of the efforts they made, the successes they achieved as a unit of three, it was the private moments that Maddy loved the most. Her intimacy with Aaron, the nights where they held each other and discussed not only their pasts, but their futures as well. Those were the moments she cherished above all else. Her need for vengeance and her pursuit of justice were nothing compared to the moments when she was pulled tight to his chest; when she was wrapped within the heat of his body and within the safety of his arms. She didn't feel the need to hide anymore, didn't fear the world as deeply as she had before. She'd slaughtered the demon, and by doing so, she'd ended the tyranny of the worst kind of evil in her and Aaron's life.

The path Maddy's life had taken was a complicated course, one that most would not believe possible. Unbelievable as it may have seemed, however, out of Maddy's worst nightmare, the most pure form of love had bloomed. Aaron still struggled against his quickness to kill, his enjoyment of the feel of steel against the flesh of his enemies, but he was no longer consumed by the anger and rage that had almost destroyed him, and it was because of the love she'd returned to him.

Madeleine saved herself when she was abducted. Taken while she was a scared woman, one who'd once been viewed as nothing more than weak and easily controlled, she'd proven that she had the heart of a lion, that she had the spirit of a

356

warrior, that her strength didn't exist only in her ability to fight, but in her ability to endure, in her ability to survive.

Most importantly, through her strength and her bravery, Maddy had not only saved herself, but also, Aaron: By opening her eyes and discovering that hidden deeply within the recesses of the executioner's soul, there was goodness, there was compassion, there was love and there was honor; but above it all ... deep within that infinite darkness ...

There was light.

The End

Future Books in this Series will be:

"Hope Restrained" ~ Coming January 2014

She was meant to be his assassin
A forced player in a rivalry within The Estate
Yet her loyalty was to no person, but herself

357

When Hope is taken captive by Xander Black
She becomes the one thing that can ensure Aaron's
reign

Raised within a rival crime network, Hope Delacroix wanted nothing to do with The Estate. A fierce warrior, Hope is given no choice but to kill Aaron Carmichael. Caught in her attempt, Hope is captured by Aaron's top guard in an effort to discover who sent her.

Ever loyal and protective, Xander Black's sole objective is to defend Aaron and Maddy. Willing to do whatever necessary, Xander gives in to darkness in order to force information out of Hope.

As Xander enslaves Hope to break her down completely, he learns that in the two years since Joseph Carmichael's death, dissension still exists within The Estate.

"I find it ironic that your name is Hope...especially considering that you have none."
~ Xander Black

Acknowledgements

I want to give a huge THANK YOU to my family, friends, blogs and fans who continue to encourage and support me as I write.

In particular, I have to thank my husband for his continued effort in taking care of the house and kids, which is a huge contributor to my success. I should also thank him for putting up with my moodiness while writing emotionally exhaustive scenes. Love you babe!

To my number one minion, sounding board and cheerleader, Gina Chiappini; as usual, I would not be able to do this without having you to pull me back from the depths of book insanity. Thank you for grounding me, for believing in me and for not being afraid to sit among strangers and discuss horrific plots and events in my book like we were talking about reality. I'm not sure how many people we have scared through the past couple of months by our conversations, but I'll never stop loving the looks on their faces.

To my fans: Stephanie Phillips, Crystal Marie (AKA the bestie's daughter), Stacy Nickelson, Gladys Gonzales Atwell, Marisa Rose-Shor, Danielle Sanchez, Lori Westhaver, Laura Voss, Jennifer Hensley, Adele Romas Camper, Mandi, Chris BlogEmporium, Gillian Pemberton, Cathy Quenzer, Karen Wonsor, Michelle Tanksley, Rosemarie Mckenzie, Echo Hill, Tbird London, Shona Reid, Stacey Clark, Suzie Cairney, Ebony Simone McMillan, Shelby Mead, Brandy Jellum,

359

Zakirrah Razaq, Mary Tater, Maria Barquero, Megan Noel, Nicole Voss, Angel Burrage, Brandi Rohr-Sandlin, Liz King, Miranda Johnson, Kristin Elyon, The Blushing Reader, and Arianna McWilliams, ALL OF YOU have inspired me to keep going and not give up. Without your support and love of books, I wouldn't be able to do what I do. I greatly appreciate each and every one of you and I'm overjoyed with having had the opportunity to meet you and get to know you through my career as an author. There are truly some amazing book lovers out there and all have you have become a family to me in our shared love of all things literary. There are not enough words I can say that would adequately express how thankful I am.

Finally, to my editor, Issac Stolzenbach – thank you for taking the time that you took on Madeleine Abducted. It's good to have someone to keep me from sticking my foot in my mouth. You did an amazing job and it's been enlightening to work with such an avid wordsmith.

M.S. Willis

If you are interested in reading additional books by M.S. Willis or would like to know when new books are being released, M.S. Willis can be found at:

Website:
http://www.mswillisbooks.com

Facebook:
http://www.facebook.com/mswillisbooks